ENTANGLED SOUL

THOMAS S. IRELAND

Copyright © 2017 Thomas S. Ireland
All rights reserved.
ISBN-10:1548070912
ISBN-13: 9781548070915

DEDICATION

To my wife, Sandy, who believes in me, encourages me and repeatedly read this book to me in its entirety as we worked together on editing and revisions.

OTHER BOOKS BY TOM IRELAND

How To Write A Great Information Technology Strategic Plan – And Thrill Your CEO

How To Create A Great Information Technology Vision – And Thrill Your CEO

Information Technology Leadership Excellence

CONTENTS

ACKNOWLEDGEMENTS

With great thanks to my best friend, Paul Smith-Goodson, who has guided me in the art and incredible challenge of writing a novel and has taught me so much about so many things over the last thirty-seven years.

Cover art by George Grie © www.neosurrealismart.com

Characters In This Book In Order Of Introduction

Teo Eyers – Father of Inara Eyers. Caretaker of the jungle planet Inara was raised on

Jira Eyers – Mother of Inara Eyers

Inara Eyers – A major character in the novel. A complete synesthete

Dr. Pren Bodhi – Physician who first recognized Inara's special set of talents. Became a close friend of Inara's family. Came to be regarded as Inara's uncle

Kieren Llot – A major character in the novel. A Controller Scientist. Close friend to Inara

The GuideTakar Cillian – Leader of the Pilgrims at the time of this novel

Malk Kring – A devout Pilgrim captured by the Five Families

Sean Lee – Minor character, scientist and explorer

Ali Xang -- Minor character, scientist and explorer

Alice -- Minor character, scientist and explorer

Bill Reynolds -- Minor character, scientist and explorer

Carlos Brown -- Minor character, scientist and explorer

Kezia Mang – A devout Pilgrim and associate of Malk Kring

Harq – A devout Pilgrim and assistant to Kezia Mang

Aulika – Spy for the Five Families

Yin Xang – Five Families committee chairman in the early days of galactic exploration

Horace Baker – Major member of the Five Families in the early days of galactic exploration.

Fritz Barnhardt -- Major member of the Five Families in the early days of galactic exploration.

Marianne Schmidt – Chief Scientist of the Five Families who initially harnessed entanglement for biological matter transport.

Ruqayah Nkruma -- Major member of the Five Families in the early days of galactic exploration.

Innes Nold – Minor character and Pilgrim

Malin Nowl – Assistant to The Guide Takar Cillian

Monty Spea – Minor character and member of the Five Families

Dean Dammar Corday – Mentor to Kieran Llot. Major member of the Controllers

Edric Yan – Controller Secretary-General of Telescence

Controller Takarn Rah – Minor Controller member

Proctor Har Ith -- Minor Controller member

Tra Llot – Kieran's little sister

Arnet Llot – Kieran's father

Paya Lachlan – Controller Secretary-General of Systems Integration.

Draylou Ler – Controller Secretary-General of Information Processing

Alana Perg – Controller Secretary-General

Erber Oran – Assistant to Alana Perg

Dathan Acob – Controller Secretary-General

Callum Seph – Galaxy Prime Minister

Monz Ingra – University Sector Minister

Jaidon Lothe – Deputy for Technical Systems and University Liaison to The Controllers

Gareth Frax – University President

Esha Arza – Sector Minister of the galactic region in which The Guide's Hall is located

Pope Cyril X – Metropolitan of Egypt in the early days of galactic exploration

Rabbi Cohen – Prominent Jewish Rabbi in the early days of galactic exploration

Denpo – Representative of the Dalai Lama in the early days of galactic exploration

Father Demetri – Russian Orthodox priest in the early days of galactic exploration

Gordon Bailey -- Five Families committee chairman in the days when humans were just leaving Earth

Melanie Bailey – Daughter of Gordon Bailey

Lydia Templeton – Five Families Proposal defender in the days when humans were just leaving Earth

Yori Tanaka – Five Families Proposal defender in the days when humans were just leaving Earth

Ibrahim Faruk – Five Families Proposal defender in the days when humans were just leaving Earth

Johannes – Marianne Schmidt's assistant

Roger Huber – Chief scientist on Marianne Schmidt's research team

Frank Simmons – Early developer of entanglement transport technology

George Simmons -- Early developer of entanglement transport technology

Frank Simmons, Jr. – Son of Frank Simmons

Quintus Gordon -- Five Families committee chairman at the time of the invention of Entanglement Transport

Akinji Simmons – Wife of Frank Simmons, Jr.

Jacob – Senior member of the Five Families at the time of the invention of Entanglement Transport

Samto Habib – Guide during the period of recovery

Demetrius – Assistant to Guide Samto Habib

Before Quanta

Good permitted the imbalance. Then the disturbance in nothing exploded into something before settling into a steady expansion. The micro and the macro engaged in a dance that would allow uncertainty and randomness to operate within the otherwise structured framework.

Good tweaked the randomness and angels joined Good. And they loved Good and Good's works.

When the right set of conditions presented themselves Good stirred matter in one small place and life began.

Uncertainty joined with randomness to allow angels and life to have Free Will and the opportunity to make real decisions unfettered by past constraints. All was one in this living Soul that was Good.

Then ambition and hubris evolved from the slowly dawning knowledge that Free Will permitted the ability to make almost any decision.

Evil was born as some of the angels separated themselves from Good causing pain in this Universal Soul that was in everything that Good had created. Free Will became the parameter within which the health of the Soul would be determined.

Inara

"Teo, I think it's time for someone to help us understand our daughter's behavior," Jira Eyers commented after watching eighteen month-old Inara throw grass and dirt in the air in different directions for over an hour. It was the intensity with which Inara studied the drifting pieces that attracted Jira's attention.

Jira's tall, rugged husband stopped his work on the transparent transport pods used to carry visitors on tours through the marvels of their planet. With amusement in his voice, he said, "I wonder how many times a wife has said that to her husband in the one hundred thousand years since we left Earth and tamed the galaxy." The look he received in return was predictable.

From the minute she was born it was his daughter who truly and completely captured the heart of this strong and intelligent man who intensely loved his family, his work and the jungle planet they lived on.

He went over to where Inara was sitting in the grass with her pet cheetah cub who always seemed to be at her side. As Teo quietly watched her for another fifteen minutes or so it seemed to him yet again that there was a pattern in the way in which she threw the grass and dirt in the air.

"Inara, what are you doing?"

"I'm making numbers and colors, Daddy."

"How are you doing that?"

Inara picked up a handful of dirt and threw it to her right. "That's a bright red seven with darker red stripes. It tastes like milk and feels scratchy. Can't you see it?"

Teo and Jira were used to answers like that. The research they had done made them wonder if she was one of those extremely rare people, maybe only a thousand of the quadrillions spread across the entire galaxy, with senses that were cross linked to some degree. That factor, in combination with her obvious genius, made her both a joy and a challenge to her parents. Because of the carefulness of her family and their isolation on their jungle planet no one outside of her parents knew how totally special Inara was. Others just saw her as exceptionally smart.

"And what are the other dirt clouds that you are throwing?"

Inara picked up a couple more handfuls and threw them with deliberateness in other directions. "That's a yellow three and that one is a purple eight. But, here is the real fun, Daddy. I just learned this today." She then picked up two more handfuls, swung her arms wide and threw the clouds high into the air in front of her so that they came together before drifting to the ground. "That one," she said gesturing to her left hand," was a red three and this one was a white eight." Now they are a pink twenty-four."

Teo's first thought was "Pretty cool for someone eighteen months old." Then he wondered if Inara really understood what had just happened or was just observing. He began to explore more deeply than he had previously.

"Inara, what if you throw two handfuls over there?" Again, the numbers Inara called out representing the individual clouds and merging into the combined cloud were multiplied together.

Five throws later Teo asked, "Do you know how to multiply numbers?"

"I don't know what you're talking about, Daddy."

Quite a bit off balance, Teo asked, "Inara, what if we both throw two handfuls in the air? What will happen?"

Inara giggled with pleasure at this new thought and grabbed two handfuls of dirt. Teo did the same. They both threw their arms wide and tossed their dirt into a single cloud in the air. Inara yelled out, "Five, seven, twelve, thirty-thee. Whee! Orange, polka dotted one three eight six zero, and it tastes like grapefruit."

Happy and apprehensive, Teo paused then took a stick, wrote the numbers in the dirt. When he multiplied the first four numbers together he got thirteen thousand eight hundred sixty! He didn't know whether to be excited or sick to his stomach. After a few seconds he asked, "Do your dirt clouds always taste like something?"

"Only a little, Daddy. But the numbers all have their own taste and color. And there is even music. The music can be the best part of all."

"Real big numbers, too?"

"The size of the number doesn't matter."

3

That stopped Teo for a few seconds until he realized that perhaps she took the word size to mean something different than he intended. Then he wrote 5387201642754 in the dirt.

"Inara, how does that taste and look?"

Now it was Inara's turn to be puzzled. "What is that, Daddy?"

"It's a large number."

Inara frowned in concentration. "Say the number, Daddy."

And so the next hour went with Teo understanding more than ever that his genius daughter saw the world in an entirely different way from anyone else. He suspected that everything might have much more meaning to her than anything could possibly have for him. Jira was right. It was time to talk to a professional. They hadn't been off their planet since long before Inara was born. It might also be nice to take a trip.

As he got up to go over to Jira he paused for a moment to listen to the beautiful song Inara was singing to her ever present cheetah as she threw another two handfuls of music in the air.

* * *

Teo and Jira, after doing some research about the best professional resources decided to make an appointment with Dr. Pren Bodhi at a medical facility associated with Andromeda University. Dr. Bodhi was a renowned researcher as well as medical doctor in neurological systems. One of Dr. Bodhi's staff members agreed to take the initial consultation over a telescence channel. Teo and Jira participated from their study.

At the agreed upon time Dr. Braff's office at Andromeda appeared and merged with Teo and Jira's study. They greeted each other with handshakes. Teo and Jira invited Dr. Braff to sit with them by their bay window and have some tea. After a few minutes Inara was invited to join them. Dr. Braff spent the next hour chatting with Inara and observing some of her skills.

When it was time for him to leave Dr. Braff explained, "I came here certain that I would be asking Dr. Bodhi to examine and visit with Inara over a telescence link. However, after my time with you and her I am convinced that Inara should travel to our medical center on Andromeda. Dr. Bodhi may bring in his extended staff and will almost certainly employ analysis equipment that can only be used in his offices."

After a few more questions and discussion Jira and Teo agreed to make the trip with Inara to Andromeda. Dr. Braff stepped across the intervening light-years to his office.

* * *

Inara had been deep into the jungle around her home a few times with her father. Sometimes the family would visit neighbors or the nearby town. However, this was different. Inara had never left her home planet. She was excited about meeting the man her parents referred to as Dr. Bodhi and wondered what he would be like. She talked non-stop about the trees, animals and exquisite scenery carefully cultivated and managed by the megacorporation that owned the planet and for which Teo worked. However, Inara seemed to go into a sensory overload as they lifted off from the spaceport on their home planet to go to the local entanglement gateway on the short-range space pod.

"Mommy, Daddy, everything is a rainbow, and it is all getting softer. Oh, this is so much fun," she said laughing with glee and holding her head in her hands in total amazement. "Thank you for bringing me here."

All Teo and Jira and the rest of the passengers saw was the interior of their spherical one-hundred person space pod with its lounges each facing the vast expanse of transparent force field providing a view of their planet and the stars. The scene outside the ship was indeed fascinating but that wasn't what attracted Inara's attention. She kept touching the air and the fabric. For everyone else it was just air and fabric. But, Inara excitedly described an ever changing panorama of numbers, smells and textures as the pod jumped upward out of the gravity well of the planet.

When they docked at the entanglement gateway Inara's actions began to change. She became quieter as they walked through the corridors leading to the quantum entanglement stations that would transport them instantaneously across the light years to their destination

"I don't like it here", Inara said quietly with a frown. "This is a sad place. I like it better in the ship. Hold me, Mommy."

Inara cuddled closely to Jira as they entered the small entanglement room lay on the family cot that was inside. Tears formed in Inara's eyes as they made the transition to the distant star's transport node. When they left the biological gateway Teo asked her why she was so sad.

"It tastes bad here, Daddy. The numbers are not pretty. The music is ugly. Space is unhappy. It hurts."

"Do you mean that you hurt, Inara?"

"Yes, I did hurt a little bit in that room we just left, but space hurts worse. Space is unhappy here. There are ugly numbers."

Teo and Jira knew better than to question something they could not even begin to understand. Instead, they just accepted what their clearly exceptional daughter was saying and held her while taking the local space transport to the medical center on the fourth planet of the star system where they had just arrived.

Inara broke her unusual silence when they landed on the planet. "Mommy, daddy, space didn't always hurt, but it has been hurting for a long time. Someday it is going to hurt much more."

* * *

All went well on the trip between the planets spaceport and the medical facility. They had a couple of hours before Inara's appointment with her doctor, so they stopped to have a light lunch at the nearby restaurant. They took their time wandering around the medical campus which at ground level was a large open garden. There were beautiful wooded and green areas with many lakes and waterfalls on the surface. The medical campus was highly populated and designed in such a way as to keep it comfortable and beautiful by putting almost all buildings underground. Inara giggled with pleasure as she watched people seemingly pop out of and into the ground as they moved between the gardens and the underground campus and medical complex via vertical transport shafts.

Each buried building was designed with interior wall, ceiling and floor surfaces that could make the office look and feel like it was outside or even floating or flying through the air. Garden scents and breezes wafted through the rooms. While all locations in the galaxy had some of these luxuries, all of the university, research and medical centers had this full set of features.

At length it was time to meet with Dr. Pren Bodhi with whom they had made Inara's appointment.

To the relief of her parents, Inara's sadness seemed to leave her completely as soon as she saw Dr. Bodhi. She looked up at them and said, "He's a nice man."

Teo and Jira had already discovered that Inara seemed to know instinctively whom she could and couldn't trust. They could only assume that her special sensory perception gave her extra insight into people. After introductions and a perfectly enjoyable conversation, her parents watched Inara happily and willingly go with Dr. Bodhi to meet the rest of the medical team.

* * *

Pren Bodhi returned with Inara about six hours later to brief Teo and Jira. Inara was clearly bubbling over with joy. Dr. Bodhi was smiling and enjoying Inara but he was also a bit quieter than he had been earlier.

After Inara told her parents about all the neat things she had done, Dr. Bodhi began to tell Teo and Jira what he had learned. Or, at least thought he had learned.

Dr. Bodhi began, "I had an educational and interesting day with Inara. As you can see, she thought it was great fun which makes me happy. Let's get the suspense out of the way by telling you my conclusions which I see as good news for you and for her as she matures. You already knew that she is far above average in intelligence. In fact, she is a genius. She is clearly in the top one hundredth of one percent of the population in intellect. And she is extremely well adjusted for which you can accept the credit."

He paused apparently collecting his thoughts. "I have learned, much to my surprise and reluctance to believe, that Inara has an almost unheard of total cross linking of all of her senses. You already knew that she has some unusual and beneficial integration across her senses. However, I want to emphasize that this is a total, not just a near total or partial, cross linking. It is absolutely complete synesthesia."

Dr. Bodhi looked at Teo and Jira intently as he continued. "For Inara, all of her senses are essentially discrete but completely integrated with each other. For us, touch is only touch. For her, touch is also vision, hearing, smell, taste all rolled into one. She, or maybe it is more accurate to say her brain, knows that the combined sensation may have originated with touch but an explosion of connections with all centers of her brain simultaneously cause a sensory integration that none of us will ever understand. We will never comprehend it in its essence any more than any of us will ever understand the detailed significance of smell to a snake or electric currents in water to some fish. There are people in the galaxy now, and there have been those in the past, who have this sensory integration to some extent. However, we know of no one with such complete integration as I have found in Inara. And not only does she have total integration, she is also a genius and extremely well adjusted. She is, without any exaggeration at all, unique in the galaxy and perhaps unique in all time."

Teo and Jira were speechless. They tried to absorb what Dr. Bodhi was telling them while Jira held Inara on her lap.

Finally, Jira asked Inara, "How did you like your time with the doctors?"

"At first it was boring. Lots of questions about what I was thinking and feeling." She paused. "Then I just played while Dr. Bodhi looked at my brain while it floated in the air."

Inara and Teo looked at Dr. Bodhi for explanation.

"Inara's answers during the first part of our session gave us some clues but my team members and I had some significant trouble agreeing if her answers were real and what they meant. We soon learned that her answers were real and honest", he quickly said as they all noticed a pout begin to form on Inara's face. "We just were so surprised by them that we had trouble absorbing them.

"Then I took a bit of an unusual step. I asked the rest of the doctors to leave and set up a strong privacy field around the laboratory."

Alarm bells went off in Teo's head and he asked a bit testily, "I assume, doctor, that you have an excellent explanation for that?"

"Please understand. I recorded everything. Here is a copy of the recording," he said as he handed it to Teo.

"I'm waiting for an explanation," Teo pressed.

Dr. Bodhi continued, "I'm not a man of strong intuition. I may have pushed that out of my life. As a result of the clinical approach I have been trained to take I tend to replace intuition with attention to detailed analysis. So, I pay attention to strong feelings of intuitive warning when they rarely occur and forcefully nag at me. As the session continued I began to feel uneasy exposing such a special person as Inara to a team of scientists aggressively on the way up their career ladders. As I just mentioned, Inara is unusual to the point of possibly being unique in the galaxy and in all of time. Professionals can sometimes be too ambitious for the good of the patient. I didn't want anyone to be tempted to take advantage of her to the benefit of their advancement. And I didn't want her to be put in danger."

As Teo began to speak again Jira squeezed his hand and said, "Let's hear what the doctor has to say."

Dr. Bodhi then asked, "Would it be alright with you if Inara went to play with some of the other children who are here?"

Jira looked down at Inara, "Would you like to do that?"

She squealed, "Yes!" in clear delight.

Dr. Bodhi called a droid to take her to the play area. When Inara was gone he turned to Teo and Jira and continued. "I realized that I had to watch what was happening inside her brain as we worked and played together. So, I set up some real-time scans and projected the results in four dimensional space-time. We also collected other dimensional data which I will examine later in more detail. Sometimes Inara watched the projection with me and sometimes she didn't. The projection is what taught me about what was happening in her brain. All of this, by the way, is on the recording I am giving you."

Dr. Bodhi expanded his explanation. "At first I gave Inara things to do and to play with. I gave her objects to touch, see, hear, smell and taste. When she sensed something, I noticed that the sensation sparked activity in the appropriate centers. However, the activity was precisely mirrored on both the right and left sides of her brain simultaneously. Then the energy exploded through her entire brain much more rapidly than is usual. It almost always bounced to her frontal lobe where it was integrated and processed. It was staggering to watch. I had never seen this before."

Teo asked, "What effect does this have on Inara? What will she be like?"

"As I mentioned earlier, she seems to be extremely well adjusted. Frankly, I think she will probably have a great attitude toward life and an excellent and enjoyable view of all around her."

That last comment was an extreme understatement as the entire galaxy would someday learn.

Dr. Bodhi paused, seemingly lost in thought.

"Would you like to take a walk in the gardens? It's much nicer out there."

They talked casually as they walked to the end of the corridor with its transparent force field walls that helped maintain a constant temperature while letting through a modulated breeze and the beautiful fragrances from outside. They stepped into a vertical tube which seemed to have no floor but gently speeded them upward about two hundred feet to the gardens exit. They walked for a bit down a path between some roses before coming to a beautiful spot with a small bonsai tree. "I'm so busy that I don't get the chance to visit this spot as often as I should. It is one of my favorite places. I thought you would enjoy it. Please sit down."

Pren Brodhi made a small motion. "The gesture I just made activates a secrecy field. As a medical doctor it is frequently necessary for me to have conversations with my patients that are none of anyone else's business. Happily, we can fully and immediately cure any physical ailments, but sometimes there is a need for privacy for various reasons. Again, I have no bad news for you but I do feel compelled to give you some advice about Inara and how much others should know about her abilities.

"I know that you are both religious Pilgrims. I am talking to you now not only as a doctor but as a Pilgrim myself. Even though we are not of the same specific religion we are all dedicated to the health of the Universal Soul. Because of that we work to nurture each other. However, there are ambitious and evil people who will tear others down and take advantage of them to their own benefit. These people care little for each other and almost nothing for the Universal Soul."

By this time, Teo and Jira had moved close to each other and were holding hands. "Doctor," said Jira, "I'm curious and concerned. What is it you want to tell us?"

"I feel strongly and unusually compelled to be cautious. I really don't want to send out a consulting query across the galaxy about Inara because I don't want to attract attention to her. But, I feel almost absolutely sure that no one has ever lived who is so well adjusted with her combination of intellect and totally cross-linked senses. Not only are her senses totally cross-linked but she may be able to sense things that no one else is aware of."

He paused, seemingly caught in an inner struggle. Teo and Jira waited for him to continue in great part because they had no idea what to say or ask.

"I suggest that you keep her abilities a closely guarded secret. Happily, your life is one where that is easy to do. You live at the edge of a jungle on a sparsely inhabited planet. Thankfully, you aren't on a metropolitan planet.

"My concern is twofold. First, even in our time there are people who would see her as a spectacle, a curiosity to be put on display and inspected in painful detail. Secondly, there are those who I believe would use her abilities for their own commercial gain and turn her into a tool. Either avenue denies her the life she, and you, deserve. Take her home, love her, enjoy her, and let her develop in whatever way she will. As she grows up be totally honest with her about her abilities so she can enjoy them. Help her to learn to protect herself without becoming paranoid. She is so amazingly well adjusted that I suspect things will go well for all of you."

Teo responded, "Doctor, you seem more concerned about the careless curiosity of others and the bad intentions of some than I would have thought. Naturally, we have downplayed Inara's abilities in front of others because we didn't want to disturb her childhood. Neither of us expected what you are telling us today.

You are mixing what might be excellent news with a message of extreme caution. It is going to take a little time to absorb."

Dr. Bodhi said, "You will all do well. Inara is the great person she is in part because you love her so much, and you are such good parents. I hope we will visit more as time goes on."

* * *

Inara and her parents stayed at the hospital visitors' center for the rest of the afternoon. Dr. Bodhi invited them for a quiet dinner at his home that evening. As sometimes happens between good people with a focus of interest they found themselves at great ease with each other. So much so that the evening went quickly as they all moved to a first-name basis. While Teo and Jira found themselves fully enjoying Pren Bodhi they also took their cue from Inara who readily climbed into Pren's lap and eagerly played with his dog before the evening was half over. They all sleepily and somewhat reluctantly took their leave of each other before Jira, Teo and Inara took the pod back to the visitors' quarters.

* * *

Inara was still bubbly when they got ready the next morning. However, her happiness disappeared when their space pod arrived at the entanglement center hanging high above the planet.

"Daddy, I don't want to go home."

"You really did have a lot of fun with Dr. Bodhi yesterday, didn't you?"

"Yes."

"So, do you want to stay here or come see him again?"

"No. I just don't want to go home."

Jira, seeing where this was going, simply asked, "Why, Honey?"

"Because space hurts inside that room," she said pointing to the entanglement door. "And it makes me real sad, and it hurts me a little bit, too."

"Is it scary?"

"Kind of."

"Well, I will hold you when we go into that room. And I will keep holding you until we leave it. Then we will never come back if you don't want to."

"OK. Don't let me go."

"I won't," Jira said as her daughter's tears broke her heart.

* * *

Pren Bodhi and Inara's family kept in close contact over the next few months using the telescence technology that enabled them to merge their rooms into a joined space over the parsecs and have full sensory interaction including hearty handshakes and hugs as if they were physically next to each other. As they sat together over shared dinner tables their friendship grew. As good as telescence was they all wanted to actually be with each other again for personal and professional reasons and Pren soon accepted the invitation to travel to their home.

"Welcome to our jungle planet, Pren. It is good to have you in our home," said Teo in greeting as they met Pren Bodhi at the door to their home.

"It's my pleasure. I enjoy your company," he said nodding to both Teo and Jira. "And your planetary replica of ancient Earth before humans took it over is fascinating. I truly feel like I have traveled back in time. You and your corporation are to be congratulated. As a Pilgrim, it does my heart good to be reminded of how it all began."

With a squeal of delight, Inara ran across the room, arms flung wide, toward the doctor. As he picked her up she hugged him saying, "I've been waiting for you" almost in a tone of cute admonition.

"Well, it is good to see you, too," he responded while putting her down. "How have you been?"

"Is that a doctor question?"

"No," Pren laughed. "It is a friend question."

"Hmm. Fine."

And so began a friendship that was so close that over the years Dr. Bodhi became Uncle Pren, dear friend and a member of the family.

* * *

As they do for everyone, those years went by much too quickly. Pren Bodhi had been invited by Inara and her family to spend a final few days with them all before Inara left her home to attend university. They had just arrived at the entrance to the entanglement node serving their star system.

Jira couldn't help but ask, "Are you alright, Inara."

"Yes, Mother, I was just remembering our last gateway trip together. I was almost brand new, and I sensed so much pain from the surrounding space. Perhaps I was just overly sensitive because I was so young. But, it was horrible!"

Teo chimed in, "We can return home if you wish."

"No, Dad. I want to go to Andromeda University, and it is time for me to get on with the next part of my life. Besides, the university is on a planet in the same star system as Uncle Pren's hospital, so I won't have to take an entanglement trip to visit him."

Pren Bodhi, uncle and doctor, stood by and just watched quietly. Then it was time for each of them to enter their individual entanglement pods.

* * *

All went well until they reached their entanglement entry point. The closer Inara got to the station door the more uncomfortable and quiet she became. As the countdown to entanglement transfer began Inara started to shake but was still silent.

None of them was prepared for Inara's screaming, tearful anguish as she exited at the other end of her jump. Her parents, Dr. Bodhi and others ran to her side as she writhed on the ground yelling, "The pain is horrible!! You have to stop making the pain!"

Teo held her asking, "Where does it hurt? Where is your pain?" Dr. Bodhi scanned her for injury as did the sensors built into the walls.

"It isn't just me," she sobbed. "It is space. Space is in so much pain. It is worse than it was. We have to stop destroying space and the soul. We are destroying ourselves. The numbers, the colors, the tastes and music are all wrong. It is ugly, putrid and sick here. We have to stop."

The proctor controller of the gateway was called, and he ordered a full class one check on all systems. Everyone who was leaving a gateway was given a complete scan and asked if they had felt anything unusual during their transfer. All systems and all people were found to be well. Dr. Bodhi quietly asked the proctor controller to link all of the information that had been gathered to his laboratory at the medical center. He used the connection to run detailed scans of every part of Inara's body and brain. He found no physical problems at all, but Inara's chemical makeup in her brain showed what was surely an almost unbearable sadness and intense pain.

It was days before Inara started to recover.

While her studies at the university went well it was months before she again became anything like her normal self. It was at the end of that first year of studies that she decided to become a Pilgrim Priest and dedicate herself to the care of the Universal Soul.

* * *

Over time, Inara came to enjoy the university environment almost as much as her home planet. That was good because she had resolved to never take another entanglement trip. Inara advanced through her courses easily using the full range of her hidden talents to absorb information from a wide variety of disciplines. She acquired a number of doctoral and post-doctoral degrees collecting them as if it was a hobby to her. Knowledge came easily for Inara as did the ability to do research. Discovery after discovery brought her attention and acclaim over the years, and she rose high in the university ranks. Opportunities were offered to her from all over the galaxy, but she always turned them down saying that she was happy right where she was. Only Pren and Inara's parents knew that she was imprisoned by the entanglement gateway.

* * *

Inara and Dr. Bodhi were sitting together at dinner one evening when Pren said, "So, you seem to have made a special friend. I'm surprised that he could beat his way through your crowd of male admirers. What makes this one different from the dozens of others you have been with over the years?"

"Come on, Uncle Pren, it hasn't been dozens."

"You are evading my question."

"What if I told you it was none of your business."

"Then I would call your mother and have her ask you."

"You are a pest."

"That is my job as uncle. And you are evading my question again."

"You aren't really my uncle."

"It is your fault that you made me that way. Now tell me about this fellow. I need to know if I must have him exiled to one of the outer fringes of the galaxy."

After a pause, during which Inara pushed her food around, she said, "He is unusually special. All my senses combine to tell me he is one of the kindest, most loving, most sensitive men I have ever met. Furthermore, he is a scientific genius. He is a lot like you."

That last statement caused Pren to pause. Finally, he said, "Tell me more."

"His name is Kieran Llot. He is here for about a year on a research grant. He is an expert on entanglement and spatial dimensions."

"Oh, entanglement. One of your favorite subjects. Does he know about your problem with transport?"

"No. I can't talk to even him about that. Everything tells me it is too dangerous for anyone to know."

"Hmmm. Not even Kieran, huh?" he said sarcastically, which got him the death stare she inherited from her mother and only women can give.

"No, I just tell him I love it here and will never leave."

They were both quiet for a while. Finally, Inara said, "He is such a good person. We care about each other. I will miss him when he leaves. There is always the possibility of telescence visits but even those are not the same as being physically in the same few small feet of space with a person you love so deeply. It seems like it could eventually be more like torture than comfort. This hurts so much, Uncle Pren."

"I can tell. I'm sorry."

"So am I. I know he will miss me, too. Maybe he will visit from time-to-time. I hope he will understand when I don't visit him."

The Guide

Years later it was an amazing day for Pren when he and Inara together attended a lecture by the leader of the Pilgrims known as The Guide. It wasn't just Guide Takar Cillian himself, or the message he had to impart that was so special. It was Inara's response to the man and his presence.

"Pren," she said and with quiet passion "this is an incredibly holy man. I've never experienced all of this before." She made a slight circular motion with her hand that Pren understood to mean the accumulation of full sensory impact. "You can trust him totally."

She became quiet as The Guide paused to look at her from over one hundred feet away. She was sure that he could not have heard what she said, and he had been looking in the other direction when she whispered to her uncle. Yet, he stared at her for an almost imperceptible second with what seemed like recognition even though they had never met. Her senses told her that it wasn't her physical appearance that he recognized. It was her soul.

"Inara," said Pren as they walked after the lecture through the gardens they both loved, "what happened in there? I've never heard you talk like that about anyone. Even your old flame you used to have named Kieran comes in a distant second. And I will swear that for a fraction of time The Guide looked at you as if you were a long lost friend."

"I'm not entirely sure, Pren. What I can tell you is that for the first time in my life every sense I have merged to tell me that The Guide is a man we can trust with knowledge about me with no reservation at all. He is filled with love for the Universal Soul, and he has total integrity. I actually think that in that group of thousands of students and faculty, he recognized my understanding of the relationship between the religion and the science of the Universal Soul."

They sat at a table in the sunlight. A droid sensed their need and brought their favorite drinks.

Pren took up the discussion where it left off. "Inara, I find that both surprising and interesting. Ever since you were a baby your parents and I have worked hard to hide your special sensory talents, if not your genius, from everyone. Even my team who examined you when we first met has assumed that your sensory integration was an anomaly of your early childhood and that you outgrew it."

"Thanks, Uncle Pren," Inara teased, "I guess you have had me simply relegated to the dustbin of forgotten experiments in your laboratory focused on much more important things."

Dr. Bodhi laughed in return. "Yup, I just hang around with you now because of your off-beat sense of humor. Seriously, I think something extraordinarily important just took place between you and The Guide. I know that you have a detailed ability to perceive, with no error at all, good and evil, love and hate. Are you telling me that you totally trust The Guide? Can he be trusted with your secret?"

Without any hesitation at all, Inara replied, "Yes."

After a few minutes Inara continued. "Pren, something else is happening to me in just these last few minutes after leaving the lecture by the Guide. I'm having a bit of trouble understanding it and describing it to myself. It is as if my synesthesia has grown an extra sense that attaches me even more completely to my surroundings."

Reacting as a man of medicine and science as much as an uncle, Dr. Bodhi asked, "Do you feel disoriented or confused?"

"A little bit of both. It is much like the feeling of being lost and not remembering how to get back to familiar territory. Or, it could be compared to learning a new technology in a difficult class and trying to make sense of the new concepts and how they fit together. I feel extended beyond myself and it is incredibly disorienting. I've always been a bit of an empath. I certainly can't read minds but I think I can now fully read feelings, since seeing The Guide. Uncle Pren, I now truly understand how much you love me and it makes me feel special almost beyond belief."

Then a sadness crept into Inara's eyes causing Pren to reach across the table for her hand.

"Pren, I may have made a horrible mistake and I don't think I can correct it."

Dr. Bodhi waited.

"I know now that I should have told Kieran about me. Instead I just let it end with almost no explanation. And now, star systems away I can feel his love, loss and pain. I wish I had this stronger empathic sense when he was leaving that I have gained in this last few minutes."

Pren Bodhi erected a privacy curtain as Inara began to sob.

Malk Kring's First Visit

The next day Inara's newly expanded senses brought her a new reality and an immense surprise.

The last of Inara's students had either left her lecture room or terminated their telescence links when a man she had never met entered the room. He stood quietly about ten feet in front of her until she looked up from the notes she was reviewing.

"Hello," she said. "May I help you?"

"Yes," he answered. "If you choose to do so. My name is Malk Kring. I think we can help each other. I can tell that you are reaching out to test my intentions. I already know yours."

For the first time Inara met another complete synesthete, and a bit more.

Inara staggered and sank into the chair that sensed her need and quickly materialized behind her. She gasped, "You are like me!"

"Yes," he responded. "I am much like you but there are some differences and those differences are beneficial and important to both of us. I am leaving myself open to you. Please feel free to reach into me so you will know you can trust me."

Inara used her new abilities to explore this visitor and recognized that he had that same full set of integrated senses she had. She also understood something much more.

She stated as much as asked, "You are not of this time. You are from the past?"

Malk answered, "I have been unwillingly smeared across time by evil people who have controlled and tortured me. But they don't know that their control has slipped a bit. Now, for reasons I am only vaguely beginning to understand, I am with you. If they knew that, then they would kill me."

"You're saying that you travel through time?"

"Not exactly," Malk replied. "It is more like I exist in all of time. Now, I am finding myself materialized in front of you. My travel is not of my free will. Both good and evil dictate my destinations in time and space. And now I am compelled, by the Universal Soul I think, to tell you about my experiences. I wish I knew where this was all leading."

Inara absorbed and processed all of this as quickly as she could, then wryly observed with an understatement that even she could not appreciate, "I can identify with that wish. You must understand that this is quite a surprise. I find myself wondering why you are here. More specifically, I wonder why you are here on the day after my entangled senses seem to have acquired some new capabilities. And I can tell you are terribly troubled and confused."

Malk responded, "I think I am here because this is where I am needed. I am sure the timing is by plan more than by coincidence. As I stand here, I am increasingly recognizing a strangely complete and compelling knowledge of my mission today."

Inara rose and walked toward Malk. They were both quiet for several minutes. Then she asked, "What do you need?'

"I need a couple of hours to tell you part of a story. Then it is my impression that I will be leaving again. But will be back. This is incredibly disorienting."

Inara considered, then said, "I have the entire afternoon available. I can seal off this room for privacy."

"Thank you. I will use the full telepresencing and projection capabilities that I can tell this facility has to present part of a story to you. I'll use all of my integrated senses to control the full environment. I suggest that you also use your integrated senses to let yourself be embedded in the scene as if you were there at that time. We will be in the era when humans were first learning that Earth was the single source of all life in the galaxy and were completing the first circumnavigation of the Milky Way. Let me set the stage for you so that you have the flavor, as well as the knowledge, of that period of time."

Malk began his story.

"Since leaving Earth's star system eleven thousand years earlier, building the transportation infrastructure to new stars and their planets had been a slow, tedious process that went through two stages.

"As you know, interstellar travel was initially achieved using folded space technology. This allowed journeys that would have taken hundreds of years to be reduced in time by ninety to ninety-five present. Even so, the amount of time required to go between star systems was daunting. Then, entanglement travel was perfected. But entanglement requires a transceiving station at the distant location as well as at the near location.

"So, interstellar travel was via folded space technology for hundreds of years and the expansion of humans past their initial star system was exceedingly slow using space warp engines on the first interstellar vessels. After entanglement transmission was perfected, entanglement stations were sent to distant locations on a folded space flight lasting many decades to a new outpost light-years away. That trip might take anywhere from thirty to one hundred thirty years. However, once that far-off star system was reached, the entanglement station that was sent there would self-activate to become the distant end of a new entanglement path. When fully linked into the rest of the transportation system, it was then possible to instantaneously transmit information, objects and living matter to the new station. Considering the expanse of the galaxy, it was a tedious process to put these entanglement stations in place. But it was worth this thousands of years process because when it was completed transmission between entanglement stations was essentially instantaneous.

"Using this folded space method of placing entanglement stations, humans had expanded to a sphere of space of about five thousand light-years in radius surrounding Earth. Human life, and all that humans brought with them, now extended through the entire local spur of the Orion Arm of the galaxy and into nearby sections of the Sagittarius and Perseus Arms. Along the way, a significant number of the planets and their moons were terraformed. Outposts were established that became thriving parts of a rapidly expanding civilization. However, this was still only a small fraction of the Milky Way galaxy.

"In that region of space, humans never encountered any other life of any kind. Not even a primitive virus. However, humans knew that there was still much to explore and there was great excitement about the adventure. Everyone felt certain that they would find other life in the remaining vastness of what had so far been the sole domain of the human race.

"In the last five hundred years of expansion via folded space technology, development had accelerated on a technically challenging new method of placing entanglement stations at distant locations. The old procedure was analogous to loading a boat with a huge stepping stone and sending it across a vast body of water to drop the stone at the appropriate place so people could take the next giant step without getting wet. By contrast, the new method was like setting up a large slingshot on the near shore and accurately throwing that stepping stone to the proper location. It involved using two existing entanglement nodes to act as the widely spaced arms of the slingshot. A third entanglement node in the middle of those two contained the station that would be thrown to the distant location. This slingshot method had been tested thoroughly within humanity's sphere of habitation. Now, it was time to test it at the fringe of that sphere and throw a new station into unexplored territory."

Malk asked for a drink and a sandwich. He quietly said, "It has been a long time since I've been able to make my own choice of refreshment. It is a nice taste of freedom."

After a bite and a sip he continued. "I've told you all of this just to plant firmly in your mind the environment at that time for the human race. Now I'd like to ask you to pull a telescence scene from the historical archives that helps define the spirit of adventure in that era and the effect of that adventure on the human psyche."

Inara replied, "Anyone without the sensory perceptions that I, and you, have would not have trusted this discussion to start much less continue. But it is clear that what you are telling me is important. Give me the reference code and I will pull what you want from the Galactic History Archives."

From the Galactic Archives

Sean Lee waited for all systems to be ready. He was in a fifteen-person control station at the edge of a star system in the Sagittarius arm of the Milky Way Galaxy, five thousand light-years from Earth. Out of the half-trillion humans in the galaxy, he had been selected to lead the team that would accelerate their expansion across the Milky Way. It was a humbling and heady assignment for which he knew he was fully qualified.

The station computer announced that all technical systems were ready. It was time to check with his teams in the other two locations on either side of him.

"Ali, are you ready?" asked Sean Lee.

Fifteen light-years to one side of Sean Lee, Ali Xang nodded his readiness over the entangled transmission link. "Yes, Sean, everything is ready for our first interstellar, single-ended placement of a new entanglement node at the edge of the human domain."

Sean chuckled to himself about Ali's official-sounding response. Ali clearly knew that more than half of humanity was probably watching.

"Alice, are you ready?" asked Sean Lee.

Alice was about fifteen light-years to the other side of Sean Lee, which put her about thirty light-years from Ali Xang. Alice Perkins responded, "Yes, Sean. All is ready here."

The transport node which was to be thrown outward was at Sean Lee's station midway between Ali and Alice. That station was managed by Vlad Marin, who also responded in his turn that all was ready.

Sean then checked one more time with his local controllers just a couple hundred yards away from his command console. The controllers also assured him all was in readiness.

"In that case we are ready for transport in five, four, three, two, one, transport."

That command gave Sean the privilege of flinging an entanglement transport node ten light-years outside humankind's current region of occupation. This was the first time a piece of equipment of any kind had been sent using entanglement technology beyond the area occupied by Earth's pioneers. It was logical that it would be a transceiving station because the only way to test if the transmission was successful was to be able to go to the distant location to check it out.

Once the transceiving station had been thrown to its destination it was time to test it. Sean turned to the entanglement chamber just a few feet away from him. Inside that room was a one inch square block of aluminum with distinctive etchings on its surface.

"Bill, please send the aluminum block to the new transceiving station."

Bill Reynolds transmitted the block, waited one minute, and then commanded the new station ten light-years away to send the block back. Bill removed the returned block from the pod for examination.

After an hour of detailed examination that over the millennia had become the standard routine, Bill reported, "Sean, there is absolutely no distortion present in the block. We are ready for the next step."

"Thanks, Bill. Please continue."

Bill then placed a remotely controlled observatory with a full set of spectral analysis equipment and imaging systems inside the pod.

Five minutes later, Bill advised, "Sean, the next set of equipment is in place. We are ready here for transmission to the new entanglement node."

"Thanks, Bill. We are transmitting in five, four, three, two, one, transport." After a short pause, Sean reported, "We have confirmation from the distant end that the equipment has arrived. I'm activating the system. We should be receiving video and spectral images in about one minute."

It was an extremely long minute for the teams at the three locations involved in the experiment as well as those at corporate headquarters back on Earth. This process had been tested so many times within their current five thousand light-year sphere of occupation that there was extremely remote doubt of any failure. The new entanglement transceiver was almost guaranteed to work.

However, this method of sending a transceiver to a distant location using entanglement technology itself rather than sending it on a long bent space journey was something that would dramatically accelerate humankind's movement across the galaxy. It had taken eleven thousand years to travel five thousand light-years out from Earth in all directions. Now they could jump ten light-years or more after just a few hours of testing. It was heady, breathtaking stuff and every one of them involved, and all of humanity, understood the implications. The galaxy was now theirs for the taking. In addition, there was the increased opportunity, as well as the adventure, of meeting any alien life they felt sure they would eventually encounter along the way.

Sean alerted the team and the billions who were watching. "The first visual images and spectral analysis are arriving." A short pause. "There is no doubt that the distant transceiving station is in the correct location and is operating properly."

Cheers instantly and simultaneously erupted across one million cubic light-years of space.

He continued. "We will now let systems tests run for about an hour. If those tests are fully successful, we will transport a chimpanzee to the distant entanglement node. I suggest that, as planned, we all take a one hour break and then return to our stations for the next phase."

As the hours went by, all phases of the testing were successful. It was time for the first human to settle onto the pod couch and jump ten light-years across space to an area humans had never visited. The system permitted transmission between any two nodes in the entanglement system. So, theoretically even a person from the corporate headquarters on Earth could have made the leap across a total of five thousand light-years to the new node. And there were corporate executives who greatly wanted to be that person. However, it was finally, and inevitably, decided that the person had to be someone from the experimental teams operating at the edge of civilization.

Sean Lee gathered the team together over an entanglement conference. "As you know it has been decided that one of us from our three entanglement stations will have the honor of taking the first trip out to the new node we have just established. The selection will be made by random computer drawing. The name of the person selected will appear simultaneously on our video systems at each of our stations. I'm executing the selection program now. The person is Carlos Brown."

Carlos was a member of Alice Perkins' team. Cheers for Carlos went up all around, especially at Alice's node. While all others were disappointed at not being chosen, Carlos was one of the best-liked team members. Alice went over to Carlos and gave him a warm hug. "Congratulations, Carlos. I wish it was me, but I'm also happy that you were chosen."

Carlos couldn't stop grinning. They were all experienced entanglement travelers as well as experts on their systems. He had perfect confidence in the technology and in their team.

Carlos made the round trip without incident.

Circumnavigation of the galaxy would now proceed at a much more rapid pace.

Malk Continues His Story

Malk Kring finished the last bit of his drink and sandwich and stood. He walked a few paces from Inara to take in the projected view of the campus buildings and the grounds. He was quiet for a considerable time before he turned to face Inara. "Please excuse my silence. It has been a long time since I've had the freedom to just enjoy beauty."

Inara replied, "You know that I can fully sense what you are feeling. Much more so today than before yesterday when my sensory horizons seemed to expand after being in the presence of The Guide. So, you don't have to apologize. Just take your time."

Malk smiled wryly as he replied, "Time is what I have since I seem to be spread across so much of it. Or, put another way, since it is all compressed to an instant for me depending on what state I am in. Perhaps we will have more opportunity to talk about that. Also, I understand that your senses have only recently been outward and more deeply into the Universal Soul. I know that it is the result of only recently being in the presence of The Guide. I suspect that it is because of what you experienced yesterday that I am here today. It is interesting how it all works.

"Now, let me give you a second catalog number from the same time period. You will learn about the early Pilgrims, about me, and even a bit about yourself."

THOMAS S. IRELAND

Another Archive Story

Pilgrim Kezia Mang and her assistant, Harq, sat in amazed silence as they watched the implementation about five thousand light-years away of the new slingshot method of placing entanglement stations. Finally, she said, "Harg, I sometimes think I should have been a technologist. I'm fascinated by what these people are doing. It seems now that the vast expanse of the entire galaxy will soon be within our grasp."

Harg pulled his attention from the holographic news display in the center of their table and looked intently at Kezia with great seriousness. "You would be intuitive enough to do that work. I'm thinking that all of us might be better served if you simply spent more time with technologists."

"Harg, do you ever lighten up and just enjoy all of this?"

"It's not in my nature. That's why I am so good for you."

With a heartfelt sigh, Kezia responded, "What are you trying to tell me?"

"I'm simply stating what is obvious. The problem you are working on seems to have some relationship with technology. So, you should be spending more time with technologists. They may have some of the answers you are looking for. I know that you are working with them a bit, but you need to focus more of your energy in that area."

Harq concluded, "Now, let's keep getting ready for your meeting. We only have an hour left."

As sometimes happened during conversations with her assistant, Kezia didn't know whether to feel like she had just been lectured or advised. At any rate, Harg was right. They were running out of time before the meeting. She had let activities five thousand light-years away distract her from what was soon to happen in the great hall next to them.

* * *

Kezia felt small as she stood behind the podium facing ten thousand Pilgrims gathered in the Earth-based sanctuary in the European city of Munich on Earth. Various religious services had just ended in the scores of alcoves around the perimeter. Some of the services were led by the heads of religions; some by the other holy attendees. She reflected on how these meetings had changed over the millennia and how unified they had all become while maintaining their distinctions. She loved this assembly of holy people.

"I felt humbled when you asked me at our last meeting to act as your pilgrim guide until the end of this session. Nothing has turned out the way I thought it would when you first gave me this honor and, frankly, this burden.

"I stand in front of you, like many before me, a confused person seeking clarity. In the last three years, I have met with the leaders of all of our religions. As a result, I have recommended to you, with the help of our spiritual council, an agenda for the next two days. Some of it is the tedious burden of administrative details, which I am sure none of us will enjoy. We will get through that agony this morning. This afternoon and tomorrow morning we will discuss spiritual items of mutual interest, most of which have become easier to discuss over the long time we have held these meetings. Because of our long history of differences and periodic conflict, a few of the subjects are still difficult for us. However, if we do our jobs well these items may fall into the easy category for those who follow us in future centuries. Perhaps they will feel the same gratitude to us that many of us feel to those who have worked on these challenges before us.

"We will reserve tomorrow afternoon for the subject that causes most of our confusion. That is 'The Pain' which has afflicted some of us for so long and which we still don't understand."

That day's sessions continued with an extensive agenda covering a wide range of subjects of interest to all who were gathered there. Over the millennia, the various religions represented had grown much closer to each other and developed an increasing degree of mutual respect. There were still some difficult issues to cover but, through these meetings, they were brought into the open and becoming ever closer to resolution.

* * *

The next afternoon, Kezia again faced the group. "I've met with the eighty-three people we know about who suffer the most from various amounts of The Pain. During those meetings, I've traveled across almost all inhabited sections of the galaxy. I've experienced a lot but am not certain what I've learned. My goal today, aside from our normal business, is to tell you what I have seen - and felt.

"I have mixed emotions about being back here on Earth. It is always good to return to the birthplace of all life in this part of the galaxy. What a special place this is! On the other hand, this is where I feel most uncomfortable, and it is where the eighty-three people I've visited sense the most pain. It's interesting to note that they seem to have a tendency to feel The Pain more during entanglement transport. And The Pain seems to be generally greater at the more heavily traveled entanglement nodes. When The Pain is greatest, each of the eighty-three also has a terrible sense of evil -- of foreboding. Like something dreadful is happening. A few have a sense that something catastrophic is going to happen at some undefined point in the future. I have begun to experience more of The Pain myself and a growing confusion about where it comes from. One of the eighty-three, Malk Kring, who is clearly the most perceptive of all of us, is here today. Malk is going to try to explain what he is experiencing in the hope that together we may shed a little more light on what is happening."

* * *

It was Malk Kring's first time on, or even near, Earth and he found it disturbing.

"Thank you, Kezia."

Reaching for a glass of water, Malk said, "I must tell you all that I'm nervous and that is unusual for me." Malk took a small sip of water and a deep breath before continuing. "Many of you know that I'm a synesthete. For those of you who haven't heard that term before it means I have interlinked senses. For example, words have a certain color for me. I have an advantage in spelling because if a word is spelled wrong, then the wrong letter will be the wrong color within the word. Sometimes I feel like I'm cheating because it is virtually impossible for me to misspell a word once I have seen it spelled correctly. Not only will the color not be right, but it won't even taste or smell good."

Malk had said this last with an inflection of humor, and it evoked the response he was looking for. In reply, he said, "Thank you for changing the room from green to a bright yellow with your laughter." That brought surprise and bit more recognition of what Malk was explaining.

Looking around the room, he said, "The orange tinge in the air tells me that you are catching on to what I am saying. You should know that I can also taste and smell the change, perhaps like a snake does. Sometimes numbers appear that represent what I see and what is happening.

"There are even moments when I think I know, in vaguely general terms, what the future brings. Right now, standing here before you, I must confess that the future scares me. I don't know why. At any rate, complete synesthesia of all senses like I have is extremely unusual. I think I may be the only one in the galaxy who also has a touch of precognition.

"That precognition is strange to me. At times, it seems to mix the future with the past and it is even difficult to separate it from the present.

"When I take all of this together I become absolutely certain that good and evil have always been with us. Ancient writings, many of them in our religious books, tell us about a battle between good and evil that happened before the birth of any kind of life on Earth. Some people take that as truth. Others feel that this event is a fiction developed by the earliest writers. I will tell you that I have no doubt that this particular battle has been with us since the beginning of time, will continue into the future, and is happening throughout all of space, even beyond the space we inhabit. My perception is that all time is blended into the present so the ancient writings may be about a battle that happened in the future. Yes, I deliberately blended tenses in that last statement.

"Kezia, you indicated a growing confusion. I am mired in confusion. My human limitations are seemingly trying to grasp something I can sense in many ways but have no framework for understanding.

"The most important thing I have to tell you is something all of you, or perhaps almost all of you, know. There is good and evil in everything in the universe. All is intrinsically good but evil springs into existence spontaneously and sometimes takes root and grows. As I perceive it, in our part of the universe, in our galaxy, its root is here on Earth. It is not easy to recognize because the evil itself is intangible. I told you as I started to speak that I'm nervous. I'm now fearful. I sense evil here on Earth far more than I perceive it anywhere else I have been."

Malk took a deep, calming breath and continued. "There have always been those who feel The Pain of evil, to some extent. Their history is regrettably incomplete. We would know much more about evil today if that history was more detailed and objective. However, we do know that The Pain increased dramatically about the time of humanity's departure from Earth. Other than that, there are too many variables to connect The Pain with anything in particular. And, in the centuries since humankind's expansion into the galaxy, The Pain has changed only an immeasurable amount in intensity. So, correlation with events has become even more difficult.

"What I have to offer on this problem that is new for me is my perception that this planet harbors the nucleus of the evil that creates The Pain. We must find it and destroy it before it destroys our civilization at some point in the future. Or, at least what we all perceive to be the future. Time merges a bit for me for a reason that seems to reach back from the future.

"You might feel that I am delivering a more aggressive message than most, but certainly not all, of the religions gathered in this room might be used to. However, it is the message that I feel compelled to deliver."

The rest of the day was taken up in passionate discussion about Malk's presentation. Any time he was involved in one of these discussions, he insisted to the group he was talking to that they must tell the leaders of their various churches about his message because he knew without any doubt at all that he was right.

* * *

At the end of the day, Malk and Kezia met alone in a quiet room.

"Kezia, there was someone in that room today who is not really one of us. He calls himself a Pilgrim, and he has been part of our organization for a long time. However, everything I sense about him tells me that he is a spy sent to check us out."

"Who is it, Malk?"

"All I can tell you," replied Malk "is that he was on the right side of the room toward the back as we were facing it from the podium. As I worked with the various people in the afternoon I couldn't narrow it down much, but I'll go through my notes tonight and give you a list of people in a couple of days."

In the meantime, I have been asked by the Roman Catholic Pope to visit him tomorrow along with his representative here to let him know what we have learned. He is going to be meeting with a couple of senior Mullahs next week and wants to compare notes with them. I'll keep you posted."

"That's fine, Malk. I'm on my way across several light-years this evening to meet with a couple of other people. We'll talk again in a few days."

"Kezia, I need to tell you that I sensed overwhelming evil from this person I just told you about. I wonder if he has something to do with The Pain."

"You could sense that from across the room?" asked Kezia.

"Yes. And I also sensed a bit more as well. I think I let my focus stay on the area near him for too long. I wonder if I am in danger from him."

Malk Introduces the Next Story

After the archive scene ended, Malk said to Inara, "I'm now going to show you something that is not in the galactic archives. It is from a secret library that can normally only be accessed by about one hundred people in the galaxy It is an event that took place during the meeting I just showed you. Here it is.

"This is Aulika. I have two names for you to pass to the right people. They should both either have accidents or disappear immediately. Their names are Kezia Mang and Malk Kring. I am transmitting a full report with this message."

Malk Kring stopped that short segment and commented, "Inara, it turned out that my fear about being in danger was well founded. I'm going to show you another presentation which will reveal the reason for my concern.

"However, before we get to that I've noticed that you seem to be almost embedded in what I am showing you. I was sure you would find it compelling but I didn't expect to sense that you would be essentially present in the scene."

Inara responded, "I didn't think about it earlier but this might be your first direct personal experience with telescence projection using technology that wasn't this highly developed in the time in which you originated. If you and I were meeting with each other, even though separated by light years, we would be able to interact as if really next to each other. This projection is almost like that. It is tuned to each observer participant so that they are indeed embedded in the scene. I can adjust it so that you have the same sense."

For the first time Malk Kring laughed. "I don't mind watching a projection of myself but I don't want to be beside myself. That is just a bit too much even for someone with the kind of experiences I have had."

"You're going to tell me about some of those experiences, aren't you?" asked Inara.

"I am", responded Malk. "What I am going to show you next comes from an archive that has never been seen outside of an exceedingly closed and evil group. It is that group I just mentioned to you. These are people who are part of five families that gathered together for the first time long before humans left Earth and when horses and wagons were the fastest form of transportation. Spears and arrows were state of the art weapons. Leading members from these five families captured and imprisoned me. That organization still exists today and maintains a full, accurate and objective documentation of their entire history.

"I can get to that archive only because of the state in which my captors have placed me. Please don't ask me to explain that because I can't other than to tell you that it is a result of being statistically scattered across space and time.

"The higher ranking leaders of the five families believed that only they could control where and when I am. They thought after their last session with me that they had killed me. In a sense they did.

"My physical body now appears to be present only when needed. Today is an example. I'm aware that I am spiritually fully one with the Universal Soul and that I am a periodic conduit with you for a purpose I don't yet fully understand. What I do know is that I am supposed to impart knowledge to you.

"Now, I am being compelled for a reason that is good to tell you another piece of the story. It takes place a few thousand years after the last scene I showed you.

"As I mentioned, this information comes from an archive that is not available to you because it is not part of the public historical record. It is instead from the extremely accurate, private history of an immensely evil and powerful group that call themselves the Five Families. They have believed from the start of their existence that they could only be successful if they learned from their mistakes as well as their achievements. So, they have always used the best technology available throughout their history to record all they do with great thoroughness. Their detailed accounts are devoid of the normal bias recorded by winners. These are fully objective archives.

"Because of my quantized time and space state I can access all of their libraries. This is important information for you to see for two reasons. You need to know how terribly evil these people are and how devoid they are of any conscience at all. Some of this is very disturbing to see. You also need to know how my role in all of this began.

"I sense that I am being drawn away from you now but you will still be able to view this information."

Malk's Prison

Family Historical Reference Code: Ps^95Dz%E9%d

Yin Xang had the current privilege of being the chairman of the "Committee of Twenty-Five" which was the top planning organization of the Five Families. They were meeting in one of their floating enclaves about fifty thousand feet above Earth's Mediterranean Sea just south of the boot of Italy. The room they were in was totally transparent and hanging tethered to the main body of the enclave. As always, rigorous security was in place. Everyone in the room could clearly look out, but no one could peer inside. All the furniture was transparent almost to the point of being invisible except for the comfortable chairs they were sitting in. Those, as had been traditional since their first meetings in North Africa, were made of the finest soft leather. The effect was magnificent. It was as if each of them and their chairs were floating without visible support high in the air.

The weather was perfectly clear, as they had arranged. Each could see almost the entire extent of the Mediterranean. The turquoise water along the southern Turkish coast was especially beautiful.

The meeting started in the traditional manner. Today, there were five randomly selected "guests". Each was caged in an individual air lock spaced around the edge of the conference room. Until ten minutes earlier, the air locks had been heated to the same temperature as the room. They were soundproof so the frantic screams of the people inside couldn't be heard but their agony was fully visible. At the moment, three of them were pounding on the walls. Their faces were contorted in fear of what was going to happen next. Two were seated and rocking while they cried. All were naked for the amusement of the Twenty-Five and also to make sure they had nothing available with which to kill themselves.

Yin Xang walked over to the chamber farthest from him and smiled at the screaming man inside. By now, the temperature had been lowered to twenty degrees above zero Fahrenheit, and the man was shivering uncontrollably. Yin Xang brought the chamber back up to room temperature for one minute and then hit the decompression button. Soon the man was gasping for breath and once again freezing. At the point where the man was almost dead Yin Xang opened the floor of the chamber, and the man fell about five thousand feet before being totally incinerated without a trace by an invisible energy beam. By this time all four of the remaining guests were screaming. Yin Xang went to each one and repeated the same sequence.

He then returned to the head of the table, faced the other twenty-four and said with unbridled joy, "It is indeed thrilling to have this kind of power." There was a standing ovation.

Yin Xang then started the business part of the meeting.

"If there is a concern at this time, it is about the general malaise that has fallen over everyone everywhere. While we are probably about one thousand years from sending humans to all parts of the galaxy, it is clear from our probes and observations that there is no other life in the Milky Way. That is great news for our families. Our concern since leaving Earth has been that we might encounter alien life that would upset our long-term plans. That is something we don't have to worry about any more.

"On the other hand, the vast majority of the galactic population continues to suffer from a depression that varies from mild to profound. Almost all humans are experiencing a disappointment that other life has not been found. It is expressed as a loneliness in a vast expanse that is unshared. That is a situation that our family ancestors of long ago didn't anticipate in the plan. The result for us has been a slowdown in productivity. However, given the extent of our riches and power, that slowdown is only a minor inconvenience.

"Another general result of this loneliness has been a gradual and steady increase in religious fervor. A new closeness has developed between humans and what they believe in as a God. This closeness is such that the most popular manifestations are a belief that their God permeates everything, and each person is, in essence, one with their God because their God made them especially to be part of Him. They have centered around the

Pilgrims who continue to be a small but growing sect of peaceful people.

"Their major focus has been on shared basic beliefs with an undulating undercurrent of trying to understand what they describe as a permeating pain felt by small numbers of their sect. They are increasingly drawn to concentrating on what they see as great commonality in ancient religious teachings such as "the body of Christ", Indra's net, and Huayan interconnectedness. This oneness with the universe seems to be helping these people be less depressed than the rest of the population. This is of some financial benefit to us. It seems reasonable to not interfere with them but to watch their actions.

"There may be a concern for us about this thing they call "The Pain". The Pilgrims seem to connect it with a manifestation of evil, and a few of them react to this pain strongly. It may be nothing, but a few members of our families, including some of our Patriarchs, wonder if it may be a cause for concern of some type. It is always important to be cautious and suspicious. As you already know, we will be joined by a Pilgrim guest later in our meeting. We will explore this subject with him.

"While this galactic depression has generally slowed activity for most it has also provided the opportunity over a long period to reexamine the structure of our corporate state. Horace Baker will present his summary of a minor restructuring and outline the distribution plan for our new major product, gene regeneration."

* * *

Horace began, "I stand before you as a man of great privilege in every way someone can imagine except for immortality. An interesting benefit of being chairman of infrastructure for the galaxy's ruling families is the opportunity to test new technologies. I am one of the first in the galaxy to be the successful recipient of gene regeneration. I guess I need to stress the word successful. I took a bit of a risk and there were many failures. However, I was young and stupid and willing to take the risk. I'm glad I did because the process has worked for me. I had my first regeneration about three hundred thirty years ago. At that time, I was one hundred fifty-seven years old. Gene regeneration was applied to only a few select members of the family. Almost all of them are still alive, including some of you in this meeting. There were also a few regretful failures. I received regeneration again one hundred seventy years later. I am now about one hundred fifty years into this second regeneration and still have the physical and mental energy of a young man. In addition, I have the personal knowledge and experience of three long lifetimes. I'm one of the twenty oldest people in the galaxy.

"The experiment has been viewed as safe for quite a while now. Regeneration is available to the entire inner circle of the five families and has been a well-guarded secret. That secrecy is ending.

"Regeneration is being announced within the next few days as a product of one of our closely held corporate-states and will be released to the general population. Naturally, there will initially be a hefty charge. It is planned that several other corporate states will soon "invent" their own competing regeneration product and everyone will have a choice of whom to buy it from. Our families will increase our fortune and power through control of this 'competitive product'. Eventually, gene regeneration will be an earned privilege. Those who perform well in life will have their genes regenerated and earn bonus lives. It looks like the limits of this technology, for reasons we don't fully understand are about four bonus lives giving a maximum life expectancy of about one thousand years.

"I'm enthusiastic for the future but won't be around long enough to see much more than about another one hundred years. As has always been true for our families we have a plan that will take us far beyond my lifetime.

"There are two major elements to that plan.

"One is a change in our organizational structure that will put us at the invisible head of what will become a much more integrated and formalized organizational galactic business structure. We will still permit, and promote, some competition and inventiveness on small entrepreneurial scales. At the same time we will develop a closer integration among our ten already tightly controlled corporations into a single, extremely efficient organization that will be in charge of virtually all commercial activities.

"The members of this single large corporation will be collectively known as the "Controllers". So, instead of there being many corporations working cooperatively behind the scenes and controlled by various members of our five families there will be one corporation with what we are terming Secretariats in charge of various operational elements. The Secretaries-General in charge of these elements will believe that they are at the head of their part of the enterprise. In truth, they will rise to these positions only because of our invisible manipulations in combination, of course, with their considerable talents.

"They will not know that our five families exist. Those visible to the Secretaries-General at the distant fringes of our families will be perceived as extremely intelligent with a background dossier of old money. They will provide advice and guidance and subtle control, and the partial truth will help to avoid any questions. Anyone who breaks through this cover at our distant fringe will be dealt with quickly, but subtly, in the usual manner that has always proven effective. Horrible accidents do happen in this galaxy that still has hidden dangers.

"The other major element of our plan is for the Controllers to give formal recognition to the religious fervor of the Pilgrims. Now, as we have all discussed, the purpose of this is definitely not to lend credence to their superstitions or their belief in what they call the Universal Soul. However, the population gains a positive emotional benefit from their beliefs, and it does us no harm. We intend to make it look like the Controllers are a major, but distant and relatively quiet, supporter of the Pilgrims.

"In addition, the Pilgrims have done something interesting that could be of great value to us at some future time. They have developed a technical research arm which is totally focused on studying the basic structure of the universe and its integration with the soul which they insist exists and pervades everything. Perhaps their pure research which has not delivered, and is not intended to deliver, commercial result or product can be of use to us as we continue to delve ever more deeply into the nature of things for our financial benefit. Getting this research for free will improve our profitability."

* * *

Yin Xang resumed control of the meeting.

"Naturally, we are keeping a close eye on the Pilgrims, and we have people who have penetrated their organization. Some of these people are long duration spies, essentially what amounts to deep agents. Others come and go. One of our deep agents, named Aulika, was in a meeting where she heard a presentation by a religious person named Malk Kring, a monk who is almost a total synesthete. Through some of our surveillance systems, our agent learned that this person could discern hints of our existence and that there was someone in the room whom Malk Kring felt was dangerous to them. Malk Kring told the meeting leader, Kezia Mang, about the presence of a deep agent.

Yin Xang then commanded, "Have Mr. Kring join the conference."

A transparent room containing Malk descended from the invisible ceiling to one side of the meeting. The area in which Malk was imprisoned contained a bed, desk and toilet facilities as well as a guard armed with a weapon designed to incapacitate but not kill. A guard was present with Malk all the time, and they rotated their duty every hour so that they would be fully alert.

"Mr. Kring has had the opportunity to see and hear all of our proceedings today. You can see that he is more than a bit agitated."

Malk screamed in apparent anger and frustration but couldn't be heard through the one-way sound barrier.

Yin Xang continued, "Yes, I know that Mr. Kring was only recently placed on our agenda for today. The opportunity to meet him came up only in the last few hours. The Patriarch's thought it important that he be brought before this group for our education because he is so unique.

"With the agreement of the Patriarchs, Mr. Kring will be kept alive for our amusement and entertainment far beyond what has become our normal life span using a new technique we are being briefed on today by Fritz Barnhardt. It is also helpful for you to know that Kezia Mang, whom you received some information about, was killed during entanglement transfer to a distant star system. We will discuss Mr. Kring at greater length later in our meeting.

"Now it is time to hear from Fritz.

* * *

"Fritz Barnhardt, chairman of technology, nodded to Yin Xang and began.

"At three hundred thirteen years old I feel like a youngster compared to you, Horace. Thank you for setting the stage so well for my summary. My teams continue to delve into the details of the structure of the universe and life. Our work on the composition of the universe has become more tedious.

"For example, I will candidly tell you that we still do not understand, any more than Marianne Schmidt did, the reason for the ancient Schmidt constant which in its early days was showing slow change.

"To refresh your memories Dr. Schmidt included this constant in her equations when she developed the initial mathematical solutions for entanglement as a tool for communication and travel. At that time the "constant" was really a variable that changed over time as entanglement was developed and used in its earliest years. As time went on, the constant stabilized and has now settled into the same characteristics as the rest of the universal constants. We continue to examine it, but I must report no progress in understanding the reason for what is clearly a "fudge factor" since it was discovered so long ago on Earth's moon. Someday, it will become clear to us.

"The good news is that our research has enabled us to build much faster computers on a wide variety of structures. Through sub-quantum computing, we have arrived at the point where we can now integrate all computers across the galaxy into the same telecyber network. This has enabled us to make our information and matter transport systems much more efficient thus improving our control and profitability. We are using this fully integrated processing power, and our knowledge, to transform planets across the galaxy quickly into habitats totally suitable to Earth-originated life forms.

"We are also making great progress on gene regeneration. Standard non-regenerated lifetime is now two hundred to two hundred fifty years with all of that spent in perfect health. We know how to regenerate genes twice to permit a total lifetime of six hundred or more years. Even with our new amazing processing power, work on gene regeneration is proceeding at a measured pace and seems to have an eventual limit.

"As we dig ever more deeply into various technologies we keep running into the Schmidt constant, or relatives of the Schmidt constant. You all already know the background on this and have heard Horace's endorsement. The Schmidt constant also creeps into gene regeneration and seems to define a wall past which we can't go and, which also makes our work more complicated the more regeneration we do. Our projection is that within the next two thousand years we will be able to regenerate genes four times to create a total life expectancy of one thousand to one thousand two hundred fifty years. For the foreseeable future, immortality will elude us.

"Another technology we are working on is the human stasis field. This is in the earliest stages, but development is beginning to come along nicely after a series of failures with our human test subjects. The stasis field allows us to put people in what you might think of as suspended animation. This is not a chemical or hibernation type of suspended animation. Instead, it is an application of what can best be described as self-entanglement. Rather than using entanglement to send a person across the galaxy, we use it to capture the exact state of every subatomic particle in their bodies and replicate that state across time instead of across space. In effect, it is a form of time travel but only into the future. When perfected, it will permit those of us who wish to do so to push our lives into the future without aging."

* * *

The floor returned to the meeting chairman.

"Thus the course is set for the future. The only thing remaining to be addressed is the prospect of alien life. We occupy most of the galaxy, and we can so closely observe all remaining regions that it is nearly certain that there is no other life of any kind in the Milky Way beyond that which originated on Earth. This discovery of other life is now so improbable as to be almost beyond comprehension. However, the search continues. We are now focusing much of our effort outside of our galaxy at the Canis Major Dwarf Galaxy, the Sagittarius Dwarf Spheroidal, the Large Magellanic Cloud and the Small Magellanic Cloud. The priorities are in order of their closeness to us. So far, we have discovered nothing.

"With our single ended technology, we should be able to throw an entanglement node as far as the Canis Major Dwarf Galaxy and the Sagittarius Dwarf Spheroidal Galaxy. However, the characteristic of space-time between our Milky Way and our neighbors seems to be such that we have been unable to make a successful throw. We will keep working on it.

"Because this is such a concern for us, a special department has been established called the extra-galactic exploration team. This team has two purposes. The first and most important is somewhat defensive in nature: keep looking for alien life. The second supports the economics of expansion and simply involves exploration for resources and new places to live as we sell our products to a growing population.

"Ruqayah Nkruma is leading this team and will now quickly brief us on what she and her team are learning. Ruqayah, you have the floor."

* * *

As Ruqayah began the presentation, she used the transparency of the room to great effect. She pressed a spot on the inside of her left wrist, and a vast image of the Milky Way appeared over their heads extending from the front to the back of the room and past the transparent walls into the cold air outside.

"Thank you," began Ruqayah. "This is an extremely short briefing. You are all familiar with the map of the Milky Way. At the edge of the galactic disk is our primary target for exploration; the Canis Major Dwarf Galaxy. It really isn't that far away and pieces of it, as you know, have been absorbed over the last few billion years by our galaxy. We have explored some of the debris from that encounter and have found nothing unusual about it. What is strange is that as we attempt to fling transport nodes toward the main part and closely associated streamers of Canis Major Dwarf Galaxy, our systems act like they hit a wall. Most interesting is that we have been unable to catapult entanglement nodes, or any other equipment, more than about fifteen to twenty light-years beyond the Milky Way in any direction we have tried. In the direction of Canis Major Dwarf, we can't go beyond about three light-years. We don't know why but we are still doing research and exploring."

* * *

Yin Xang announced, "Now we bring our attention back to Mr. Kring."

The guard inside the transparent prison sprayed a calming mist over Malk.

"I should tell you all that the drug that Mr. Kring was just given leaves him calm but fully alert mentally. He has heard everything we have said, and he can now participate in our meeting.

"Malk, in your Pilgrim meetings you describe what you call The Pain. You also talk about experiencing great evil in the galaxy. We have let you know about our families. What do you think this pain and evil are?"

Malk turned in his prison holding his hands out as if feeling the room. He took time to sniff the air while looking from person to person.

Impatiently Xang pressed, "Come, Malk, don't hesitate or try to lie to us."

In clear anguish, Malk groaned, "You killed Kezia Mang."

"Yes, and you must stop avoiding my questions," commanded Yin.

Sweating, trembling and with clenched fists, Malk strained to ask, "What about my family?"

Surprised at Malk's tolerance to the drug and at his emotional strength, Yin replied, "They will continue their lives, and you will never see them again. They will not know what happened to you. Now, you must answer my questions, and you must not lie to me."

Malk was silent and Yin Xang was patient.

Malk finally quietly said, "You and I know that the drugs you have given me make it impossible for me to lie to you. Everything I will tell you is the truth."

"Then out with it. What is the evil that you sense? What is this thing you call The Pain?"

"That is two different questions" replied Malk. "Evil is something that has always been with us. The Pain that some of us feel is new, and we don't know what causes it."

"So, we don't need to fear this evil?" asked Yin."

"We all need to fear evil and fight it."

"Then tell me what it is."

"Various people say it is different things. Some see it as a real demon. For others, it is a spiritual demon. Many see it as just the cumulative result of bad intentions. I personally don't know."

"You aren't much help."

"You know that I am compelled by your drugs to help you if I could. I really wish I knew the answer."

Yin pressed on. "As we spread out across the galaxy, we are surprised that we haven't encountered alien life yet. Is that undiscovered alien life the evil you describe?"

Malk paused for a long time looking around him at things the others couldn't see; feeling, hearing and smelling things that didn't exist for anyone else. Finally, he said, "Perhaps. I just don't understand and don't know. The only thing I can tell you for sure is that the evil and The Pain are connected, and you should fear them."

"Do the Pilgrims fear them?"

"Yes."

"Do we need to fear the Pilgrims?"

Another pause. "No, the Pilgrims could actually be your salvation from The Pain."

"But we don't feel The Pain."

"Someday you will."

In exasperation, Yin concluded, "Then we will make sure you are there to feel it with us. You heard our discussion about our new technology called stasis. We are going to put you into stasis and wake you when we need you again. Good bye, Mr. Kring."

The transparent prison that held Malk returned to the ceiling.

Yin Xang then took center stage and again projected above and around them the image of the Milky Way that Ruqayah had used.

"When humans first left Earth our ancestors conceived and executed a plan to replace geographically based governments with corporate governments. This was a genius idea that continues to serve us well. A borderless planet allowed the corporations we control through a variety of threads to manipulate the populace in any way we wished. Wars that we started and finished at will were fought without traditional boundaries. They morphed physically and philosophically giving us great ability through the media we owned and controlled to spread our "truth" about the reasons for these conflicts. Loyalty was, and still is, to the corporation. Loyalties follow money.

"We set the stage for this new perspective by subtly, gradually and deviously changing the attitudes about a small but influential group of the population about the sanctity of life. This group, over time and with our help, came to be regarded as the elites of society. With no lack of hubris at all they became convinced that they were a privileged class and progressive thinkers. We used one of our fringe members, Peggy Ranger, to introduce our ideas to these people, as well as the general public, about population control, euthanasia, and abortion. At our direction, Peggy's doctrines were focused on what she defined as eliminating the undesirables in our society; low producers and what she described as inferior groups. Once the ball was rolling, primarily through the universities, we disguised her initial message by moderating its intensity and letting it morph into a new background of ethics. Over a few decades we achieved our goal and many of the human race were willing to accept this new position on the value of human life. It became their perception that it was to their benefit to do so even though it was detrimental to so many others. Loyalties follow self-serving power.

"All of this has made it much easier for us to steer the direction of society.

"That plan remains in place. And now we know the galaxy is ours to control without interference from alien life. We can build on this plan with a structure that takes full advantage of how society and technology have evolved under our geographically borderless rule.

"We are now ready to execute the next stage of this plan as it has been developed over the last hundred years or so.

"We will now complete the establishment of three large organizations in the galaxy which, unknown to them, will obviously be under our discreet and direct control. Each of these organization headquarters are being set up in their own star system. They will be spaced one-third of the way around the galaxy from each other. Each will be close enough to the center of the galaxy to see the beautiful and awesomely impressive effects of the massive black hole that is the engine of the Milky Way.

"One organization is the galactic government. Of course, it will continue to have governing power in name only since corporations and the puppet media have the real power. It will essentially be an infrastructure organization responsible for care and feeding of the galactic population. Police will still rest with corporations, all of which are under our extremely discrete control through a wide variety of mechanisms.

"The second organization is one we are now creating and will be called The Controllers. They will be an extension of, and the umbrella agency for, the technologists who develop and manage the entanglement technology that has become the backbone of our civilization. Entanglement will continue to be the conduit through which we pipe energy across the Milky Way, transport goods and people at will through any two points we wish, and communication between distant locations. The Controllers will be the most elite corporation in the galaxy with the strongest police force. The best technologists will be employed by them. As their reputation builds they will be revered by all as the greatest and most reliable corporation in the galaxy.

"We will enhance this reverence by providing them with a truly massive and magnificent edifice which will be called The Cathedral. This will be their central point of governance.

"The final group is The Pilgrims. I know we have had a lot of contentious discussion about this. However, the Patriarchs of our Families, after much deliberation have decided that The Pilgrims can be a great tool for us by providing a perspective about the universe that is much different from ours. Additionally, we have learned over many centuries that suppressing religion is a fruitless, self-defeating endeavor. Let them have their beliefs. It will save us a lot of grief. Their leader, whom they call The Guide, will be located in their star system in a structure of interconnected spheres called The Guide's Hall.

"The galaxy is ours. We now know that we don't have to share it with any life other than that which originated on Earth.

"Assuming there is no further discussion this meeting is over."

End of Archive Ps^95Dz%E9%d.

***

With
the departure of Malk Kring, Inara had a thousand questions but no one there to ask. However, she had a lengthy discussion with Pren Bodhi the next time she saw him.

Inara's Quest

It was eight years later when something happened that sent Pren on a quest to find some way to have Inara meet The Guide.

Without any announcement, Inara established a telescence link with Pren. The room on her nearby planet merged with Dr. Bodhi's. An unusually distraught Inara rushed toward her uncle and held him in a strong embrace. Her words rushed out. "Uncle Pren, I don't feel well. Please come visit me right away. I need you."

"Of course. I'm on my way, Inara."

Some requests don't need any question or discussion. Just immediate response. Pren signed off and quickly left his office.

Dr. Bodhi ordered his home to pack some bags for a few days journey and took the transport pod at the end of his building to the spaceport just ten miles away.

It took only a day for Pren to reach Inara's adjacent planet. He immediately went to her home. Inara grabbed him in a long hug as soon as they met. She looked stressed, but in better control than she had shown the previous day. After a moment she said, "Thank you for coming, Pren. We need to talk." As was their custom she asked, "Can we take a walk?"

Inara was uncharacteristically quiet until they arrived at the path close to the lake near their favorite bonsai tree. Suddenly tears welled up in her eyes, and she grabbed Pren's arm as they walked. He just looked at her waiting to hear what was wrong.

"Remember when we went to the lecture by The Guide?"

Pren nodded.

"I had never felt such goodness." Inara paused catching her composure.

She continued, "I went to another lecture yesterday by a different visitor. I have never before felt such evil and horrible danger as emanated from him."

They were now sitting beside each other on the grass far from anyone else. The ducks were landing in perfect formations on the lake. It was one of those days that felt like a gift. Inara was in such emotional pain that she received no pleasure from any of it. Her senses were still overloaded by the horror she had experienced.

"What happened, Inara? Are you in danger?"

"No, I don't think I'm in danger. However, yesterday morning I felt an evil approaching our planet. That was the only time I've had that experience. What I finally understood is that the evil was in a man who had arrived at our star's entanglement node and then came to Andromeda University to meet some of the senior staff and be given a tour. Thinking back, I know now that the feeling of evil grew stronger as his spacepod moved from the entanglement node to land on our planet. The feeling was accompanied by a horrible smell and ever increasing pain. The numbers in the air became twisted at and above the spaceport and an ugly brown streak blazed through the soul along the path of his ship. I had never seen anything like it before."

She squeezed Pren's hand while staring absently across the lake for a few minutes. She still felt residual pain inside. Empty. She wanted to throw up.

"Uncle, Pren, I had to know what the source of all of this was."

Pren feared for what might be coming next.

"So, I went in the direction the feeling was coming from. I was afraid to get closer to the evil but knew it was important for me to understand what my senses were telling me. I was being drawn to the central square of the campus where I knew a presentation was being made that day. There are always visitors giving presentations, and I hadn't paid much attention previously to what it was. As I got closer there were a number of students and faculty going in the same direction. I overheard conversations about a visit from a rich benefactor and a gift he was giving to the university. As I reached the square, he was standing with the chancellor.

"I couldn't believe what I saw. The Universal Soul stopped at his skin. It didn't enter him at all. I could barely make out his face because everything about him was twisted. He was pure evil. I felt like I was going to pass out but somehow found the strength to sit casually on a nearby ledge and act like I was just one of the viewers. As I watched, I saw almost invisible threads coming out of him streaming in many different directions. I think the threads were linking him to other sources of evil." She paused, then said reflectively, "There are others like him. No one can see what they are except me."

Pren's question was urgent. "Did he see you or notice you in any way?"

"No, it was just the opposite of what it was like with The Guide who knew I was there. This man was cautious, but fearless and self-centered. I was at the edge of the square far from him. He didn't have a clue about my existence. I would have known."

Pren trusted Inara's senses completely even though he didn't even come close to understanding her full capabilities. If she said this evil person didn't know about her or what she perceived about him, Pren knew it was so. Above all, he didn't want anyone who was evil to know about Inara. Even good people periodically do bad things to hurt others. He didn't want to take any chances with anyone as evil as Inara had just described.

In that moment, he determined to follow through on an idea he had thought of eight years ago after Inara's experiences with The Guide and Malk Kring. It was time for a solo entanglement trip to visit an old friend who was an executive priest in the Pilgrims and had his offices in The Guide's Hall.

The Guide's Hall

Dr. Pren Bodhi and his friend, Innes Nold, listened in respect as The Guide, Takar Cillian, finished his Mantra.

"We believe that all physical life in the galaxy is sacred because it is the fruit of the First Seed from the original planet. All living and non-living things in the galaxy are permeated with one soul while being distinct in their existence. There is one soul and one original seed of life for our entire galaxy. We have learned that in all of our galaxy there was no life except on Earth. With this knowledge comes the obligation to protect and prolong each life because of its uniqueness and the uniqueness of the origin of all life. We will treat all things, living and non-living, with respect because they are all part of the one Universal Soul."

When The Guide finished, Pren Body turned to his friend to say, "And that, Innes, reflects what I came to talk about. However, I am bound to keep a confidence that I can reveal only to Guide Takar Cillian himself."

"That, Pren, is an almost impossible task. Do you know how many people each day would like to have a personal meeting with The Guide? It numbers in the thousands, and on a good day he will see three for about ten minutes each. What you are asking just can't be done."

"Innes, I must insist. And I really think The Guide will agree to this meeting."

"You seem almost impossibly sure of yourself. It's not like you to push like this."

"I'm sorry, my friend. I'm not doing this for me. And I can't tell you anything more except for this. I think if you have The Guide's assistant, Malin Nowl, say to the Guide 'A young blond woman you noticed across the lecture square at Andromeda University eight years ago urgently needs to meet with you. It is a matter of the soul', then he will agree. It is a message that is only ten seconds long. Every instinct I have tells me that it will have an eternal impact."

"Pren," Innes sighed, "I'll give your message to Malin tomorrow, but I won't promise anything. In the meantime, let's go have some dinner. You look tired, and I suspect that you're hungry."

* * *

Innes provided Dr. Bodhi an office in the visitors' section of The Guide's Hall which is where Pren went right after breakfast the next morning. Pren had to admit that the Pilgrim Inquirers, the research and technology arm of the Pilgrims organization, treated their visitors extremely well. It was more than comfortable, and he was able to get much done.

After a couple of hours of work, Pren decided to take a walk to the observation platform. He was almost there when the wall whispered, "Dr. Bodhi, please go immediately to The Guide's office. The purple cat that has just materialized to your left will guide you there."

Pren was more than surprised, while at the same time amused, that the technologists in this place would be so whimsical as to make a computer generated purple cat his guide. He was even more impressed when the cat rubbed up against his leg and purred before running down the hall then looking back and crooking its tail in the "come here" sign most people make with their index finger. Apparently some junior Pilgrim technologist was having a good time today.

It was good that he had an escort. The path to Takar Cillian's office was complex in the extreme.

* * *

Malin Nowl met Pren at the entrance to The Guide's office suite.

"Welcome, Dr. Bodhi. The Guide wants you to know how pleased he is to meet you. He told me immediately after the event about seeing your niece and you in that crowd at Andromeda."

Pren was taken aback. "Dr. Nowl, you can't be serious!"

Malin chuckled at the reaction, "Very much so, sir. The Guide has described it to me as being one of the most unusual experiences of his life. He is anxious to meet you, and hopefully one day meet your niece. You should also know that he has never talked about that experience to anyone else and has barred me from doing so as well. He has no idea why he feels that this discretion is important, except that it feels tied to the health of the Universal Soul."

All this time they were walking across Dr. Nowl's office to the opposite wall. As they approached the wall a portion of it melted into an archway past which The Guide, Takar Cillian, was waiting. Beyond The Guide was the open expanse of the galaxy.

Dr. Nowl did the unnecessary introductions. "Your Guide, please allow me to introduce Dr. Pren Bodhi who has requested an audience with you. Dr. Bodhi, please greet His Guide, Takar Cillian." Malin Nowl immediately bowed and left.

"Dr. Bodhi, thank you so much. It is good to talk to you. You, and especially, of course, your niece, have been in my thoughts almost daily for years."

Pren automatically took the offered hand and shook it. He managed to blurt out, "Thank you, Guide, for this honor. Frankly, I'm stunned and hardly know how to respond."

"Doctor, I have a feeling that the honor may be mine. I still feel the effects of that day. I hope you understand that it was for me a profoundly spiritual experience that I cannot even begin to explain. At the same time, I have this overwhelming need to keep the event secret. I have always known that it was something I should not talk about unless I was approached by you or your niece. Now, please sit down and tell me why you finally decided we should talk."

Pren looked around the room at the new and ancient collection of religious artifacts from not only the Pilgrims, but also of the pre-Pilgrim religions and those that still co-existed with the Pilgrims. "Guide, I am trusting you with Inara's life that her parents and I have worked so hard to keep normal. I hope that you will keep between us what I have to tell you today."

"You have my word. I hope that my silence over the last eight years will help you to believe that. At the same time, since Malin knows about this as well, and since I trust him with everything, I would ask that he be included in our discussion. Is that alright with you?"

"Only if Dr. Nowl swears to be as silent on the subject as you."

At that point The Guide said to the room, "Have Malin join us."

Pren and The Guide talked about the artifacts in the room while waiting less than a minute for Malin to join them.

As soon as Malin took his seat, he said to The Guide, "I have taken the liberty of cancelling all of your appointments for the next three hours. I thought that was appropriate considering your reaction to Dr. Bodhi wanting to meet with you and your behavior after returning from your Andromeda University lecture."

The Guide's face broke into a large smile as he said to Dr. Bodhi, "Now you know who really runs things around here. I'm just happy Malin keeps me around."

Pren Bodhi then began to brief both men on Inara's life, her special gift of interlinked senses, her genius and her love for, and sensitivity to, the Universal Soul. Their discussion ended up taking them through lunch and half the afternoon. All other appointments for the rest of the day had to be cancelled as The Guide and Malin Nowl became totally entranced by the story of Inara. By the time they were half way through their discussion, the three men were on a much more personal basis calling each other by their familiar names.

"So you believe, given Inara's perception of this man who was at Andromeda University recently, that there is a relationship between her reaction to him and her trips through the entanglement nodes," observed Guide Takar Cillian.

Pren responded, "Inara believes that's true. I have to take her statement as fact because of her extraordinary perceptions. She feels the soul being hurt, even damaged, during entanglement trips. In the case of this visitor, Inara feels that he has violated the soul so badly so many times that he is essentially excluded from the soul. The soul is the link between the two experiences. Furthermore, she sensed that there are more like him, and that the brown threads coming from him and leading to great distances represent linkages between him and other evil people."

The Guide exclaimed, "Pren, this is beyond extraordinary. I expected to hear a story today about an exceptionally perceptive and holy woman. Never in my wildest dreams did I imagine what you are describing. No wonder you have kept her genius and talents a secret."

Pren elaborated, "She was taught from an early age to enjoy her sensory gift, but to hide it from others because they might find her weird or make her an object of ridicule. However, she, and we, have never hidden her genius, and she excels at everything she does. Of course, it doesn't hurt that she has a lot more tools to use than we have. For her, five times seven is solved through color, smell and feel as much as anything else. It is crazy and interesting."

Malin chimed in, "And you think that this man who Inara describes as evil doesn't know her perception of him?"

"Inara is certain of that. Remember, Takar, when you perceived Inara in the large room of over a thousand faculty and students? Inara calls that a connection through the soul. By the way, that is the only one she has ever had. She has always felt that the connection between the two of you had a purpose which someday would be realized. That perception was not available to the recent visitor to Andromeda University because he is outside of the soul. Inara could see the brown haze and the distorted numbers surrounding him and smell his putrid scent from a distance. But he sensed nothing in return."

"Pren, it is perhaps time to realize the purpose of that connection between Inara and myself," Takar observed. "Do you think she would come here to work at this Hall? Here we can give her greater protection and she can work on any project that she believes best serves the Universal Soul and humanity. She can be on Malin's direct staff and she would work on projects that he will oversee."

"It might be the only thing that could persuade her to take another entanglement trip," enthused Pren.

"Well, Pren, if the Universal Soul is all we profess it to be, and if she is as connected to it as she seems to be perhaps we can help her along the way."

After the meeting was over, Pren Bodhi immediately returned to the star around which Andromeda University and his medical center revolved.

* * *

With massive trepidation combined with great happiness, Pilgrim priest Inara Eyers readily agreed to take a promotion to join the Pilgrim Inquisitor team at The Guide's Hall. At the same time, Dr. Pren Bodhi was offered a senior research position on the Guide's Hall medical staff.

Inara's parents went to Andromeda University to spend a week with her, wandering the grounds and having dinner with people who had become Inara's friends over the decades. Almost all of her friends were Pilgrim priests who recognized her genius, greatly enjoyed her company and were genuinely happy for her. Pren Bodhi joined them all the day before Inara's departure. Inara had decided to spend a month on vacation at her parent's jungle home before going to The Guide's Hall.

At breakfast the next morning, they discussed the special prayers that were being said for Inara that day by millions of Pilgrim priests all across the galaxy. The Guide had announced that he needed help in the form of a meditation for the well-being of the Universal Soul. While the reason for the meditation was accurate in general terms, no one knew the specific reason except Pren, Takar, Malin and Inara's family.

An hour before Inara and her parents stepped into the entanglement node the mediations began, and they continued for three hours after her arrival at her parent's home star. It seemed to work. To the surprise of Inara and her family, she felt some pain and nausea during the entanglement transition, but nothing more.

Inara turned to her parents and Pren at the end of the entanglement journey while walking to the local shuttle. "I don't feel well but I also understand that I'm being protected. It is strange. At the same time, I can sense in every way possible that this transport node is sick in only a vaguely technical way. Perhaps no one would find a system problem if they were to examine it. However, things here are worse than before. And the things that are wrong push farther into the surrounding space than previously. I'm worried for the future."

* * *

Pren stayed with Inara and her family for a couple of hours at the entanglement terminal. Then he went on to his new position at The Guide's Hall and to help with the preparations for Inara's new assignment. Inara and her parents took the short shuttle ride to their home planet.

Soon after he arrived at The Guide's Hall, Pren had a short meeting with The Guide and Malin. They sat together in The Guide's study. A large window took the place of the wall opposite Malin's adjoining office. A view of a dual star sunrise could be seen through the window with a herd of deer on a rise of ground just next to a forest. Birds could be heard encouraging the suns to rise and the deer to come into the field. The three men were eating a light meal as they talked.

After pleasantries, Pren finally launched into the subject that had him so concerned.

"Gentlemen, shortly after we arrived at the transport node near Inara's home planet she expressed great concern about a sickness surrounding that node. She felt that perhaps no one would find a technical problem if they looked for it. She went on to say that there was something wrong with space around that node, and that she was worried about the future."

Malin observed, "We know that Inara suffers greatly both mentally and physically during entanglement travel. Perhaps she was just having an emotional response to that suffering."

"No, Malin, the prayers offered by all of you must have had a profoundly positive effect on her. While she had some discomfort it was surprisingly mild. She asked me to express her gratitude to you."

Takar cautiously asked, "Then you think that Inara's observation is something we need to take within a broad framework?"

"That's partly why I came straight here on my arrival. You see, while Inara loves all that is around her, she is also able to be quite objective. There is something seriously wrong and she can see and feel it even if she can't quantify it."

Takar responded, "Pren, Malin, I'm not sure where fate is leading us but our job is apparently to just go where it takes us. This young woman who we have decided to bring here to study the Universal Soul and the balance of good and evil may do more than we have anticipated. I think we may be embarking on an unusually interesting journey with Inara as our real guide."

* * *

Inara spent a beautiful month at her parent's home where Pren joined them during her last few days there. She took special advantage of their isolation at the edge of the jungle to openly and without reservation engage all of her senses in absorbing her home world. After her previous entanglement trips she had felt like she might never leave Andromeda University to see her home again. She was determined to enjoy the grass, jungle and all of pristine nature to the ultimate. Even for Inara it was almost a sensory overload. For her parents, it was overwhelming happiness to see their only daughter this way.

Pren commented, "Inara, I haven't seen you like this in decades. You look so happy and relaxed."

Inara hugged her uncle. "Pren, there have been times during these last few days when I wonder why I ever left. This is home. For me, it is the most beautiful place in the universe. I am part of it and it is part of me. You being here with my parents and me makes it complete."

She paused. "Thank you for everything you have done for me. Maybe you aren't my uncle by blood but I have always known you are a good and honest man and that you would give your life for me if that was necessary. I would do the same for you."

Pren was speechless and could only marvel at this family that had made him their own. He was indeed a lucky man.

The night before Inara and Pren were to leave for The Guide's Hall Inara turned the conversation serious. "This will sound strange but I'm worried about the galaxy. Not just the soul that permeates the galaxy, but the galaxy itself. Even here in this place that I love I can feel an almost imperceptibly slight change. Not in the numbers or scent or music or any of those other things that I sense that I know you can't. It is extraordinarily vague. I sometimes wonder if the feeling comes from the future instead of now."

That surprised all of them because Inara had never talked about a sense of the future. However, they remained quiet and listened.

"Mom and dad, I want you to buy all the power generation that you can. You can say that it is for development of the jungle domain. Burrow down into the ground to where the mantle is several hundred degrees so you can have a source of heat and energy. Create artificial light underground for growing things. Prepare for a long time without any kind of supplies. Do this in total secrecy. I don't know precisely why I'm telling you this, but I know you must do it or you will die. You should start as soon as possible."

All three of them were stunned by Inara's words. Finally, Teo broke the silence by simply saying, "We will do as you say."

The next morning Pren and Inara said their good-byes and left on the local transport for the closest entanglement node. Once again, The Guide put out a request for meditation for a special cause that he left unnamed. No one connected the timing with the entanglement trip that Inara and Pren were making to The Guide's Hall.

Except for some nausea, all went well on the trip for Inara.

* * *

Guide Takar Cillian gave Inara a couple of days to rest and find her way around The Guide's Hall. She was officially assigned to create a new research team whose job it was to fully understand the structure of space-time and its relationship to entanglement. As with all assignments within the priesthood the purpose was simply to do research and gain understanding. Inara was to be given greater than usual latitude in her work and couldn't have greeted the assignment with more enthusiasm. She knew she would receive the task of working on the structure of space. However, this was even more than she could have hoped for. The other researchers were thrilled to have a person of her genius on board.

Three days after Inara's arrival at The Hall, Guide Takar Cillian stood in his office anxiously awaiting the meeting with Inara. Malin had already sent him a signal that Inara had just arrived in Malin's office. The Guide was now just waiting for Inara to be ushered into his chambers. There was no doubt at all in his mind that Inara was a special person. He knew that she was a genius, that she had fully integrated sensory ability, that she was religious and in spite of, or maybe because of, all of this she was also an unusually caring person. But what interested him most was that unexpected connection over a distance eight years ago at the Andromeda University. While over the years it had come to mind from time to time it surprised him to learn from Pren Bodhi the strong reaction it had also raised in Inara. Now, he was about to meet her again.

* * *

Malin brought her into the room. Inara was dressed in the traditional Pilgrim technologist robe common within The Guide's Hall. It was the type of robe that The Guide had once worn when he was a younger Pilgrim. The Guide waited for introductions as he should even though introductions were hardly necessary. "Guide Takar Cillian, please allow me to present Pilgrim Inara Eyers. Inara Eyers, I am pleased to introduce Guide Takar Cillian."

Though she had been briefed on proper protocols, which included walking forward to shake hands with and then slightly bow to The Guide, Inara was frozen in place. All of her senses were in overload individually and in combination with each other. It perhaps could only be best described as the complete opposite of what she experienced when traveling through an entanglement node. The Guide was a symphony of sensory perception. Everything about him was in greater harmony with his surroundings than she had ever experienced with any human being. The most profound effect was that, while he clearly was distinct unto himself, he seemed to blend with everything around him. She wondered if she was perceiving a blending of body and soul. She vaguely felt Malin put his hand gently under her right elbow to encourage her to walk toward The Guide. In the few steps that it took to reach him Inara recovered enough to shake his offered hand and bow.

"Thank you, Malin" said Takar Cillian. "I will let you know when we are finished." With that statement, Malin knew that he would be cancelling appointments until Inara and The Guide walked into his outer office.

"Inara, please sit down here." The Guide pointed to a comfortable chair over against the side wall of the room. The Guide sat in an identical chair that was about two feet away. Refreshments were on tables in front of and between the chairs.

"Thank you, Guide." Inara walked over to the offered chair and sat down as she looked around the room.

The Guide made a motion with his hands that was supposed to be interpreted by the room as a command to sense the emotional state of his visitor and create an environment that would be most pleasing to her. Inara understood what the Guide was attempting and chuckled as the room blinked quickly through a series of scenes in a vain attempt to understand Inara's complex set of emotions. "Thank you, Guide. This has happened before with me. I think I would like to sit in the fields by the jungle on my home planet." The room changed, and Inara and The Guide found themselves with a wooden floor under their chairs and table and slightly raised above the grass. The sun was warm about halfway down the sky to their left. There was a slight breeze.

After a short silence to enjoy the view, the Guide asked, "Do you have any objection if my assistant watches our meeting from his office?"

"No, I already understand that I can trust Malin."

The Guide responded, "Good, we will each respect your confidence and fully understand your concerns about your safety."

The Guide then observed, "Your home is a beautiful place. Do you visit it often?" Immediately, he regretted his words as he thought about The Pain she experienced with entanglement. He was uncharacteristically off his game.

Inara correctly interpreted his discomfort. "Guide, I know that you are a bit off balance because of the sensory connection that you feel between us. I was at first also. I didn't understand it on Andromeda Campus, but I understand it now."

She continued, "I sense not only the physical world but also the spirit. That is because I have the advantage of knowing without any doubt that they are one and the same. You have been chosen Guide because of your strong belief in and connection to the Universal Soul. Consequently, you and I have a sensory connection to each other through the soul. It is something that I can accept easily because of my integrated abilities. It is new to you, and perhaps you just have to accept it for what it is, just as you accept your brain interpreting a certain frequency of the electromagnetic spectrum as blue."

"Hmmm. Thank you, Inara. I will try to understand that. But, tell me more about your sensory abilities and your life."

The Guide listened in rapt attention for the next ninety minutes as Inara unfolded her life story and her range of interlinked sensory abilities. She concluded by describing how she saw the galaxy in relation to the Universal Soul. It was this last part that compelled the Guide to ask many questions.

After extensive discussion The Guide said, "Inara, I have long believed that everything shares a Universal Soul. That is the basis of our spirituality and I know you believe the same thing. I think I hear you saying that you would like to learn as much about that as you can. I also would like you to do that and share your knowledge with us."

In her excitement Inara interrupted The Guide. "Yes!, she exclaimed I would love to do that."

Laughing, The Guide continued, "Inara, how would you like to have complete freedom here to explore the Universal Soul as a scientist and Pilgrim?"

Inara paused for a second as she analyzed the question. "What exactly does that mean? How far can I go with that work?"

"You can go as far with it as you wish, Inara. I had hoped to have you join us here to understand better what makes you special and to give you a chance to feel safe while researching the connection between science and spirituality. Our discussion today makes me want to do more."

The Guide stood up, and then stepped down off of the wooden floor to the grass surrounding their platform. He bent down to run his hands through the grass and the dew clinging to the blades. Then he turned toward Inara as he continued. "I want you, if you wish, to learn as much as you can about the Universal Soul, how we affect it and how it affects us. You already have a good background in this area, and even though you have stifled your ability a bit over the years by hiding it, I suspect that, with the right team, you can teach us more than anyone in the galaxy. I am offering you whatever laboratory space you want, and as much staff as you need so that you can learn and teach the rest of us."

The Guide held up his hand as he noted the concern on Inara's face. "I know you are afraid because of the visitor you saw at your campus. What you experienced frightens me also. You have described a person who is essentially outside of the soul and is connected on those thin brown lines to others like him. If that is a correct conclusion, then I hope it is something that you can help me to understand instead of remaining a mystery."

Taker went on, "I think what you observed might be as close as we can get to pure evil. The rest of us can't see it as you can." The Guide returned to sit beside Inara. "If you agree to my offer, then you may choose your own staff, and I hope you will use the full extent of your talents to make that selection. You will work in a carefully controlled, sealed-off section of The Hall. You will report directly to Malin who will brief me as necessary on your progress. Please understand that you will have full research freedom and total security. Do you accept my offer?"

Inara was literally shaking with excitement. Nervously, she answered, "Yes, Guide, of course I do. It is more than I ever imagined would happen in my life. Thank you."

"You're welcome, Inara." The Guide then made a gesture and the platform on which Inara was seated extended itself to the door to Malin Nowl's office. She and The Guide stood and shook hands. Inara turned and walked toward the doorway and her new life.

* * *

Malin got up from his seat. The desk that had been in front of him dissolved, and The Guide's assistant walked through where it had been toward Inara. "Inara, as you already know I observed all that happened in your meeting with The Guide. It looks like we have some work to do"

Before Inara could comment, Malin continued, "Please understand that The Guide has given you a tremendous opportunity and a massive responsibility. I think you understand the opportunity, but you may not yet understand the responsibility. That understanding will come with time. You must be ruthless in selecting your staff. You must use all of your integrated senses, your intellect and judgment to decide who is going to work for you. I will work with you to find an assistant. You and your assistant will then choose your research staff. Choose as if your life depends on it, because it seems to me that it does. And perhaps, your life is the least important thing that your decisions depend on."

Inara stood for a few minutes looking directly at Malin. Then closed her eyes. She opened her eyes again after a minute and looked around the room. She reached out her right hand slightly as if feeling something that Malin couldn't see. Then, while looking a little off to Malin's left she walked toward him and touched his chest with her left hand. This was all surprising and strange to Malin and he obviously felt confused to be approached in that manner.

Inara finally responded, "In the last few minutes I have come to understand that the assignment I have been given, and accepted, is important to The Guide. It is also important to me."

Then with a firmness that impressed Malin, she said, " My assistant will be Pren Bodhi, so I won't need to take your time with that. However, he will need a small staff to keep up with me and my research team. Naturally, I will personally interview everyone who is involved, but Pren and I will need your help to point us toward excellent leaders who will work directly for Pren."

"OK, Inara." Then speaking directly to the room, Malin said, "Provide Inara and Pren Bodhi with full access to my files on the best leaders we have in the Guide's Hall. Give Inara a hologram guide of her choosing to lead her toward where these people work. Also, give me -- no, give Pren Bodhi and Inara a layout of available space in The Guide's Hall for the creation of a laboratory research facility of her design." Then speaking to Inara, he said, "I assume you will be going directly to Pren's office?"

"Yes, Dr. Nowl."

"Inara, from now on in private please call me Malin. Only in public will we be Dr. Nowl and Dr. Eyers. You should please understand that you and Pren Bodhi are now part of a new and totally discrete inner circle with The Guide."

Speaking again to the room, he directed, "Let Pren Bodhi know that Inara is on her way to his office."

"Inara, do you have a preference for a hologram guide?"

"Yes, a cheetah cub."

A cheetah cub instantly appeared and momentarily sat attentively staring at Inara. Then it walked toward the door of Malin's office.

"Malin, that looks like my cue to leave." With great sincerity she said, "Thank you", and followed her cheetah cub to Pren Bodhi's office.

***

Over a snack Inara told Pren about the meetings with The Guide and Malin. Pren was as thrilled as Inara was with the turn of events. He reflected that if Inara had never seen the evil visitor to the Andromeda campus or The Guide years earlier, they wouldn't be here today. Strange how things turn out. "Or is it", he wondered.

"Inara, we have a lot of work to do. I suggest that we press on immediately with choosing my administrative staff and your technical team. As soon as your technical team reaches critical mass you can start work."

Using the files that Malin provided to them, they went to work right away. Together they first interviewed for Pren's administrative staff, which would initially be three people. Using the combination of Pren's executive experience and Inara's special talents, they were able to pick three people who were excellent administrators and managers and who Inara confirmed were fully trustworthy. Inara then picked thirty researchers who would work directly for her. The thirty researchers were divided into three teams who would each specialize in different aspects of the science of the Universal Soul and report to three lead technologists who coordinated work among each other. They had the responsibility for technical leadership within their teams, assuring cohesion among the teams and collaborating with Inara on reaching the goals she established. Pren's administrative staff worked quietly and subtly to overlay their executive experience on the operation. All were experts at what they did. Then Pren and Inara and the three lead technologists created what Pren called a strategic vision with a linear tactical path to that vision. Consequently, everyone knew what they had to do. The three lead technologists, Pren's administrators, Inara and Pren were the executive team. Inara and Pren reported to Malin who informed The Guide about progress.

* * *

About three months into their work, with much equation development and laboratory simulations behind them, Inara walked into Pren's office.

"Hey, boss," Pren said. "You looked like you have the weight of the galactic soul on your mind."

"It's interesting that you put it that way," she retorted. "If I thought the soul weighed anything, then I would say you are right. However, it weighs nothing, and that is actually what brings me in here."

"Wow, Wizard, I'm almost sorry I brought it up. Tell me more."

"Pren, can something that weighs nothing have inertia?"

"Like I said, tell me more."

"I wish Malk Kring would visit me again. He is the one who gave me the information that has put me on the path to what I think we are discovering.

"The space time equations that were derived one hundred thousand years ago or so, and which have been greatly refined since then, always take into account each of the constants that define the fabric of space time. Malk reminded me, through one of the presentations he displayed, that when entanglement first started being used, a constant was derived that, according to the ancient archives, was called the Schmidt constant after Dr. Marianne Schmidt. No one ever could explain the constant, but it has been assumed over time to just be something that had to be inserted and represented a function of space-time that we simply had yet to figure out."

Inara leaned forward for emphasis. "What is most interesting is that in the beginning years of entanglement the Schmidt constant was changing slightly over time until it reached a point of stability. Once it reached that point of stability, the assumption was arbitrarily made that the initial measurements of the Schmidt constant were simply inaccurate. In retrospect this could be seen as scientific laziness.

"Now, Schmidt was by all reports the great entanglement and space-time scientist of her time. She was also egotistical and strangely practical in a non-scientific way. Once the Schmidt constant stabilized, the scientific community started using that final number ignoring all the well-documented work that came before about the changes in that figure from the beginning to the point of stability. Entanglement transport worked, and no one pursued the anomaly of the Schmidt constant. It wasn't the first time in scientific history that happened, and I am sure it won't be the last. Accepting that number made things work and avoided the necessity of digging further."

"Inara, are you going to tell me that you have discovered something more in the last few months?"

"I am, Pren. And what I am learning is both unsettling and rewarding."

"Can you just give me the bottom line? As a scientist you have me in great suspense."

"Here it is. The Schmidt constant is the first indicator of something that could be called space-time-soul. No one fully understood it because soul didn't enter the equation at all for them. The Schmidt constant is the first scientific indicator of a direct relationship between space-time and the Universal Soul."

Pren Body shifted position in his chair as he paused to absorb this information and its implications. He then asked, "Are you telling me that there has been equation-derived scientific proof of the existence of a Universal Soul for one hundred thousand years and no one knew it? That you and your team are the first to recognize it?"

Inara reached for a drink of water. "It looks that way. However, there is more work to do."

Pren took a deep sigh. "I assume that you have told me the rewarding part of your news. What is the unsettling part?"

"I think that the Schmidt constant really did change in the early days because the use of entanglement had an effect on the Universal Soul that spilled over into space-time. Finally, a new balance was reached and the Schmidt constant became stable. What is truly unsettling is that I think we are discovering that a new point has recently been reached at which the space-time constant may start to change again with unpredictable results."

Pren asked "Do your other team members agree with you?"

"It doesn't show up yet in a rigorous scientific manner although our teams are finding hints of it."

"Hmmm. How does it show up?"

"In color and scent and music chords that aren't quite right."

"You know, if you said that to more than about five people in the entire galaxy you would be sent for neural rehab."

Inara laughed, "Well, Uncle Pren, that is why you are the first to know."

"Put it in terms I will understand. Make me believe you."

"When I was a child entanglement travel was painful, scary. I sensed it was more distressful to space than it was to me. As I became older, it became even more painful to space, or more correctly, to the Universal Soul, and to me. I only made it through the last two trips with the prayers and meditations of the Pilgrims. I felt this pain in the same way I felt the goodness of The Guide the first time, as well as the visitor on Andromeda who I am absolutely convinced is extremely evil.

"Pren, remember the conversation I had at home with mom and dad? I gave them that warning to build a survival shelter. I gave that warning not just out of a reaction to the muted pain of my entanglement trip home. It was because I sensed a deterioration that I now think will be increasingly damaging to space-time-soul, as I and my team have now come to know it. The soul part caused a change to the space-time part at the beginning of entanglement travel. I am sensing in a subtle way that it is happening again. In simple terms, the new balance that space-time-soul reached a couple of hundred years after the beginning of entanglement transmission is now changing. There was a broad region of balance that had been achieved. That region balance is now being exceeded and will reach imbalance. I sense that the imbalance may be catastrophic for humanity."

Inara paused. She could tell that, while Pren was following her, she wasn't really presenting a convincing argument, only an idea.

"Pren, I see the universe differently than anyone else I know. While the number is probably in the single digits, there are others now living in the galaxy who, like me, have fully integrated senses. However, just as some people are oriented toward the sciences and some toward music, I am oriented toward an intense interest in systems integration. I love both science and music. While I want to know why music is music, I also can simply appreciate music without analyzing it. I see all the pieces as part of the whole. To put it in even more abstract terms, I can't hear what a dog can hear. My ears don't work that way. But, I can smell and taste what a dog can hear so I know why a dog is reacting a certain way even when others don't. That in great part is because I am a genius as well as having fully integrated senses. I know how that sounds, but it is simply true. I didn't do it. I was born that way. In addition, I was raised on a quiet planet by religious Pilgrims. Knowing the Universal Soul is natural to me. It is easier for me than most because of my parents, and also because I sense space-time-soul, not just space-time. I have the gift, for all of these reasons, of a unique perspective. I see all of it, and can put it all together, in ways that no one else can."

"OK, Inara, I accept what you are telling me. What are you going to do about it?"

"I just started my team to work on that perspective, but all of this will be difficult to prove. I have to find a way to put this in the form of equations so everyone can truly understand it. There is another aspect to this, Pren. I hate to bother him, but it is time for us to have a meeting with The Guide."

Pren responded, "I'll set it up."

ENTANGLED SOUL

* * *

The Guide, Malin Nowl, Pren Bodhi and Inara were seated in a semi-circle in comfortable arm chairs with padded seats and backs. There was a matching oak table in front of them with refreshments. All of this was positioned on the floor of The Guide's office which was presented as being semi-transparent. Inara created the scene to make it appear as if they were in space above and outside of the plane of the Milky Way. They were looking up at the spiral arms wrapped around the black hole at center of the galaxy. As had been long established, The Guide's Hall, the Controllers Cathedral, and the headquarters of the galactic government offices were equally spaced one-third of the galaxy away from each other and about ten thousand light years from the galactic center.

In short order Inara launched into the discussion. "I chose this scene, which I have also shown to my staff, because I want you to sense the galaxy as much as possible in the same way I do."

As she said this, they were immersed in a mixture of aromas. There was an overall scent. However, as each of them looked at a different section of the galaxy, they were individually provided with a set of smells reflecting the area they were looking at. In the same way, they saw a cascade of translucent numbers all around them that changed subtly as they watched. They sensed each other, the chairs, the galaxy in front of them, space around them as sounds without hearing sounds, touch without reaching out and feeling, taste without having anything in their mouths, and smells that changed with where they looked. Taken together, it was a cascade of information that fully defined what they were looking at and which was almost overpowering. Inara had programmed the room to turn up the intensity of the experience and then to make it slowly disappear over the course of about one minute. Inara waited for their reaction.

Pren said nothing because Inara had already given him a preview of her presentation. Malin and The Guide were clearly overwhelmed into temporary silence.

Finally, The Guide could ask, "Inara, is this what you experience all the time?"

Inara explained, "This was only a little of what I sense. And I'm not sure I can give you the full experience. It is like drawing a three or four-dimensional space on a two-dimensional surface. It can be shown to you but the representations can't be picked up, touched, rotated or tossed in the air.

"Now I want to show you something else."

This time the images of every person in the room became smeared at the edges. Each of them melted slightly into their surroundings, melding with their clothing, the chairs they sat on, and the floor. Inara had programmed the presentation to give just a slight effect at the beginning with the intensity again increasing over a few seconds. The galaxy in front of them became slightly fuzzy as if there was a halo around each object. Everything was distinctly itself yet also merged into its surroundings. As the presentation neared its climax and end they all noticed that The Guide's image was fuzzier than the rest and that he and his surroundings had merged more than the others. Inara brought their environment back to normal by ending the presentation.

"That is another perspective on how I see things. The first was kind of a space-time representation. The second was as close as I could come to space-soul representation. Guide, you can see why your image affected me so strongly on the Andromeda campus. I had never seen anyone merge with their surroundings the way you do. You are blended strongly with the soul.

"Now, I am going to show you something else that you will almost certainly find massively disorienting and confusing. I will watch each of you closely to make sure you aren't terribly overwhelmed"

This time Inara blended the previous two presentations so that her perception of space-time was integrated with her perception of space-soul. The effect was as she anticipated and so impactful that she stopped it after only a few seconds.

After giving each of them some time to recover she said, "What I just showed you is how I see and sense everything around me all the time. It is what I understand to be the full integration of space-time-soul and I believe this integration can be defined with equations."

Again, Inara paused waiting for their reaction.

At long last, The Guide, visibly shaken, was the first to speak. "Inara, you are telling us that the soul and space-time are so interlinked that we really have something that you are calling space-time-soul."

"That is exactly how I understand it, Guide. In fact, my team and I have done some work along those lines to determine how space-time-soul can be defined by equation.

"I had in the past sometimes thought the pain I have felt during entanglement transfers since I was a young child was perhaps just psychological because of my ability to sense the twistedness of space-time that occurs during that transport. I didn't always fully accept that it was real emotional and physical pain that was being inflicted on me. More importantly, I also didn't understand that I was sensing the great harm that was being done to space-time. It is more accurate to say that it was harm that was being done directly to the intrinsic soul of space-time."

The Guide was deep in thought. Obviously, all devout Pilgrims believed in the Universal Soul and that it penetrated everything. However, he had never thought of it as being fully integrated with space-time in the manner Inara had just described. He wondered what she was on the verge of teaching him during this discussion and in future discussions.

The Guide asked, "Inara, can you show me what you sensed when you saw the visitor to your campus who you describe as evil?"

"I can," she responded. The man was then projected in front of them inside a brown haze with tendrils snaking off to the distance. He did not merge with his surroundings at all. Inara showed the soul stopping suddenly at the fringes of the haze. There was a disgusting smell with distorted music, and he was physically painful to look at.

The Guide then commanded the room, "Replace the generic male image that Inara is using with that of Montgomery Spea from my personal file. Present him in his normal form without the surrounding effects that Inara has added."

Turning to Inara, he said, "This is the man you saw on the Andromeda campus. I had him researched after you described your experience to me. My research was extremely discrete and through a long chain of contacts. I don't know who the people are toward the end of that chain, and they don't know where the query came from.

"Monty Spea was, at one time, senior in the Controllers organization. He rose through the ranks quickly. He is the son of people who were also higher ranking in their organization. He is on his fourth life and left his position in the Controllers about halfway through his third life. He is now a consultant for them and travels extensively. His home base is in the Earth sector of the galaxy. He is known as a benevolent person with an extremely engaging personality and is still well connected within the Controllers, the galactic government, and apparently within the Pilgrims. Almost everyone who meets him finds him enchanting. I have never met him and no one above five layers down into the Pilgrims has ever met him. He has never been to The Guide's Hall."

All became silent for a while as Inara stared in clear fascination at Monty Spea's image. Then she got up from her chair and walked through Spea to stare at the presentation of the galaxy. She turned to face the three men."

"Since you invited me here, Guide, I have followed Pren's suggestion and strongly exercised my integrated senses. I can absolutely trust those senses and so can you. I have been able to use them all the time to their utmost while in the safe area of my laboratory. They have become stronger and more integrated. What I showed you today is just a fraction of how I sense things."

Inara then gestured toward the galactic image and magnified a section of it in about a thirty light-year circle around Earth. "Montgomery Spea is in this region right now." She magnified the region more thoroughly, then made an overlay which, because of her previous presentation, she knew would make sense to the three men. "The brown clouds in this region represent evil and sickness in the Universal Soul. Mr. Spea operates only at the fringes of that evil. Others who are much more evil direct his actions. I don't think he knows who they are. And this will sound strange to you. These people, and their intentions, are the reasons space-time-soul is deteriorating. I can't tell you why that is happening, but it is the most important thing in the galaxy for us to understand."

Inara continued, "Just one more point. We are just researchers. We don't operate the entanglement systems. Consequently, we don't know the detailed equations that describe the intricate operational elements of entanglement transport of data, things and living matter. The changes that I am seeing in space-time-soul will, I believe, start showing up soon in the entanglement transport systems. The controllers who operate the systems might already know that these changes are taking place. In fact, I will be surprised if they don't know. What they may not know is the extent of the effect. What I am sure they don't know is that space-time-soul is a single entity, and if they are only working the problem from the limited perspective of space-time they won't fix it.

"It may also be worth noting that all of us, including myself, might be in a similar quandary. Some say perception is reality. However, perhaps our human perceptions are so limited that we don't have a clue about reality. Sharks and some other fish can sense, and make sense of, electromagnetic signals to capture prey. Snakes can use their sense of smell to 'see'. If a simple primitive radio had a brain, it would be fascinated by the fact that humans can see light and process it into images."

Inara concluded, "The trick is in understanding what we can't perceive."

THOMAS S. IRELAND

Kieran

The planet's winds flailed violently at man's carefully positioned musical monuments clinging to the planet's surface at the edge of numerous caverns. The ever-changing currents created always-new melodies on subtle themes that labyrinths transformed into a symphony and carried to the research cloister hundreds of yards below. There, Controller Researcher Kieran Llot struggled feverishly one more time through a revelation as haunting as the music that never quite brought solace to his troubled spirit.

The source of his emotional distress long pre-dated the technical problem that he was working on in his advanced research laboratory. In many ways, that personal distress was the impetus for the fevered research that kept his mind focused on more clinical thoughts. However, in a cruel twist of fate his technical findings were threatening to cause a new mental torment focused on events far beyond his own personal existence.

In an uncharacteristic move, Kieran growled in frustration and pushed over the virtual telecyber module at which he was working. The table skidded on its side across the floor sending the computing devices against the far wall. The ocean display on that wall dutifully swallowed the virtual debris with a larger than usual shore wave leaving the room clean. Kieran was left drifting in the peacefulness of the ocean view, the sound of the surf and the background melodies until his mind settled.

Finally, with hunger beginning to disturb his rest, Kieran conjured up a garden scene with a fully prepared dinner table. As he ate, he resumed working through his analysis making periodic gestures to throw his thoughts in a graphic form against the air.

As he did so, Kieran finally accepted that he wasn't making any new errors. As with any complex work, he had over the weeks certainly made some errors in technique, math and physics. However, he had learned from his mistakes and then come up with a conclusion that led him to even greater frustration. His experimental measurements were undeniably correct, and they were producing results that overturned ancient theory and newer discoveries.

The anomaly that started Kieran on the path to frantic nervousness appeared in the fifty-third decimal place. Matter transfer and telescence, though, required precise definition to at least fifty-five decimal places. Controllers had dedicated entire lifetimes seeking that absolute precision required for the transmission of matter, energy, and especially people, around the galaxy!

Errors in transmitting people were almost unheard of. The last major one had occurred over three thousand years ago. It resulted from coincidental quantum events of spontaneous creation and extinction too complex to formulate. However, a new set of programs had been written to abort activity if such a set of simultaneous events showed evidence of emerging. The results of these few transmission errors would always be catastrophic, but they had become avoidable through the work that had been done.

But this situation was much different. He wasn't finding evidence of one-time anomalies. He was concerned to the point of frantic disbelief because each of his new trials produced a deviation in experimental result that was infinitesimally greater than in the previous trial. It was as if the experiment itself was a devil feeding the anomaly. Reluctantly, Kieran finally admitted to himself that there was no fault in what he was seeing. The challenge would be in convincing others of what seemed to be a catastrophic truth.

* * *

After dinner, Kieran leaned back in his field cushion. As his computerized environment sensed his need for a few minutes of relaxation it triggered for Kieran a three dimensional projection of the instruments on the planet's surface vibrating soothingly with the music. The feedback between his mind and the computer-controlled projection quickly led him to a healing thirty-minute slumber.

A gentle chime and pleasant female voice interrupted the holographic sonata. Kieran's scheduled telescence session with his mentor and academic counselor, Dean Dammar Corday, would start in five minutes. He had scheduled the meeting a couple of days earlier. At that time his only objective had been to give a periodic progress report on his academic work. Now, Kieran needed the meeting even more to share his troubled thoughts with a trusted old friend who also happened to be his boss. He was going to have to report what could only be seen as the ultimate in unsettling findings.

He didn't want to pull Corday into the controversy he knew his findings would create. The two held almost identical conservative approaches to science, building on previously established fact and moving cautiously forward one excruciatingly detailed step at a time. Only his recent discoveries and the rumored work of others over the last six months could have moved Kieran to question so much of what he had learned during his career. Kieran was certain that Corday would strongly question his analysis.

Kieran was better with academic argument than political challenge. He also knew that political challenge often buried truth. Experience made him wary of those who maliciously took advantage of mistakes made by others so they could further their own careers or earn a bonus life cycle.

The music faded, and the female voice announced that his room was being prepared for the telescence session. An energy veil hid the current remaining set of laboratory equipment behind a view of the wind-sculpted cloister gardens. Kieran stood in respect to greet the Dean as the far end of his room was presented as an extension of the Dean's study in the nearby star system.

In keeping with custom, the Dean's image was grade eight in size and enhanced to near perfection. Full perfection isn't permitted for Deans. Kieran could sense Dammar Corday's environment and white-robed image in every way even though the Dean was five parsecs away on the Galactic University campus adjacent to The Cathedral. Kieran's image was similarly presented to the Dean but Kieran was permitted only the grade four size and quality of a Researcher. Each was an expert user and Controlling keeper of the technology which permitted them to deliver the full sensory impact of their images to each other so that they could interact as if really together. It was part of the glue in their trans-galactic civilization. The Dean and the Researcher were sworn, as members of The Controllers to protect telescence's secrets and integrity.

The Dean was seated behind his desk and in front of a free space model of a particularly scenic section of the galaxy. The effect was to make it appear that their integrated room was traveling through space at high speed. At the moment, they were passing a triad of distinctly different planets orbiting around each other and a bloated red giant star close to collapse.

"Hello, Kieran. I'm sorry that it's been so long since we've met with each other. Several teams around the galaxy have been asked to work on a special problem. I've taken the unusual step of personally heading one of the teams and that has kept me terribly busy."

"Please, Dean, don't apologize. I've accomplished a lot. As a result of some conclusions I am just reaching this is really a good time to discuss what I'm doing. I do need some help though. What are the results of the committee's review of my work?"

The Dean's room sensed the need to avoid distraction. The star field was replaced by an antique study. Kieran briefly marveled at the ancient titles of the leather-bound volumes on the oak shelves. In addition to his technological vocation Kieran also had a consuming interest in ancient history. The books hinted at the opportunity to lose himself for hours in old writings. The musty smell of the paper compelled him to run his hand over the collection nearest to him.

The Dean responded, "I'm sorry to say that I haven't personally looked at what you've done but the scholastic and technical review committees agree that there must be an error in your work. Your research is in such a new area, though, and contains such original thought that they don't fully understand what you are doing. I guess we aren't much help to you."

Corday got up from behind his desk and walked over to Kieran reaching across the light years to extend a warm arm around Kieran's shoulders and continued, "My friend, it's not like you to get stuck like this. And I sense from your eyes that there is something you haven't told me." As he spoke his image changed to match the size and enhancements of Kieran's signifying a discussion between friends.

Kieran shrugged his lean shoulders under the comforting embrace of his friend. "You're right. I think I finally understand what's happening. But, you aren't going to like it. I don't like it. It's a strangely uncomfortable truth."

"Truth is often uncomfortable. Sometimes we are afraid to hear it. Sometimes we are afraid to say it. Unspoken, it can become a barrier. Between friends, a difficult truth is often a bridge. We've been friends a long time. Trust me."

"This is tough. Because of our friendship, I'm reluctant to involve you. Because you are my boss, you must know. If you weren't my friend I might even consider delaying telling you for a couple more days. However, some new discoveries I am making could be creating a necessity to tell you now. So, I have to tell you because of our friendship. It's a terrible contradiction."

"Kieran, you're giving me a headache. Try getting to the point before I pull rank," Corday said with a chuckle.

Kieran took a deep breath. "In spite of what your committees say there is nothing wrong with my results. In fact, if I choose to reason that I'm not making an error in experimental procedure, then the data lead to the conclusion that I'm uncovering a normally imperceptible anomaly in space. I'll need a few more weeks to be certain. Here are my summary findings."

Kieran called up a high-speed free-space holographic presentation of the most critical elements of his work. The green eyes under Dean Corday's bushy white eyebrows revealed a sudden increase in interest when they came to the part about the apparent anomaly becoming greater as the experiment was repeated. The Dean interrupted the presentation frequently to ask questions that displayed more detailed knowledge than Kieran expected.

As soon as the presentation was over Kieran said, "I think you see my dilemma. According to theory, and accepted proven dogma, some of these results simply can't occur."

Kieran went on, "Dammar, your strength isn't theory. It's application and operations. Where did you get the knowledge to ask these questions?"

Corday interrupted by holding up his hand. After a few moments of reflection he said, "I really do wish we had talked sooner. Your discovery is extremely disturbing."

Kieran could see that his mentor was having difficulty. He waited for the Dean to continue. "I told you that I'm working on a special project. As Chancellor of Operations Research I've been asked by Secretary-General Edric Yan to find the reason for some minor disruptions which have recently crept into our transport systems. Our focus has been on control system errors. We haven't found anything. Now I think I understand why."

The Dean paused. Now it was his turn to be concerned about a friend. "Kieran, I'm impressed that you have enough focus to be this precise and thorough. How are you doing?"

Kieran warmed under Dammar's concern and felt thankful for his kindness. As always, though, he hardly knew how to answer. While considerate of others, Kieran still felt uncomfortable when the consideration was extended in his direction. The loss of the family he loved had occurred years earlier. The obliteration of his planet in war only weeks after he had left it had been devastating to him. The residual sadness and pain were an ever-present backdrop to his life. He suspected that they always would be. Dammar was one of a only a handful who knew the details of the loss of his family and had helped him through some tough emotional spots.

"As you know, it always helps me to stay busy. I'm concentrating better these days, and I think it is because I have a passion for this work. You can help me best by keeping me busy."

Corday's heart went out to this man whom he loved like a son and had known since he was a boy through his association with Kieran's father. He knew the depth of Kieran's losses, his hard-earned rediscovery of real emotion when he met Inara years ago, the crushing blow of their parting, and the effort it sometimes took to face each day. Corday was there as Kieran repeatedly worked to chisel cracks into the hardness that had initially helped him survive but eventually became a barrier to life and a love that once almost happened at Andromeda University. With a sigh he replied, "I can at least do that for you, Kieran."

After a short pause, he added, "I remember when you were much younger that you had fire in your heart. Now you have fierce determination in your mind. Determination that may be masking your true calling. I am concerned about that for you. But, more than that, I sometimes wonder if the fire in your heart has changed to a bit of ice in your soul."

Dammar Corday's image reverted to that of a Dean. "Continue your theoretical work. Believe your experimental results. In particular, concentrate on your anomaly supposition. Don't waste time doing any more experiments since the work would probably be redundant. Please be available for me to call you later today. Thank you, Kieran."

* * *

Without waiting for further comment the Dean broke the connection.

Dammar Corday continued to study the space Kieran's laboratory had just occupied in his office and cursed himself for being such a fool. Unconsciously raking a hand through his hair, he turned slowly to scan through Kieran's latest calculations. For months, Dean Corday had been monitoring and guiding the work of several special teams. He had assembled them at his Secretary-General's direction to concentrate on the most critical problem facing The Controllers.

Until now, he had seen it as an annoying technical issue that was critical, but not threatening, to essential operations except in the long term. Now, as a result of his conversation with Kieran, he was putting together pieces that made him uneasy. His other teams had not seen an accelerating time line. In fact, the problem had looked like it would not manifest itself in even a minor way to the general public for a few hundred years or so and not have a major impact for long beyond that. In the interim, he had been sure that the masses of experts, of geniuses, working on the problem would understand the cause in time and create a cure.

However, based on Kieran's analysis, the problem would occur in a serious form much sooner and have a noticeable impact on their civilization. He had already been under increasing pressure from his Secretary-General to understand the slight discrepancies that were cropping up in their operations at varying degrees across the galaxy. In his desire to guide the task force to a quick solution he had focused on obvious causes. In the meantime, the brightest of his students, his friend, had for other reasons made the breakthrough he was seeking.

As he continued to scan Kieran's equations, he realized that he would need more time and a lot more help to understand what Kieran was learning. He would like to digest the information and share it with the task forces before passing this new knowledge up the chain of command. However, Secretary-General Edric Yan had asked for an immediate personal update if there were any new discoveries. He would need to report Kieran's findings immediately.

Executive Order

The Dean sang the special authorization code supplied by the Secretary-General to be used whenever it was necessary to request an immediate, full override telescence session. When he finished the intonation, a unique priority signal was sent to Secretary-General Edric Yan. Without announcement, and before Dammar was fully ready, Edric Yan's presence from his Cathedral office had replaced the opposite end of the Dean's room. This was the third time that the Dean had made direct contact with a Secretary-General and the size ten perfect image still left him a little off balance. As he studied the Secretary-General's materializing image he wondered if anyone ever got used to such an imposing presence.

The image crystallized into absolute presence. Secretary-General Edric Yan's wide-set blue eyes and flaming red hair seemed to pierce directly into Dammar Corday's soul from across the Cathedral. The slowly shifting glow from a wall of fire formed a backlight framing the Secretary-General with an aura of strength and energy that complemented the presence of what Dammar believed was one of the most powerful persons in the galaxy. The Secretary-General betrayed his anxiety by foregoing any greeting. "Dammar, your use of the special code leads me to assume that one of your teams has found something that can help us with our problem."

Dammar was taken aback by the energy of the Secretary-General's agitated response. Edric Yan had apparently shut down all emotion and content filters on his end of the telescence session.

"Actually it was someone not on the teams, Secretary-General. We have a bright Researcher on his first life cycle who has been working on his postdoctoral thesis at one of our remote cloister laboratories. He has been developing a theory he has long held about how to enhance our transport systems by modulating the carrier simultaneously in several of the higher virtual dimensions. In the process, he found an anomaly. Frankly, his results are a surprise. I had no idea that he might shed some light on our problem. I just talked to him five minutes ago and his report has left me a little shaken. Within a few weeks we may know how to apply his work to our problem."

"Dammar, we don't have that kind of time. New information reveals that events are moving much faster than we thought at the time I sent out my broadcast message initiating the special effort your teams are involved in. It's hard to believe that this is happening so fast, and that we still don't understand why."

Edric Yan paused. Dammar could tell from the tilt of the Secretary-General's head that the reason for his pause was to listen to information being fed to him by another source. Dammar took the opportunity to absorb this new knowledge before Edric Yan continued. The sudden reddening of the Secretary-General's face made Dammar uneasy.

"Dammar, I have to be blunt. Every sensor here tells me that you know something important and disturbing. You must have equipment there designed to mask emotions you don't want revealed. However, your emotions are so strong they are leaking through anyway. I think you have had a recent shock and are afraid of the consequences of truth."

Corday quickly repeated his conversation with Kieran to Secretary-General Yan who listened impassively and without interruption. Even after Corday finished the Secretary-General remained quiet, obviously lost in thought and staring at a spot somewhere over Dammars' left shoulder. As the Secretary-G eneral swiveled to the left in his chair and began to talk to someone else his image frosted over as a signal for Dammar to wait.

After a few minutes, the frost cleared and the Secretary-General returned to the conversation. "Dammar, clearly your young Researcher has a history of being precise and conscientious. Our situation is serious and we can't ignore his findings, even if they seem out of sync with other efforts. At another time, I might be outraged and be tempted to say that his work had to be incredibly sloppy because the findings were so unbelievable. But other new evidence suggests that he may be right, and that he could be one of our primary hopes in solving this problem. Tell him that his physical presence is required at the University Campus. I want him to be there tomorrow afternoon."

"Yes, Secretary-General. What should I tell him the reason is?"

"Tell him that we have a better laboratory there where he can continue his work. That should temporarily satisfy his youthful curiosity. Don't tell him the full impact of our problem. He'll be fully briefed when he arrives. Dump his entire file to my chief of staff."

On impulse Corday blurted, "I can't do that, Secretary-General. Kieran's findings can be viewed as threatening to the positions of some powerful people. He is my friend and I won't compromise him. I'll only send his files to you coded for initial review by you only when you are alone."

The Secretary-General's blue eyes flashed in anger. The Dean, to his own surprise, remained calm and impassive. Seconds slogged by. Edric Yan's round face turned thoughtful; his voice suddenly filled with fatigue. "It's accelerating, Dammar. The first evidence led us to believe the growth was linear. Now everything points to a faster expansion. If that's true we'll need a solution a lot sooner than we thought.

"I understand that Researcher Llot has been your protégé for several decades. Clearly you are also personal friends. You have an excellent history of choosing and guiding talented people. You also have a history of good judgment so I will honor your request - your demand. Send your file to me coded for private review."

* * *

Kieran was surprised to see Dammar Corday again so soon.

Without preamble, Dean Corday said, "Kieran, I've just briefed Secretary-General Edric Yan on your work. I told you earlier that we're working on a problem which your study turns out to be related to. The problem is worse than we thought, and we are facing a much shorter timeline than we realized. We think that your work may help us to understand, and hopefully solve, the problem. We can provide you with better facilities and a team to work with here at University Planet and The Cathedral. The Secretary-General wants you to come here immediately so you can use our laboratory and computers. We'll expect you here tomorrow afternoon. I can't tell you more right now."

Seeing the concern in Kieran's eyes he continued, "You're protected, my friend. Don't be concerned."

First Major Event

As was normal before a long trip Kieran slept poorly. He awoke dreading the agony of the day's travel. No matter how exotic some thought it to be, Kieran still considered travel to be more hassle than pleasure.

During his time at the Cloister he rarely ventured away from his subterranean apartment. There was no need to since the Cloister's information and support systems put everything he needed for his studies and subsistence at his fingertips. He surprised himself with the realization that he hadn't been outside since he had arrived two years earlier. He also understood that he had deliberately, even if unconsciously, isolated himself from non-essential direct contact with people. Now, he was supposed to immerse himself in humanity to travel light-years across the local sector of the galaxy the next day.

There was a time when he loved the excitement of travel. There was a time when life itself was exciting all the time. But that was when he was younger. And then again for a short time at the Andromeda Campus. Now he felt like life had many more downs than ups. The only reprieve came when he could, for hours each day, immerse himself in his work.

The ground transport pod stopped at, and connected itself to, his apartment door a few minutes after he had finished his breakfast. He walked through the energy door that automatically dissolved as it recognized him and his approach. His bags put themselves in the compartment provided for them. As soon as he settled into his seat the vehicle began to move along the natural rock underground corridor serving the widely separated dormitories of The Controllers Cloister.

The pod reached the surface of the planet and shook almost imperceptibly as it was buffeted by a hurricane force wind. Kieran jerked in surprise as white particles radiated from a point in space in front of the pod like a vicious meteor shower. It had been summer when Kieran arrived. He hadn't thought of a change in the seasons or anticipated the snow which had started overnight. The wind didn't surprise him. It was always windy on the Cloister, and the surface had been beautifully sculpted by nature's smoothing forces. Other students in land surfers were zipping along and leaping over the undulating grooves rising and falling and twisting and turning along the hills and valleys. The more skillful riders of the wind could reach speeds of over two hundred kilometers per hour and perform awe inspiring aerial and surface acrobatics. He stared through the force field that blocked the wind and snow, admiring the view as he moved quickly toward the space lift.

* * *

Before long, the pod arrived at the space lift and matched speed with a moving walkway. A local robot took his bags away to be checked. Kieran stepped into the stream of people on the walkway. He was soon moving along at about fifteen kilometers per hour. The unfamiliar breeze felt pleasant on his face.

He was in a new section of the terminal. Most of the other travelers were hurrying. Some were going to distant places on the planet or traveling to other planets in this star's system. Others, like Kieran, were going to the entanglement gateway farther out in this planetary system. In any case, few looked like they were enjoying it, especially the parents of small children. Soon the walkway brought Kieran to a central terminus where he followed private audio cues to another section that would take him to the interplanetary terminal and the gate to the space lift. His travel had been booked on a small regional carrier that gave discounts to students. The security androids at the gate droned their way through checking the boarding pass of yet another faceless traveler.

Kieran grimaced when he found that he was seated next to a grossly overweight man whose left elbow jammed into his arm. It would probably be almost impossible for him to enjoy the study materials he had brought with him. He knew that the standard entertainment on the ship would bore him to distraction. Only the slightest of bumps let him know that they were on their way.

Kieran was cramped and irritable when he got off the ship at the entanglement gateway space station. He became even more disgruntled when he found that his bags were on the wrong ship destined for another planet in this system. He wondered how in this day and age semi-sentient bags and transportation companies could continue to get it so wrong! At least he was now at a Controller gateway in an environment that had been a part of him since he was born.

* * *

Entering a gateway base was like returning to the home Kieran once knew. It was bittersweet. The telescence bases that he had been raised on were no longer his residence. Entering the gateway as a traveler brought a longing to belong to the core of the telesence transport teams. It was for that reason that he had asked for, and received permission to, retain his reserve officer commission in the Telescence Corps. At the same time, he loved his research work in the university environment. He reflected that he should just take more time to be thankful for all he had at the moment that he had it.

The sight of about three thousand people milling around the central hallway reminded Kieran that this was the high season for religious pilgrimages and that this sector was strongly devout.

Kieran noted that the crowd was not moving with the usual entanglement gateway efficiency. Contrary to the experience at local transport systems, gateway passengers rarely experienced delays. The system could efficiently handle capacity crowds, but he noticed that the travelers were standing in groups or sitting on the floor of the large room. The food generators were running at capacity and many of the groups sitting on the floor were eating. Children were running everywhere, some crying and fighting with their siblings. Mothers were sitting on the floor nursing babies. The normally near antiseptic terminal was filling with trash and dirt faster than the cleaning machines could collect it. There were extra human and android police and guards. The human ones looked nervous.

Kieran jumped as someone gently gripped his elbow. "Are you Telescence Corps Commander Llot?"

Kieran irritably turned to see a tall lean man, rather young and clearly on his first life cycle. He wore the robe of a Local Node technologist. The design and color of his belt told Kieran that this was one of the Controller interns in training at this gateway. "Not any more. I am only a reservist now and a Researcher. What's happening here?"

The intern's anxious brown eyes darted nervously from Kieran to the crowd, then to the guards and back to Kieran again. The young man tightened his grip on Kieran's elbow. "Please come with me. We were told you were coming. We need your help with a problem. I was told to bring you immediately."

Kieran followed the intern through the milling crowd. They found it difficult to make their way. Several pilgrims asked what the reason was for the delay. Each time the intern pleaded ignorance and continued to push through the knots of people toward the side wall.

They were stopped at a small door by a non-human security guard carrying a stun ray and programmed to be officious. He checked their identification making it an artificially complex task. Finally, he opened the door and waved them through with a syntheskin-covered hand.

Kieran and his escort were now in the baggage storage area. At the far end, Kieran could see a row of twenty gateway exit doors. He knew that behind each door there was a small room wit field pods on which to recline. These were the gateway rooms and the passageway to the only method of interstellar travel.

Under normal circumstances the gateway doors would randomly open about once a minute as travelers left the transport system to pick up their bags which had preceded them. The doors were all closed. The only activity was from a cluster of Controllers and the gateway Proctor. They were gathered around a piece of baggage. As Kieran approached, the Proctor detached herself from the group to greet Kieran. The local node technologist who had been escorting Kieran made introductions.

"Commander Kieran Llot, I am Controller Takarn Rah, and this is our Proctor Controller Har Ith." Kieran started to speak but Controller Ith, raising a hand, interrupted, "I think I can anticipate some of your initial questions. Let me describe what's happening. I hope you can help. By the way, Researcher, or should I say Commander, you have been temporarily recommissioned during this emergency." The strain showed in Controller Ith's voice. Thin beads of sweat on her forehead and upper lip reflected the room glow. "Forgive me for not taking time for the social protocols, but you'll soon understand why."

Proctor Ith turned, and Kieran followed her to the group over by the baggage exit in front of its associated biological transport door. The group parted as they arrived and Kieran saw a piece of baggage twisted into a strange shape with portions of the contents embedded in and sticking through the surface. Controller Ith told him "This arrived about two hours ago. When it came in we thought we had experienced a multi-thousand year anomaly. Then we found those within the next two minutes."

Kieran looked at the next baggage tray and saw two more pieces of luggage in similar condition, and a third which was just a mass of unrecognizable matter.

Kieran, still examining the residue of the transmission, said, "I assume that you shut the system down after receiving these and that explains the reason for the crowd."

"That's part of it, Researcher. However, there is more, and it is much worse."

Controller Ith took Kieran to the biological gateway associated with the first bag and opened the door. One of the accompanying Controllers grabbed Kieran's arm to steady him as he gagged and his vision swam. The human who had come through the gateway from a distant location was a grotesque misshapen parody of a man or woman. He couldn't tell which. The limbs were terribly distorted, and parts of the torso were twisted beyond belief. The face was something out of the most terrible of dreams. Kieran stumbled outside the door, sat on the floor without dignity and became sick to his stomach. It was the first human transport anomaly in three thousand years.

* * *

Kieran's little sister Tra leaped into his memory. His mind was back at seven years old, and he was playing in his father's laboratory. Kieran's father had also been a Controller Researcher and worked on ways to simplify the encoding process to transmit inanimate matter between two points. The research was important to the Controllers because simplification led to less energy use, which meant less cost. Even miniscule savings per node meant great savings per year over the total number of nodes in the galaxy. Consequently, simplification was eagerly sought.

Kieran's father, Arnet, was one of the best at developing little refinements. His concentration when working was intense and his mind was always a little on his work no matter what else he was doing. His attention to the technology left him absent-minded in other areas of life. Others, including his adoring wife, forgave him his absent-mindedness and accompanying eccentricities because he was such a gentle, compassionate and, in his own way, caring man. Arnet loved his children and they often accompanied him to his laboratory where they played in a corner protected by force fields from his often-esoteric experiments.

On the particular day which Kieran was remembering, Arnet was bouncing a dense metallic sphere between two transporter nodes that he had set side by side in his laboratory. As the sphere transported between the nodes Arnet would take measurements. Then he would tweak the parameters of the control field, sometimes grunting with satisfaction as he encountered minuscule successes or gained new knowledge. Tra giggled with excitement as the sphere entertained her with its high-technology game of peek-a-boo. Kieran was too absorbed in building something to pay much attention.

Eventually, Arnet, still in deep concentration, left the laboratory. In spite of being so absorbed he was careful to re-engage the force field after he left. He paused to chuckle with Tra at the sight of the bounding ball, seeing it much differently through her eyes. Then he bent over for a few minutes to talk with Kieran about what he was building. Arnet was a contented and happy man.

Arnet left to walk down the hall. After a short distraction took Tra away from the bouncing ball she looked up at it again caught in deep thought. She remembered that the last time she had visited the laboratory her father had given Tra her own code to enter the lab. She had been thrilled to look at the recognition plate and say her name so that the force field would drop and she could walk into the experiment area.

Arnet had done this as a game and immediately took steps to erase her access code as soon as the game was finished. While they had been going through those erase steps an alarm sounded alerting Arnet to a critical activity taking place in a weeks-long experiment. A trans-dimensional threshold had been reached which Arnet knew was coming and wanted to observe. The threshold event demanded massive amounts of processing power to record all activities and a real-time explanation of what was going on. Arnet, as well as the entire processing power of the laboratory, was suddenly caught up in this critical event. As a result, the computer didn't immediately finish confirming the deletion of Tra's access code and reserved the action, and Arnet's confirmation, for a later time.

Tra ambled over to the doorway, looked at the faceplate and said her name. She smiled as the force field dropped and rushed in to play with what she saw as a bounding ball. Tra had just reached with both hands for the ball when Arnet returned just in time to see her forearms and hands momentarily disappear and reappear as twisted appendages. Arnet screamed in horror. Tra shrieked in pain. Kieran looked up to see Tra faint and then die after a couple of minutes of excruciating agony from the neural shock. Kieran couldn't take his eyes off of the things at the end of her arms. Arnet could only hold Tra and scream in his anguish of guilt and loss.

Life was never the same after that. Arnet, in spite of intense counseling and therapy simply didn't recover from his guilt. Kieran's mother, in her mental anguish, blamed Kieran and Arnet for not watching Tra closely enough and became emotionally distant from both of them. As the years went on, it was as if they were no longer a family. Arnet lived in agony with his guilt and spent all of his time in the laboratory, never again producing at the level he once did. Kieran's mother immersed herself in books spending most of her time alone studying history. Kieran sometimes wondered if she thought she might turn back time through her history books. None of them had much conversation with either of the other two. Inadequacy in Arnet's marriage and in his profession finally piled on him so deeply that he took his life years later in his laboratory.

Kieran tried to escape his pain and guilt by immersing himself in his studies. He had a consuming interest in the same entanglement technology that intrigued his father and killed his little sister. He used his studies as a way to hide the pain and loneliness of losing his family and essentially most of his childhood.

Kieran wasn't an uncaring person. He truly liked other people and enjoyed life. However, he had buried the true capacity for deep emotion. Few others knew of his withdrawal because he used any ability he had for empathy to be sensitive to, and emulate proper responses to, various situations. He ended up spending a great deal of emotional energy pleasing everyone else and never really taking care of what he truly wanted.

Kieran advanced in his career. His dedication combined with a superior intellect brought him attention from several research scientists in the Controllers organization. One, in particular, was Dean Dammar Corday, a friend of Kieran's father, who aided Kieran's career by guiding him toward active military and research assignments at a variety of educational and development facilities around the galaxy. Kieran eventually left his active military role to become a Controller reservist to focus more intently on furthering his telescence work.

It was during one of these research assignments that war broke out among several of the planets in his home sector. Kieran never understood the reason for the conflict. All he knew was that it killed his mother and destroyed his planet.

* * *

Kieran returned to the present.

He looked up at Controller Ith in horror and asked, "Were there others?"

"Yes," she replied quietly. "There were three others who came through at the same time as their baggage. This one and two of the others died in transit. The third lived for a few minutes. It was horrible. One of the Controllers shut the system down. You saw the resultant chaos in the main terminal."

She paused as much to compose herself as to give Kieran a minute before she delivered the next critical and devastating piece of information.

"Researcher, I also have to tell you that similar anomalies have occurred at about ten percent of all the gateway stations across the galaxy. The anomalies are greatest at the most heavily-traveled stations. All entanglement transport of animate and inanimate matter has been stopped everywhere in the galaxy. Only energy and information are being transmitted now."

Kieran sat on the floor in stunned silence and emotional turmoil for some time before he could bring his mind to sort logically through what he had seen as well as the additional information he was being given. Finally, still silent, he stood to face the others.

"Researcher", Controller Ith said quietly, "we called the local Administrator after shutting the system down. Naturally, he and many others reported each of their situations all the way up to the Cathedral. He called back to say that you were on your way and to show you everything. He said that your recent work might give a clue to what happened here."

Her voice was tightly controlled but tinged with anger as she added, "Researcher, was this predicted?"

Kieran, still recovering from his shock worked hard to regain his composure. He was aware that as the ranking technologist, the others, including Controller Ith, would naturally look to him for leadership. This responsibility gave him the strength he needed to move the group to action. His personal strength would become the group strength they all needed to get through the next few hours. While beginning to formulate his technical approach, he thought about the growing crowd behind the wall. Others would have to deal with that. He seized on the clue embedded in the information provided by Controller Ith as well as his own recent research.

With command authority in his voice he said, "I'll need access to your computer and dimensional distortion equipment. Please put your best programmer and technician under my direct supervision while I'm here."

"All right. Controller Aul Kins and Controller Hedril Fra will assist you. Our command center is over there." She pointed to a green door fastened with huge hinges to a reinforced frame and enveloped by a deliberately visible, shimmering force field. The guard by the door looked like he took his job seriously.

"Thank you, Har. You're still in command. I just need some time to complete my analysis. I'll work more quickly if I'm not bothered."

"I understand, Commander."

As Kieran motioned to the others to come with him he knew that he wouldn't have to worry about interruptions.

Two hours later Kieran and the two Controllers emerged from the control room tired but satisfied. Controller Ith, looking totally haggard, asked him what the situation was. Kieran responded, "I understand what happened and you can soon resume normal operation. I've made some changes to your programs that I should clear with the executives and the system integrators at the Cathedral. Your Controllers will explain them to you. They did a good job."

Relief showed through the fatigue in Controller Ith's face.

* * *

"Thank you, Researcher. 'Upstairs' has been calling to see how you're doing and when you'll be finished. Because of the distortion we've been experiencing it was hard to tell who I was talking to but I'm afraid that I may have told one of our senior Controllers who insisted on interrupting you to 'Go to Hell'.

In response to Controller Ith's grimace Kieran said, "Let's return that call together. Maybe I can get you off the hook with that senior Controller. We should be able to set up a good telescence session now."

Kieran almost totally lost his composure when he realized that the person they were talking to, the person who had been asking for status from Proctor Controller Har Ith, was Secretary-General Edric Yan. As the session began Kieran wondered if he and Har would survive the discussion with their careers intact. He thought Har might really be in trouble when the Secretary-General asked her to leave the room as soon as the link was established.

The Secretary-General began, "Researcher, I'm pleased to meet you. Dean Corday and I have talked about your work. It's fortunate that you were available to help."

Kieran knew that the Secretary-General had excellent aids who worked hard to keep him well informed so that he could add personal touches to conversations. Kieran mistakenly assumed that the Secretary-General's niceties were the result of good staff work.

Secretary-General Edric Yan continued. "The Cathedral computer staff is checking your work. It appears you've made a modification to get us around this problem. Good work."

"Thank you, Secretary-General, but the patch is just a temporary one."

Kieran paused, looking earnestly at the Secretary-General of Telescence. "Secretary-General, this is terrible. If what I've learned here is true, then we're in serious trouble."

The Secretary-General never lost his composure. "I know, Kieran. Your research has confirmed a problem we knew was developing. We didn't know it was going to happen so soon. We thought the problem wouldn't occur for a few hundred years and we felt we could find a solution within decades. Now we need your help. Is it safe to put your gateway and our other gateways back into operation? Can you leave immediately for the University node?"

"Yes, Secretary-General, but the operation will be at less than normal speed. I've put in some additional safety measures and adjustments to support biological transport. The people being transported won't notice the difference, but there will be additional processing load on all of our gateway systems."

"OK. Just get to the university as quickly as you can. Your work will continue there. The Secretary-General began to signal a sign off then paused. "Kieran, please tell Har Ith that she did a good job protecting your time. However, she shouldn't get into the habit of telling a Secretary-General to 'Go to hell'." Then he signed off.

* * *

Kieran took some time to meet briefly with Proctor Controller Ith and her local node Controllers before continuing on his journey to the University. As soon as he was satisfied that the system was operating properly Kieran started toward the main terminal to get in the queue with the throng of people waiting to get to adjacent nodes. Controller Takarn Rah, who had met him on his arrival, stopped him. "Researcher, as soon as you're ready you may leave for the University."

"Thank you. I was just going to join the others waiting in the terminal."

Controller Rah looked at him in surprise and a little amusement. "I guess no one told you, Researcher. Secretary-General Yan has directed that you be booked through with Secretary-General priority. You won't have to wait. By the way, we found your bags. They will be transporting just ahead of you. Please come this way. You're leaving through gate eleven."

Controller Rah escorted Kieran to his bags that had been waiting for him just in front of the biological gate. The apprentice controller also scanned into Kieran's neural chip his new boarding pass stamped with Secretary-General priority. After saying good-bye to Controller Rah, Kieran, with poorly disguised hesitation, turned to the biological gateway door for the next part of his trip.

The Fly

When the door to the entanglement pod opened, Kieran stepped inside to lie down on the transport field. No sooner had he relaxed than a voice that seemed to come from inside him began to take him through the transport sequence.

"Researcher Kieran Llot, we are beginning the formulation required to assure your safe transport to the University node. Scanning has already started and formulation will be complete in about five seconds. Once formulation is accomplished you will be transported to the University Node". A pause. "You and your baggage are now at the University Node. Please leave the same way you entered. Thank you for traveling with The Controllers."

For the first time ever when traveling via a gateway, Kieran checked himself over before walking out the door.

Kieran's appreciation for Secretary-General travel priority grew after he left the gateway room. He was met by an apprentice controller who already had his bags. He greeted Kieran by saying, "Researcher, I am instructed to take you immediately to the executive regional interplanetary pod. Please follow me."

The young apprentice controller took off at a brisk pace and led Kieran to the executive terminal where he directed Kieran to step into a four person private spacecraft. Kieran was the only occupant.

"Researcher." the apprentice said, "this spacecraft has been programmed to take you to University Center about one hour's travel from here. You will be met when you arrive. The pod will sense when you are ready to leave. The ship will then depart as soon as you have traffic clearance. Have a safe trip."

The small four person spacecraft was almost identical to the pod Kieran had used when leaving the Cloister. In fact, the development of standards had long ago reached such a high level that each of the ships could have performed the other's task with only one hour of transmutation to interchange the drive modules.

Kieran settled in for the last leg of his trip. As the little craft lifted off, Kieran began to review the day's activities and the unusual turn of events. Only this morning he had been a simple research student. Now he was traveling with Secretary-General authority after saving major sectors of the galaxy from prolonged isolation.

He was preoccupied by the coincidence of having his recently gained knowledge be the factor that played the major role in overcoming the disruption. He finally accepted the coincidence and put it out of his mind as he brushed away a fly that was buzzing around his head. He wondered momentarily where the fly had originally come from and where it would eventually end up.

His thoughts went to the reason for the failure at the university node. A feeling that he was overlooking something nagged him. He leaned back in his seat deep in thought as the small ship continued toward its destination.

Half an hour later the fly again annoyed him as it suddenly dive-bombed his head. He cursed the fly under his breath looked for something to swat it and wondered why man ever let flies leave the Earth in the first place. They were a pestilence that moved with man in his tiny ships and his sophisticated transport systems.

Suddenly, Kieran sat bolt upright in alarm. That's it! Why hadn't he thought of it before? Just as man was transporting flies across the galaxy, the disruption was being transported from node to node every time energy or matter was exchanged between them. The distorted space in one location was being transported with each transmission to the other network node in the transmission link. In this way, humans were causing the disruption to spread across the universe similar to the way this fly had been accidentally, and perhaps repeatedly, transported across the galaxy. Just like in his experiment at the university, each transmission increases the distortion in the transmitting location's space. Now he recognized that the node with the greatest distortion also increased the rate of distortion in the adjacent space. The rate of growth must be phenomenal he thought.

He frantically used his computer to modify his previous work with his new thought. After about another ten minutes of travel, he had set up the model and developed a graph showing disruption in a multi-node system over time. First, he graphed the situation of one node. The growth over time of the disruption was linear and would not have a practical impact for millions of years. The growth became nonlinear with a two node system, but the effect was still negligible and wouldn't reach critical levels until man's present inventions had long since crumbled to dust and been replaced by new technologies.

As he added more nodes to the model the curve grew upward at ever-sharper angles once the amount of distortion reached a critical level. Kieran then drew a model that took into account the growth in the transport system over time from the activation of the first node pair linking Earth to its nearest star to the present system. The crucial level was reached in one hundred thousand years putting Kieran and his generation right at the critical time. Kieran added data from the work he had just done to restore the transport system to operation and was shocked by the result.

They were out of time! Sweating and heart racing he looked at his hands that trembled with the rush of adrenaline caused by his excitement and fear. He noticed the fly sitting on the top of his computer and no longer had the heart to end its short, suddenly significant life. He tried to compose himself, but couldn't. He knew he had just seen how man's civilization would end. He started to make a call then stopped. It was only another five minutes to the University Campus. He would selfishly keep to himself that time which had suddenly become so valuable.

The fly continued to buzz but Kieran no longer cared.

The Council

The planet called University is considered by many to be the most beautiful in the galaxy. Great care had been given from the time of its first visitors to taking advantage of its initial rugged state when terraforming it for human habitation. As was true on every planet in the galaxy, other than Earth, there was no native life of any kind. Plant and animal life had been imported over thousands of years. Robot gardeners now tended a proliferation of worldwide gardens, jungles and parks in a climate that varied from tropical to frigid. All buildings and roadways were underground with the transportation network only rising above the surface on almost totally transparent structures to cover the great distances between the cities and provide travelers with awe inspiring views of beautiful terrain. University was also one of the most self-sufficient planets in the galaxy for a body that wasn't Earthlike. Its relatively low population of arguably one of the five most creative and intelligent collections of minds of any planet in the Milky Way put few demands on the carefully constructed ecosystem.

Furthermore, a keen sense of history and a recognition of the accidents and misfortunes that befall even the seemingly strongest of societies encouraged the planet's leaders to establish a Defense Force that involved spherical layers of protection reaching beyond the outermost planet of its stellar system and past the major adjacent entanglement nodes. This was made easier, and more imperative, to accomplish since University was also host to the Council of Secretaries-General and was the guardian planet of the only transportation access point to the Cathedral; home of the Controllers.

As Kieran was settling in at University, the Council of Secretaries-General was urgently meeting at the Cathedral.

No one ever tired of the Cathedral. It stood alone in space, five hundred million miles away from the star of its guardian planet. The Cathedral held itself in place between that star and the center of the galaxy. This archaic looking, but extremely functional, structure with spires ten miles tall and a main hall one hundred miles long by fifty miles wide stood alone in space. A man-made world, it housed the heads of the various technology standards committees and their one hundred fifty million members. The ornate front with its heavy double doors at the top of a flight of stairs ascending from nowhere faced away from the center of the galaxy. The other end was open to space and the galaxy's central kaleidoscopic black hole destroyer of stars. Anyone standing inside the five mile high first floor had an unobstructed and awe-inspiring view out of the two hundred fifty square mile end of the cathedral. From there they saw streams of spaghetti-like matter and energy spiraling in rainbow colors into the galaxy's central maw.

The Council of Secretaries-General always met at the Cathedral. More specifically, they met between the Cathedral and the black hole at that point in space where the end of the building would have been had it not been deliberately left uncompleted. Their chief purpose was executive management of the Controllers organization and development of the Galaxy's Technological Systems.

Recently, the subject of spatial disruption had dominated the meetings. The initial report of a potential problem at the galaxy's entanglement transport nodes had at first been skeptically received. The extreme, and emotional, reluctance of the Council of Secretaries-General to believe these reports from a creditable source had threatened to end that technologist's career. He was one of The Controllers' brightest minds and had demanded his right to full analytical review. He was vindicated after his findings were verified.

At that point, the Council had no choice but to report this unsettling news to the government leaders who needed to be informed, and whose duty it was to determine how support infrastructures would survive if the entanglement systems were to collapse. The Council of Secretaries-General then met in special session.

Back then they thought they had more than sufficient time remaining to find a solution to the problem. Today, they were meeting again in the Cathedral on the same subject.

Whenever they met, each of the five Secretaries-General executed a traditional 'leap of faith' by stepping out of the massive open end of the Cathedral into what looked like empty space to walk the one-half mile in the direction of the black hole and their reserved chairs floating between the deliberately incomplete human structure and God's inferno. The contrasts were not lost on any of the Secretaries-General. This meeting place had been deliberately staged by their long-ago predecessors to remind them that the total power they wielded by human standards was, in reality, no power at all.

Tradition and mutual respect required each of the Secretaries-General to simultaneously leave the end of the cathedral to walk across the invisible path stretching to their chairs which were arranged in a slowly rotating circle. They had already made this walk and were seated in the chairs they normally used.

While tradition was still being closely adhered to on this day, the tone of the meeting did not reflect the usual, if sometimes artificial, respect.

Paya Lachlan, the Secretary-General of Systems Integration, started the discussion. None of the Secretaries-General was devoid of ego, but hers was easily the most powerful. Everything about her appearance was studied perfection. Even in the shadow of the galaxy's central engine she exuded strength and overwhelming confidence. A born economist, she controlled the purse strings of the systems she managed by manipulating the granting of systems interface approval in a sometimes-arbitrary manner. She was the most vocal opponent of what was commonly and unflatteringly referred to as the proprietarian technologists. She, and the other Secretaries-General, felt that proprietary initiatives were frequently at cross-purposes with their precise and cautiously evolutionary system integration efforts. Since the dogma of systems integration was so integral to the beliefs of The Controllers, she normally found her systems integration positions and attacks on proprietary solutions easy to defend. Today was a rare exception.

"Edric, I can't believe you actually gave this Researcher permission to proceed without consulting the rest of us. What's going on? "

Edric fired back, "Come on, Paya, you know what's going on. We had an emergency situation involving the loss of life and property and the total breakdown of most of the entanglement transport system. I did what I had to do to get things back on track. I let you all know what happened immediately after the problem was corrected."

Secretary-General Edric Yan wasn't being entirely truthful. He believed that dogmatic systems integrators, like Paya, didn't understand the necessity to make the immediate decisions which those who have responsibility for day to day operation live with. There had been time to convene and consult but he deliberately hadn't done so because convening a committee to solve an operational problem only had the effect of delaying the solution in an urgent situation.

Secretary-General Lachlan started to respond but was cut short by Draylou Ler. While anyone in this advanced society could be physically perfect, Secretary-General Ler was naturally and ruggedly handsome. He left the few flaws bestowed by nature as they were and the effect was to make him even more intimidating than he would otherwise have been. As Secretary-General of Information Processing, he could be violently emotional in his defense of the systems for which he was responsible. He had destroyed the careers of many who questioned his strict adherence to old standards. His entire secretariat was filled with conservatives who went out of their way to frustrate those they viewed as overly aggressive or threatening to the stability they had created.

He had a conviction spanning many life cycles that telescence and transport systems were a lower technology whose value was only made possible by his telecyber systems which assured proper transport of matter or energy. He was probably on his last life cycle as evidenced by his receding, slightly wavy grey hair combed straight back from a ruddy, jowly face.

Right now Draylou's complexion was redder than usual and his blue eyes blazed with indignation. "Let's face it, Edric, your people screwed up, and you're trying to cover it up by not keeping the rest of us informed."

Looking around the circle he continued, "I suggest; no, I demand, that my group be allowed to take over this problem. Transport people do not understand processing well enough to solve this issue in the time required. The fact that Edric's researcher used a proprietary solution supports my argument."

Edric Yan was proud to be Secretary-General of Telescence Systems. While he logically understood that all elements of each of their systems were equally important he felt a special fondness for his network which he was in the habit of calling the glue of civilization. He valued objectivity, and was trying hard to maintain his own under Draylou's attack. He had always had mixed emotions about Draylou. He had tremendous respect for his intellect, but Edric resented Draylou's attitudes toward the transport technologies. He also knew that Draylou viewed the galaxy in black and white and at his advanced age would probably never change. Edric surprised himself by responding with an uncharacteristic burst of anger.

"Look, Draylou, I've had enough of your nonsense. You've done the same thing yourself when required. I even remember an independent action you surprised us with early in your career that we still haven't fully recovered from. I suggest that for once in your life you respond with some objectivity and work with the rest of us to solve this problem. Can't you even forget your self-interest in the middle of a crisis that threatens to end mankind's entire civilization?"

And there it was. While each of their staffs had been working on the problem and whispered in quiet corners about the potential for disaster no one, until now, had come out openly in an executive forum to define the potential catastrophic impact of the growing distortion.

While Edric Yan did have a latent reputation for a quick temper, it had literally been decades since anyone had seen him lose it. The vehemence of Secretary-General Yan's counterattack left Secretary-General Ler gaping in response. His small mouth with its full lips worked silently in a vain attempt to form the response that his shocked mind refused to construct.

Secretary-General Lachlan quickly jumped in. "We must work together on this because, if we don't, it does mean the end of civilization. As you know, I can invoke my 'senior among equals' position as Secretary-General of Systems Integration and place you all under my control in time of crisis. I'll do just that if you can't work together willingly."

Deliberately turning her back on Draylou Ler who was now almost apoplectic, she addressed Edric Yan who was to her left.

"Edric, you've already brought us up to date on the events at the university node. Can you describe for the rest of us what Researcher Llot did to resolve the problem? "

Secretary-General Yan was still working hard on the inside to calm himself down. He paused for a few minutes as much to collect his thoughts as to assure that he settled himself to speak professionally. As he started, his back was almost to the Cathedral. The center of the galaxy filled his field of view.

"You know from the information I've just sent to you that Researcher Llot is working on a postdoctoral project about potential enhancements to both telescence and generalized transport. We already knew that extremely minor distortions that we couldn't account for were beginning to creep into our transport systems. There was always the remote possibility that the independent work of Researcher Llot or some other technologists would give us some clues to solve the problem that we all felt was minor but had the potential to become more serious over a much longer period. However, our main effort was focused on those teams directly assigned to this project. As time progressed, the distortion, which was still minor, began to increase at an undefinable and extremely small rate. The technologists working on the problem kept encountering roadblocks to a solution. That includes Draylou's groups, my own laboratory groups and the independent technologists."

Edric couldn't resist the indirect dig at Secretary-General Draylou Ler. He was smugly satisfied that his remark elicited an intensified glare.

Edric continued, "One by one each group came to a dead end. Except, as I only recently learned, for Kieran whose work shows signs of true genius. Kieran avoided the trap that all the others fell into. While they had been assuming that we understood all there was to know about the structure of space, Kieran decided to assume that his experimentation was revealing new knowledge. His quandary, and the quandary all the experimenters had, was that the tests didn't match theory that assumed we had correctly defined space in all dimensions. Kieran decided to reexamine space and found a slight deviation in the thirteenth virtual dimension. When I was told about it I was mildly curious that it had never been discovered before. Then it quickly began to make sense.

"Until the last few months the distortion was at levels which we couldn't detect, but apparently it has been building ever since the first node was constructed at the beginning of entanglement communication. It now appears that the growth has become a high exponential. That is, the growth continued at an imperceptible rate for a long time, in this case one hundred thousand years, before it reached a detectable level. Then, just before the point at which it was detectable with our instruments, it accelerated dramatically. In just the last couple of days our projection to a serious situation has moved from hundreds of years to a much nearer future."

Edric Yan continued to elaborate, "This morning's event is a taste of what will follow shortly. We appear to be close to a total spatial breakdown in the region of our highest use nodes. The breakdown will immediately spread across the galaxy. We don't know how. . ."

Edric Yan was interrupted by the Energy Secretary-General Alana Perg who nearly came out of her chair as she exploded, "Very close to a major problem at our high use nodes! Are you sure? What the hell does that mean? How long have you known this?"

Secretary-General Yan responded, "Only minutes before I came in here, Alana. We are still building on an analysis that Kieran did while he was on his way to University after the node disruption. We have been examining Kieran's latest work as well as the characteristics of the University node and comparing them with the station that Kieran was traveling through. With that new knowledge, we have been able to work quickly back in time and find clues to impending disruptions. Disruption is dependent upon frequency of use and the volume of traffic. More heavily used nodes and their adjacent node will experience unrecoverable breakdown first.

"The University is in a low-energy section of the galaxy heavily traveled by Controllers and the most highly religious Pilgrims. Energy is constantly piped into this transport node from adjacent nodes and nearby energy sources to provide sufficient power to run the node as well as the planets of this relatively cool star. More combined energy and matter traverse this node than any other node in the galaxy. So the disruption occurred here, and at similar locations first, and quickly rippled across about ten percent of the nodes in the galaxy. Any nodal transition, whether energy or matter, adds to the distortion potential. One of the clues, just discovered today by Kieran Llot, is turning out to be a minuscule change in the Schmidt constant."

Alana sighed as she slumped back in her chair. Her thin, wrinkled face framed with its thinning gray hair showed a despair that Edric had never seen before in this astoundingly positive woman.

Alana was on her last life cycle. She had been renewed four times at the two hundred year point of each of her standard spans bringing her to the normal full life span of about one millennium. In Alana's case she had actually lived about one hundred years beyond her millennium thanks to exceptional genes on her Controller's side of her family. The renewal process was less effective with each cycle, and Alana had recently been showing some of the physical effects of old age which occur rapidly in the last few years of a person's last cycle. She had been elected to the Council of Secretaries-General during her previous life cycle and had served with special enthusiasm and competence. Edric had never seen her let anything affect her constantly positive attitude until now.

"Edric, you sound certain that you have defined the problem and you make it sound hopeless." Alana's blue gray eyes looked filmy and haunted. "How certain are you?"

"Not totally certain yet, Alana, but the evidence is mounting. We'll know more in a couple of days."

Alana sat upright and fixed him with a suddenly firm gaze that was also somehow far away. "You mean after your young

Researcher has spent some time at the prime node laboratory on University testing his new theory?"

"Yes, he has already arrived and started work."

Alana, appearing to be restored to her old self, said, "I'll be leaving in an hour to join him."

Speaking into space she said to her aid, Administrator Erber Oran, "Erber, book passage for me to the prime node laboratory. I'll have two of my bags pack and transport themselves as soon as I leave this meeting. I'll be traveling with Secretary-General priority, but I forbid any ceremony at any point along the way."

Secretary-General Ler's mouth worked but no sound came out.

Alana lectured, "For Pete's sake, Draylou, stop imitating a fish! I'm sure you don't want me involved. As a matter of fact I'm sure you don't want anyone involved but you and your people. Sometimes you are more proprietary than the proprietarians."

Turning to Edric Yan she said, "Edric, the prime node lab at University Planet is your turf so I should ask your permission."

Secretary-General Yan was both surprised and amused. "Alana, I would be foolish to refuse permission. You are welcome at any of my facilities at any time."

"Thank you, Edric. As always, you are gracious. However, now is not the time to be gracious. I think we have to be as direct and honest with each other as we know how to be. The picture you paint is grim and we will need every resource we have if we are going to find a solution. And I refuse to believe there isn't a solution. I'm going to the prime node lab because I believe I have something to contribute; five lifetimes of wisdom and experience and the best gut instincts of anyone I know. I'm certainly not going to do any good here."

Alana turned to Secretary-General Lachlan. "Paya, this is an extraordinary situation. You have no choice but to take charge. I'm putting myself and all my people under your control until this emergency is over. The rest of you should willingly do the same."

Edric immediately agreed and Draylou grimaced his concurrence.

Secretary-General Lachlan turned in silence to the only Secretary-General who hadn't spoken. Secretary-General Dathan Acob was the youngest of the five and had only been part of the council for ten years. He worked closely with Secretary-General Lachlan to set standards and assure that there was a linear evolutionary path for the development of the technologies they all managed. He also shared with Paya the oversight and coordination with other sciences and technologies used by the galactic society. Dathan and Paya were the gateways to the other technologies. Dathan's simple response was, "I agree with Alana."

All were quiet for a few minutes. By this time, Paya Lachlan was looking almost directly into the open mouth of the Cathedral. She studied its straight sides with flying buttresses and conical towers probing into space, its interior with floor upon floor upon floor of work area occupied by Controllers dedicated to promoting and preserving exactly what was falling apart around them. What would those Controllers think if they knew what was happening? What would they all be thinking or doing in what might be the immediate future if they had to shut down the systems which kept all the far flung homesteads of humanity combined into a single galactic civilization? How many people would die if they failed? What anarchy would follow in the next few years?

With an effort Paya tore her eyes from the Cathedral to look around at the other Secretaries-General. What were they thinking? Would they all do the right thing? What was the right thing? She thought about transferring control to Edric Yan. He was certainly qualified to lead them all and he had already taken de facto operational control. No, leadership had to be exerted by a person at least once removed from the problem and had no assignments. And while Draylou would follow Edric if directed to do so, at some subconscious level he might not fully cooperate.

At last, Paya Lachlan spoke with firmness and command.

"I agree with Alana. Thank you for your support. As of this moment I take full supreme command of The Controllers."

Turning to look directly at Dathan Acob she directed, "Dathan, this may result in a horrible triage situation. I want you to start immediately on a massive program to manufacture personal stasis pods here and across the galaxy. You will not be able to manufacture enough to serve all humans who will need them but each one that is produced is another life that is possibly saved. Assure that each one of them has its own source of power. My goal is that we will solve this problem. However, if we don't, then we will need to use your pods to save as many people as possible by putting them into stasis."

Paya continued, "Edric, you have full authority to do whatever is necessary to solve this problem. As of this moment you have total operational control of all of the galaxy's technological systems. All other Secretaries-General will report to you for operational purposes. I retain overall command. Use your best judgment in taking actions and keeping me informed. There are no committees for this project at our level. Don't assume that I will slow you down." Only in passing did she notice the flush in Draylou's face.

Then addressing Alana, she said, "Right now, Alana, I want you to join me in a telescence conference with the government leaders. After that meeting you can continue as you suggested."

Meeting Between Government and Controllers

Galaxy Prime Minister Callum Seph reflected on the events of the recent past. He, and all of the Galaxy's Sector Ministers, had been receiving reports from the Controller Secretaries-General for a few years about a problem they had been working on with the entanglement transport systems. At first, the reports looked routine. And perhaps, he thought, the problem really was routine at that time. However, he had never before seen The Controllers put that much technical information in their standard reports to the galactic government. As time went on, and especially more recently, the reports had taken on an edge of concern, and included what seemed to be unusually careful wording about a disruption to entanglement transport that could be caused at some undefined future time.

About a year ago, Prime Minister Seph became sufficiently curious and concerned that he initiated a rare telesence session with Secretary-General Paya Lachlan. As they usually did, the meeting went well.

* * *

At that time, and twenty-five thousand light-years apart, the Prime Minister and the Secretary-General had presented their size ten images to each other as they walked across their merged offices to embrace as full equals. Their staffs had planned a casual, yet elegant, setting for their discussion. They turned and walked together through an arched doorway in a side wall to an open glade near cloud-covered mountains where two wicker chairs and a table were available.

After exchanging pleasantries, Paya opened the subject. "Callum, it has been years since we have visited each other and as much as I enjoy seeing you we both know this isn't a social call. My staff tells me that you have some concern about the entanglement technical issues we are working on."

The Prime Minister responded, "Exactly, Paya. When I first saw your reports on the problem I wasn't too concerned, although I was curious that such a technical subject was of sufficient magnitude to make its way into a standard report to us."

Paya acknowledged, "Actually, it was something at the time that we had a hard time deciding about reporting. As you might guess, we have thousands of technical issues of varying magnitude that we are studying all the time. You can't have a system this big without something large or small always being wrong somewhere. I'm sure you have the same experience with the planetary and interplanetary infrastructures you have responsibility for. And The Controllers seldom hear about any of those issues."

Callum Seph nodded in agreement, "Of course. That's true. And that is specifically why I'm curious. If I looked at the worst case, it seems you're telling us that there might be some type of a breakdown in the entanglement systems at some undefined point in the future and at least a couple of hundred years away."

"Callum, a couple of hundred years seems to be the worst case. And we have many, many decades to understand the problem and work on a solution. We have great scientists and engineers, and they haven't failed us yet. I'm sure they will find a solution."

Prime Minister Seph was receiving direct neural hints that the Secretary-General wasn't being entirely truthful, especially about what the worst case could possibly be. And, of course, Paya would know that. So, they each fully understood each other but, as is always true in these types of situations, they let that mutual knowledge go unspoken. Callum had learned what he needed to know. That the problem was serious and the Controllers fully believed that they had time to solve it. Good enough.

So they had left it at that. After some discussion about mutual friends, they ended the session and returned to other activities.

* * *

That was a year ago. This was today and concentration etched deep furrows in the Prime Minister's high forehead.

The full Council of Controller Secretaries-General had about an hour ago requested a joint telescence session with him, his cabinet members, and all of the galaxy's sector ministers. Such a meeting had never been requested during his several lifetimes. What choice did he have but to say, "Yes"? That session was due to start in just a few minutes.

Callum Seph's barrel chest periodically heaved with heart-felt sighs in a vain, subconscious attempt to relieve the tension which had been incessantly building since the disasters across so many entanglement nodes that morning. What had happened to make the Controller's system collapse so badly? Countless people had died in transport and most of the galaxy was in panic.

The blood pulsing through his head pounded on him with a cadence matched by his long, neatly trimmed fingers drumming on the arm of his control throne. Here, in his glass domed sanctuary atop the galaxy's governmental headquarters he could normally depend upon the beauty of the view to help him relax and resolve his problems. But this time when he looked out the dome at the star field he was looking at his problem. When he used the entanglement technology that linked him to distant trusted advisors and friends, he was personally adding to the problem. When he sucked additional energy through the headquarters' energy transport node he accelerated the disruption and became part of the problem. He felt helpless because he could only be part of the impending disaster that might topple his empire; not part of the solution that could preserve it.

The information the Controllers had been trickling out to him since this morning was so outlandish, so terrible in its impact, that he at first refused to believe it. The recent galactic-wide disturbance went beyond the concerns of the technical updates. He wondered what was really happening.

How could a couple of hundred years with plenty of time to almost certainly solve a problem turn into a nearer term catastrophe with the potential loss of trillions of lives across the galaxy? They gave him no warning at all! Why didn't they tell him? They must have known and were deliberately hiding the information. Either that or they were truly incompetent. He was suddenly totally without trust. Then again, he could simply be suffering the constant suspicion that comes with power.

Callum Seph had been trained from birth to handle political and economic issues, but he had never felt fully comfortable in the role that he always secretly knew should have gone to someone else. When it came to technology, he was only a user. He had little more than a layman's knowledge of the science that supported the galaxy's infrastructure and bound its far-flung provinces together. All his life he had placed his trust in The Controllers of technology, and they had never betrayed that trust. But now, paranoid doubts about their information and abilities gnawed at him.

A vibration from his throne pulled him out of his introspection. His chambers announced, "The scheduled telescence conference with the Council of Controller Secretaries-General, you, your cabinet and sector ministers will begin in five minutes."

He immediately relayed the message to all the sector ministers and his executive staff. In a few minutes, they would be meeting.

His mind was spinning. What approach should he take? The disruption was so unexpected. So catastrophic! News of the breakdown was of course minimized as much as possible. However, it was eventually known across the galaxy within hours. Every person would surely now have their media filter set to receive news of this import while eliminating or storing off-line things that were less critical. The ministers in the various sectors of the galaxy were indicating that the disruption, as expected, was creating intense unrest and anxiety.

The minister responsible for the University sector in which the problem had been analyzed, and fixed by a Controller Researcher previously unknown to any of them, had repeatedly tried to set up a telescence session with him since the disruption occurred that morning. So far, the Prime Minister had been able to ignore his calls pleading a busy schedule. And that was only one of hundreds of requests. He couldn't dodge the calls much longer, but he had wanted to talk to the Secretaries-General first so that he could have more knowledge before attempting to respond. It now seemed that his staff and sector ministers would learn what was happening at the same time he did.

* * *

It took a minute for the Galactic Prime Minister to settle himself, after which he spoke the command that would assemble his cabinet for a telescence conference. While everyone would know that his staff was actually dispersed across three hundred thousand cubic light-years of the galaxy it would appear to every participant that his entire staff was assembled in his office. All cabinet members and ministers naturally responded that they were immediately available. He assembled them first into a quick internal meeting before responding to the Secretaries-General's request.

"Each of you has received a preliminary, and regrettably incomplete, briefing on the massive galactic-wide disruption that occurred this morning. You know that the timing and severity of the disruption were a total surprise to The Controllers." Or so they told me, he thought to himself. "They did not expect the initial disruption to be either this pervasive or for it to come as soon as it did. They anticipated perhaps another couple of hundred years and plenty of time to avoid any problem. My previous briefings to you reflected what I had been told by the Controllers.

"It now looks as though the previous information was incorrect. We are all aware of the disaster this morning, the resultant loss of life and the disruption of the transmission of people and material, but not communication, galaxy-wide. As soon as the event occurred, I asked for a meeting with the Council of Secretaries-General. We scheduled that meeting for this afternoon. We will begin shortly."

Suddenly, the Galactic Prime Minister raised his hand and a translucent privacy curtain veiled him from the others. His chambers alerted him that the meeting would be with Secretary-General Paya Lachlan alone, not the full Council of Secretaries-General. That was strange. At first he didn't understand. Slowly, it dawned on him that Paya must have taken over full control of her council, and that could only mean bad news. That changed things dramatically. He was shaking with stress and commanded the room to include a calming drug in the air around him. After about thirty seconds he reentered the conference with his sector ministers.

"I've just received notification that our meeting will be with Secretary-General Paya Lachlan, not with the full Council of Secretaries-General. We all know that her individual indication, rather than a group indication, must mean that she has exercised her option to assume the position of Supreme Secretary-General. I suspect that means that the news might be even worse. Unless there is an objection, I'll respond now to that request."

* * *

The Prime Minister noted that each of his cabinet members and ministers was composed and apparently ready to take whatever action was necessary. He wondered if they were truly more relaxed than he was, or had also taken a drug to stay calm. Inside he was in a panic, although he was no longer shaking on the outside. Enough was enough. He turned his throne to assume the proper position for a conference, and completed the channel to the person who was now the Supreme Secretary-General of the Council of Secretaries-General.

Secretary-General Lachlan appeared at the center of the screen, slightly in front and to the right of Secretary-General Alana Perg, who flanked her. The slight cloudiness that overshadowed the other Secretary-General was an indication that only Paya Lachlan would be speaking. This was clear proof that she was no longer just a senior among equals. She was now fully in command. She spoke first.

"Mr. Prime Minister, I'm advised that now is not the time for ponderous social protocols or political jargon. I'll speak frankly, and ask that you do the same with special attention to making good use of what little time we have left."

The Prime Minister responded, "If you feel that is required then proceed quickly. However, I wish that you had advised me before you assumed full authority over the other Secretaries-General."

Paya ignored the rebuke. Instead, she asked that all of the standard emotion blocking safeguards be removed for the rest of the conference. "I realize that this is an extremely unusual request normally only granted between the closest of individuals. However, by the end of the session you will understand the reason for my suggestion."

The discomfort of all the attendees, including even the background Secretary-General was clearly evident. After all, there were always emotions people were each unwilling to share. Certainly, the Prime Minister didn't want it known that he had to be sedated to maintain control.

Paya continued. "I understand your reluctance. To show my good faith I will be the first, and I am dropping all safeguards at my location right now." Immediately, each of the other attendees at all locations in the conference felt the full emotional thrust of Paya's concerns. They also perceived the massive self-control and good leadership sense that she had. In the midst of the entire sudden wave of direct emotional access to Paya they knew that she was operating without subterfuge and out of a recently understood belief that civilization was on the brink of extinction. They also saw, and felt, the random background emotions that always run through any person's mind. Without waiting for the others to follow suit, and as further evidence of her concern, she proceeded quickly through the events of the last few hours, including the fortunate availability and recruitment of Kieran Llot, and his work to adjust the transport systems to return them to full, if temporary, operation. One by one, almost all other attendees of the meeting removed their safeguards. The Galactic Prime Minister was the most notable exception.

Paya summarized the meeting of the Council of Secretaries-General that had just ended and then informed the group. "Prime Minister and Sector Ministers, as a result of what I have learned today, I have taken two major actions within my organization for which I am obviously now Supreme Secretary-General. Secretary-General Edric Yan is now in charge of all operational and development activities necessary to preserve our systems and continue them at full operation. All other Secretaries-General are reporting to him during this effort. We don't have much time and we may not succeed. If we don't succeed then we will need to save as much of the galaxy's population as possible."

That last statement increased the level of concern among all of the attendees as was clear from the anxiety wave that suddenly cascaded through the entanglement connection.

Paya then explained, "To that end, I have asked Secretary-General Dathan Acob to begin full-scale production all across the galaxy of personal long-sleep stasis pods with individual fusion power supplies. These, of course, are meant to be used only in the event that we have catastrophic breakdown of our entanglement systems."

Paya held up her hand to ask for silence as the Ministers began to ask a deluge of questions or murmur among themselves. "Yes, it is that potentially serious. No, we did not know it was possibly this catastrophic until the last few hours. Yes, we have been honest with you. Mostly, as leaders, we need to be calm! I am hiding nothing!"

The University Sector Minister, Monz Ingra, boldly executed a conversation override and quietly observed, "Paya, you will not be able to produce enough pods for the entire population of the galaxy. I offer the full services of the University Sector to this effort. But, you surely know that as soon as it becomes known that a catastrophe is certain to occur, and that stasis pods are available for a long sleep and potential survival, that riots will break out everywhere as people clamor for access."

Paya responded, "I am sadly aware of that. That is where the government police forces and the corporate military forces come into play. However, I also know that these forces may turn on the population and use the pods themselves. Perhaps our android soldiers can be used. I don't have any answers for that and it is something that has to be addressed outside of this meeting. Frankly, there may be no answer. Chaos may be inevitable. It is a horrible situation."

All were quiet for a while as the gravity of the crisis and the burden of their responsibilities settled on them.

At length, the Prime Minister leaned forward in his throne, his brown eyes focused directly on Paya. "I don't understand your technology, but it is clear that you are hiding nothing and are operating in the best interest of all. It seems you have no choice in the direction you are taking. It looks like we in the government don't either."

The Prime Minister paused while he searched for the right words and for the control he wished he had . "Paya, I don't believe in coincidence, and I'm not a mystic. I do know when to take advantage of what looks like luck, but isn't. Perhaps your Kieran Llot is the key to solving this problem. He'd better be because you obviously don't have anything else. We will work with you. Please keep me posted so that the government will know what to do to prepare the citizens."

To Paya's astonishment and his own relief, the Prime Minister immediately shut down the conference. Paya sat blinking for a few seconds at the space the Prime Minister's chambers had just been occupying.

Alana's voice broke the silence. "OK, we all know what we have to do. Unless you have an objection, Paya, I will be on my way."

"Thank you, Alana. No objection. You and I and Edric will need to keep in close communication with each other."

Activities at University Planet

University Sector Minister Monz Ingra was equally surprised by the abrupt way in which the Galactic Prime Minister terminated the telescence meeting. He immediately established a profound cloak of privacy so he could have a few minutes to absorb this new and devastating information. He was furious, desperate and determined. As the University Sector Minister he had full responsibility for management of this section of the Galaxy. He had believed the previous information that any problem was still at least centuries away and solvable. This morning's breakdown gave him no time to prepare for this ultimate of all disasters. The queue of people trying to reach him was thousands long. Many were as angry as he was and demanding explanations. He didn't have any because The Controllers claimed surprise. It didn't help that the weak-kneed figurehead Galactic Prime Minister Callum Seph had been dodging his calls.

His sector was home to University Planet, the galaxy's primary and most prestigious seat of higher learning and development. In turn, University Planet really belonged to The Controllers and was the guardian planet for The Cathedral.

One of the recipients of that learning, Kieran Llot had been the key to minimizing the morning's disruption. If it had gone on much longer many more deaths would have resulted. As it was, the failure had temporarily slightly disrupted all energy flow to the sector's life support systems as well as non-critical systems. The storage systems on each of the sector's planets were fortunately fully charged and were really only meant to provide a means of leveling the load presented to the transport systems. These storage systems could, on the average, keep the sector going for about ten hours. If the disruption had gone past six or seven hours, non-critical systems would have to be shut down so that the life-support systems could last another couple of hours. Past that point people would start dying as heating and recycling systems failed. Panic and riots would probably follow as a pampered populace panicked. Even without that more massive failure, he was being besieged by panicky constituents. Monz didn't like the few options that were available to him.

Monz had begun to suspect the worst immediately after the disruption and had quickly advised his engineers and scientists to make necessary preparations for a catastrophe. Their reaction was generally professional even though they were clearly shaken. However, Deputy for Technical Systems and Liaison to The Controllers, Jaidon Lothe, was miserable. Minister Ingra suspected that Lothe's misery was out of fear for his career instead of concern for the populace. How could he have been stuck with such a dolt? Politics!

"Minister, I'm sorry. I can't think of anything we can do to prevent catastrophe in the event of a prolonged outage," Jaidon had whined.

"Jaidon," the minister replied with exaggerated patience, "Let me explain this to you again and carefully. You shouldn't be thinking about the possibility of a prolonged outage. Think of the certainty of a permanent outage. You must prepare for the worst and hope for better."

"But minister," the deputy was almost crying, "there is nothing that can be done. All energy and all interstellar travel and communication come through The Controllers' node. We can do without travel and communication, but without energy we will all freeze within a week."

"Jaidon, stop telling me the obvious. At this point travel and communication may be luxuries. Concentrate on alternate energy sources and remember that The Controllers need this sector because it is their home. This is the home of University Planet and The Cathedral. We are the seat of knowledge and technical prowess for the galaxy. Gather the experts, put some of that knowledge to work and get back to me tomorrow with solutions. If you can't perhaps your assistant can. I don't have time to coddle ineffectiveness. Get out of my office."

Monz had watched with disgust and impatience as the shocked deputy backed stumbling out of his office. Perhaps the man's greed and ambition would incent him to come up with a solution. Certainly intellect wouldn't.

Monz had little sympathy for Jaidon, but he had to admit to himself that he was also shaken by the suddenness of the disruption. Supposedly the Controllers thought they had time to prevent it. Assuming they were being honest, and it appeared that they were, they were taken completely by surprise. They had all clearly become complacent. Millennia of perfect operation of the telescence and transport systems left the entire galaxy with no backup systems in the event of any breakdown. They had put all of their eggs in one basket. Obviously it was a well-guarded, well-designed basket, but it was the only one there was. How could they have all been so stupid and so full of technological ego?

Monz shifted in his chair as he reflected that the University sector was pocketed in a low energy part of the galaxy even though close to the center. Its stars were generally cooler and more dispersed than adjacent areas. It was simply a random result of the expansion of the universe. The planets were, therefore, artificially heated with energy imported through the entanglement systems. Consequently, the sector imported massive amounts of energy from other areas that were energy rich. In turn, the university sector balanced payments by exporting knowledge and providing research facilities.

So much for introspection. Given the information he had just received during the telescence session with the other ministers and Paya it was time for more aggressive action. He made the gesture to establish a telescence conversation with University President Gareth Frax.

* * *

Gareth Frax's notification chime sounded and a disembodied voice announced an urgent request from Monz Ingra for a telescence discussion. Gareth, sitting slouched in deep concentration in his office casually waved agreement. Gareth and Monz were best friends. Theirs was an easy relationship derived through two hundred years of association. Monz stepped across the distance between their planets to an empty chair in front of the fireplace. The room, as was customary, automatically placed a chess board with their current unfinished game between them. Gareth gestured it away. Monz sat down and picked up his favorite drink that had materialized on the table beside his chair.

Each stared silently at the fireplace, still a psychological comfort left over from the days of the cave. Gareth eventually broke the silence answering the unspoken question.

"Monz, I've just been briefed for the third time today on Kieran Llot's findings, and we have checked his work with some quick computer simulations during the last few minutes. There is no doubt that another disruption is inevitable, and perhaps irreversible, no matter what we do. We also don't understand the reason for the disruption. I've already deposited the details in your throne computer for your review. If I and our university scientists understand this properly, we are some indefinite amount of time away from a total breakdown of all major nodes in the galaxy. I've already assembled several small groups to be at your command as soon as you declare martial law within our sector. One group, with the charter of finding and managing energy sources, is ready to be put under your control immediately."

Monz nodded his agreement. He had been sure that Gareth would take the proper initiative without being asked. It was a reflection of Gareth's professionalism as well as Monz's number one leadership principle that 'people will always meet your expectations'. Monz's expectations were always positive and high.

Gareth asked, "How did your meeting go with the Council of Secretaries-General?"

Monz had recorded the session and replayed it for Gareth.

When the recording was finished the two friends just sat for a time in silence. They both suspected that humankind was moving inexorably toward a cataclysm that couldn't be prevented. Neither could predict what the result would be, but perhaps they could at least minimize the destruction in their sector.

Monz asked, "I get the impression that you feel there is no hope, Gareth?"

"None that we know of here. My academic researchers need an immediate closer relationship with The Controllers scientists, so it is helpful that you had the meeting with Paya and Alana. And it is important that Kieran Llot is here. Teaming up with the research scientists at The Guide's Hall might be a good idea, also."

"And, if I know you, then you have already made moves in that direction," Monz said with a smile.

"Naturally," Gareth replied as he stood to slowly pace across the room.

After a few more minutes of reflection, Monz told his friend, "You and I are both realists. We know that our civilization and structure as we know it may be coming to an end. You are the head of the seat of knowledge of the galaxy when it comes to generalized information. Within this sector that I control, I will shortly direct that we put all of our resources toward preserving the University planet for as long as possible. I have no doubt that The Controllers will help us. Gareth, you must be ruthless in your efforts to preserve University."

Monz continued, "Gareth, I am going to direct that all stasis pods that are built in the University Sector will first be used to put scientists and engineers and other University Planet and Cathedral people necessary to the preservation of knowledge and regeneration of civilization into hibernation. I suspect that The Guide will be doing the same thing at The Guide's Hall. I don't know what our Prime Minister is going to do. My suspicion is that he will panic."

Monz walked toward his friend. Gareth stood and the two embraced each other. Too full of emotion to say anything more they parted and Monz returned to his office. With a final nod goodbye, they terminated the telescence link. Each knew what they had to do and some of it was best left unspoken.

* * *

As soon as he was alone after the meeting with Paya Lachlan, the Prime Minister of the entire galaxy shuddered yet another sigh. As he again nervously strummed his fingers on his throne, Callum Seph finally understood what was really happening. The Controllers had been taken by surprise and lost control. Their beautiful system, with all its safeguards, that had run so well for one hundred millennia was collapsing. And they really didn't know why. While the problem, as they initially understood it, had probably taken them by surprise it was now cascading out of control. Cheap, easy energy and a flawless transportation and communications system all rolled into one had lulled them into ignoring alternative technologies in the event of disaster. He knew he was as guilty as the rest. He never even thought about a catastrophe of anywhere near these proportions. Even now he was having trouble grasping the total impact. How do you imagine the end of a galactic wide civilization built up over one hundred thousand years?

The knowledge that he had to lead forced its way through the fog of his fear. He understood that he had no time now for self-indulgent introspection. He knew he had to make the announcement he had been putting off. He wondered how his message would be received.

The news about the disruption had reached even the most remote and isolated parts of the entire galaxy. At first it was received by many as a blatant error in reporting or, perhaps a gross exaggeration of events. After all it had been thousands of years since the last previous major event.

The Controllers had always guaranteed that such a disruption was impossible. In fact, the belief in the technology was so strong that disruptions weren't talked about even in fiction.

Follow-on news reports soon confirmed the event and brought total detail to the story. Each viewer felt like they were at the scene giving them the full impact of the catastrophe and the near disaster which followed. Almost everyone in the entire galaxy watched replay after replay in horrific fascination. At some base level, even the viewers in greatest denial knew that this was a portent of some event even more unimaginable. Reporters and publicity seeking intellectuals made wild speculations that the populace immediately interpreted as learned speculation. Those knowledgeable individuals who correctly guessed the impact were so frightened by their own conclusion that they kept their own counsel out of fear of creating a panic in the whole of civilization. As it was, taverns were filled to overflowing and production requiring human supervision came to a virtual standstill. Though the local Controllers managing each node insisted that all was well, the number of travelers decreased by eighty percent.

Gathering of Forces

One of those travelers was Secretary-General Alana Perg who arrived at the University only four hours after Kieran Llot. Kieran had just finished briefing the University President and was preparing for a night's sleep guaranteed by physical and mental exhaustion when Alana entered the President's office. She had been remotely viewing Kieran's presentation as she traveled from the nearby gateway. An aide announced Alana's arrival.

* * *

"University President Gareth Frax, please permit me to introduce Secretary-General Alana Perg."

Alana perfunctorily accepted the unnecessary introduction and gracefully walked into the President's office. She nodded to the President and extended her hand to Kieran, who accepted it and bowed from the waist saying, "I am honored, Secretary-General."

She surprised Kieran and the Gareth Frax with her reply.

"Nonsense, Researcher. It is I who am honored, and I place my authority and myself at your disposal. Between you and the President Frax's facilities you have enough technical resources and intellect to be able to cope with any scientific problem. I'm here to offer my political clout so you can get things done in case anyone in the Controllers organization gets in your way. The entire resources of The Cathedral and The Controllers organization are at your call."

She paused to look Kieran over carefully. She hoped that Kieran had the stuff for what lay ahead. During the brief silence Kieran and President Frax said nothing, mostly because they didn't know what to say.

"You look tired," she observed. "I want you to forget this problem until tomorrow. The most important thing you can do now is sleep. While you do that, the rest of us will discuss how best to manage the impact of your findings." Then she said to Gareth, "May I request that you put the Researcher in quarters close to mine and see that he isn't disturbed until either he or I permit it?"

"Of course, Secretary-General."

Alana then dismissed Kieran saying, "Researcher, please excuse us now. But be ready to join us when you are refreshed."

Kieran bowed to Alana and shook the University President's hand before quickly and quietly leaving the room. He was exhausted, but not sure that the adrenaline still surging through his arteries would let him sleep. Ten minutes later mental and physical exhaustion won and he was unconscious before his head hit the pillow.

Alana resumed, "President Frax, I meant what I said to the Researcher. I've been away from our art and in a leadership position too long to think I can be of any technical use, but I am willing to lend my support and take some of the political heat off of you and the sector minister. I understand the two of you work well together.

Gareth replied, "We do. We've been friends and associates since our last previous lives."

"Good. Your friendship and mutual trust will be important over the next couple of days. What has been the response to the meeting Paya Lachlan and I had with the Prime Minister and his staff?"

The University President felt cautious but answered candidly. "I wasn't in that meeting, but I talked with my Sector Minister Monz Ingra only a few minutes after it ended. He strongly believes that the University Planet and The Cathedral are the most important locations in our sector. He has directed me to preserve and protect these locations whatever it costs the rest of his sector. I am prepared to do that and Monz believes that The Controllers secretaries-general will feel the same way."

The Secretary-General was quiet for a few seconds. How did they come to a situation in which people who were essentially strangers were thrust together in the greatest threat ever faced by humankind? She mentally sighed, hoping he was as good as his reputation. She wanted to work with him and use his talents fully.

"Mister President, we don't know each other well and I know it takes years of shared experience to build full mutual trust such as you and Monz Ingra have. But we must drop all reserve with each other and work in a trusting relationship. Through different means, we have both confirmed that Researcher Llot's projection is correct. We are probably going to lose the Galaxy's energy, matter and biological transport systems in the almost immediate future. When that happens our civilization as we know it may end.

"We all know that the Prime Minister is a morally and mentally weak man. He and his cabinet are not strong enough or knowledgeable enough to take the steps necessary to help us at least preserve something for the future. Paya Lachlan and I believe that he will probably do more things wrong than right. I'll bet Monz Ingra hasn't personally heard from him at all. My suspicion is that our Prime Minister is near catatonic with fear. Family loyalty will prevent his replacement until it is too late."

Alana continued to give her candid perspective. "The Council of Secretaries-General is ineffective for this type of problem. We are nothing but a group of super executives at the top of a bureaucracy deliberately designed to be ponderous so that we don't create technological disruption.

"President Frax, the stark reality is that we are standing at, and you are in charge of, the hub of all of humanity's accumulated knowledge. That knowledge must be preserved for any future civilization that emerges from the ashes of our mistakes. Given the realities we all face, the most important task we have is preservation of the University and the University sector so that future generations, if there are any, will have full access to the knowledge trove of humanity. I feel sure that I can persuade Paya Lachlan to turn over Controller leadership of such an effort to me. However, you must have enough blind trust in me to work with me as closely as you do with your friend the sector minister. A fully trusting close relationship between the three of us is necessary to preservation of the University and as a new starting point for future civilization."

Alana had surprised herself as much as President Gareth Frax. She wondered where the thoughts she had voiced came from and where her words would take them. Was there such a thing as divine guidance after all? She wondered what the President was thinking. Alana was almost suggesting mutiny justified by extraordinary circumstance. It was hard to imagine circumstance more extraordinary. Her next move would depend on the

President's response. Whatever his response, it would be a long night.

* * *

The Guide and Malin Nowl were meeting at the same time Gareth Frax and Alana Perg were having their discussion. The Guide had been looking through his protective field at the complex structure of the linked spheres of The Guide's Hall stretching into the infinite space. The room shimmered in the scene's glow producing the impression of a mist lifting and separating him from his surroundings leaving his features vague. He turned to walk toward and sit beside Malin. His voice, while sounding tired, was kind, compassionate and compelling.

"So, The Controller Secretaries-General have met in emergency session and have briefed the Galactic Ministers. Do you think they expected this, or that they understand what is really happening?"

"No, Takar. But then none of us know for sure what is impending. They appear to be totally surprised at the swiftness and breadth of this disruption. They didn't expect this to happen so soon."

The Guide observed, "I don't think any of us did, even including Inara."

Takar Cillian struggled for only a second or so with a decision that seemed to him to take hours to think through. A decision that was horrible, but even worse not to make. "Malin, please set up an emergency telescence session with Secretary-General Edric Yan and have Inara come here immediately. I want the session with Edric Yan to start about fifteen minutes after Inara arrives. Inara will join us in the telescence session, and I want you to attend as well. Please let Secretary-General Yan's staff know that the meeting is extremely important to us and to him, and that we will strive to keep it brief."

Malin gently observed, "If you are going to do what I think you are going to do then Pren should be here, too."

With no hesitation, the Guide responded, "You're right, have Pren attend also. Obviously, we can't tell Edric Yan or his staff about Inara. We will leave that up to her."

The Guide didn't have to wait long. As Inara and Pren entered his office, he was shocked by Inara's appearance. She was stooped over and obviously weak. She was doing her best to present herself properly to The Guide but was clearly exhausted. Pren Bodhi and Malin helped her to a chair which the room had immediately materialized for her just inside The Guide's office door.

Stunned, The Guide asked, "Inara, what is happening? I had no idea! How long have you been like this?"

"Please, Guide, it is alright. I'm actually doing better. This started with the disruption this morning. The soul felt great pain, and I'm still recovering from my reaction to that."

"Malin, have the entire Hall start praying immediately for my intention. They will stop only when I give the word."

Inara tried to interrupt, but The Guide held up his hand and simply told her, "No!"

The Guide then took Inara a drink of water and sat beside her putting his arm around her. Pren sat on the other side of her holding her hand. After a few minutes, Inara broke the silence, saying quietly to the Guide. "I know that you are going to ask me to do something that might put me in great danger. I know you have no real choice, and I will do whatever you ask. Let's not wait any longer. What do you want?"

Pren glared at The Guide who suddenly, to his own surprise, had tears in his eyes.

Inara turned to look directly at Pren and said, "This has to be done. Please help. Don't interfere."

The Guide stood and walked a few paces away from them before explaining. "Secretary-General Edric Yan of The Controllers is a devout Pilgrim. I have met with him on many occasions. He is devoted to the Universal Soul and is a good man whom I trust. In a few minutes, we will have a full telescence session with him. He and I will each present ourselves to each other at size ten. There will be no formalities and we will launch immediately into discussion. You three will be in the room with me, and I fully believe that Edric will have others with him. Inara, at the outset of the meeting I want you to tell me what you sense about each individual in the room. Before even giving any hint of your special talents I want to make sure there is no evil in the room."

Inara grabbed Pren's arm as he angrily came out of his seat. With surprising strength, she pulled him back into his chair.

Inara then quietly said, "I understand what is needed. This problem can't be fixed without the full set of information needed to understand it. You believe that a complete understanding of the linkage of soul with space-time is required to prevent a catastrophe. You also believe that The Controller technologists need to have that information to solve the problem."

"Exactly," responded The Guide. I also think that it is in the best interest of even the most evil people to solve the problem. However, I won't reveal you to evil people. So, I want you to tell me if there is anyone who is a danger to you in the meeting. I will do whatever is necessary to exclude that person."

Inara shrugged her shoulders and said simply, "Let's get started. But, you must understand something. It may already be too late to prevent a horrible catastrophe that will kill the vast majority of life in the galaxy. But perhaps we can prevent the destruction of all life. And, more importantly, retain our relationship with the Universal Soul."

The Guide looked at her and forlornly nodded his head.

In response to his thought, The Guide's throne appeared in the center of his study. The Guide sat with Malin to his left, Pren to his right and Inara to the right of Pren. After a short wait for the appropriate meeting time, The Guide waved his readiness and the size ten image of Secretary-General Edric Yan appeared about ten feet in front of him. Two others, a man and a woman, were in the room with Edric Yan. The Guide and Edric Yan rose to walk toward each other to shake hands. Malin and Edric Yan's assistant made introductions. Malin simply indicated that Inara and Pren were technologists on his staff.

Inara signaled to The Guide that something was terribly wrong. At the same time, Inara used the Guide's room to send him a neural signal that said, "The woman is evil."

The Guide turned to Edric Yan and quickly said, "Thank you for this short meeting. You know that I have a good research staff. They are at your disposal if you need them to help with the problem that occurred this morning. You have direct access to me at no notice for anything that you need. I asked for this telescence discussion so you would have the full import of my sincerity. I won't keep you any longer."

Edric Yan, if he was surprised at The Guide's abruptness, didn't show it. Instead, he simply said, "Takar, it has been a long time since we have had some time alone together. Perhaps we could have a cup of your great refreshment. Given the situation, we may never have this opportunity again."

"I agree, Edric. Will you join me in my office?

Nodding his head in agreement, Edric Yan walked across the room to The Guide and removed his two staff members from the meeting. He looked at the three with The Guide and raised his eyebrows in question.

In reply, The Guide said, "I think it is important to all of us that they stay."

The Guide paused and looked at Inara who nodded agreement. That slight interaction did not escape the attention of the Secretary-General.

The Guide then made introductions, "These are Pren Bodhi and Inara Eyers. You already know Malin. If at any time you want them to leave just let me know.

"But first, let me ask you to do something unusual. Please shake hands with my friends Pren and Inara."

Edric gave Takar another questioning look but did as he was asked. By this time both Edric Yan and Takar Cillian were at normal size. The ever protective Pren pushed ahead in front of Inara and quickly shook the Secretary-General's hand and welcomed him. Inara then walked up to Edric and looked him straight in the eye for a few seconds before reaching out her hand to shake that of the Secretary-General. She held onto it for a second or two more than was usual, after which she smiled at The Guide. She then said, "Let's continue."

The Secretary-General asked The Guide. "Will you please tell me what is happening here?" Inara nodded her agreement while Pren fidgeted.

"Edric, let me tell you about Inara, about the Universal Soul and about evil."

Thirty information-packed minutes later, Edric Yan felt like he was in overload. "Takar, if anyone else in the galaxy told me this story I would not believe them. Now the question is what do we do with this information. You have added the element of great evil to the problem of disruption. And, if I understand correctly, the one influences the other."

For the first time Inara spoke up. "In all of this that you have been told there is a backdrop that needs to be understood as well. The action of entanglement as it is being used tears only slightly at the fabric of space-time-soul. The major impact of this slight tear that we perceive is on the space-time piece. However, it also tears in a larger way, that we don't perceive, at the soul. This is because, throughout our long history, this technology was originated by, controlled by, and enriched incredibly evil people at the expense of good people. These evil people operate in a deep background and no one outside of them has ever met the core group. This tearing of the soul couldn't be seen and understood in the standard equations and so the long-term impact couldn't be predicted. This morning, in the midst of the galactic wide disruption, I finally began to put together a small piece of the mathematical side of the soul equation because I could actually see the tearing of the fabric of the soul and the associated larger tear in space-time. I think that, with some help, I could make better progress."

Inara looked at The Guide and said, "You can stop the prayers now. Thank you."

The Guide nodded.

Edric Yan offered, "Certainly. I can get that help for you with your agreement. But, Inara, let me probe something for a minute. You just said you could see the tearing of the soul. Please, I can accept, or at least do my best to accept, integrated senses combined with a genius intellect permitting you to see the galaxy in ways not available to the rest of us. While it requires a lot of acceptance, the concept is indeed fathomable. But, to see the soul actually tear. Isn't that pushing things a bit?"

Suddenly, Inara had fire in her eyes. "Secretary-General, let me show you something."

The Guide interrupted. "Inara, the Secretary-General has already been given a tremendous amount of information to take back to others he has to work with. Before you go further, we might have to ask the Secretary-General if there is anyone else who should be invited to this discussion. It will save much valuable time later."

Pren quickly spoke up with a bit of anger in his voice, "Guide, haven't we endangered Inara enough? You promised to protect her."

Inara put a hand on her uncle's arm. "Uncle Pren, it's too late for anything to touch me. Things are going to change soon. The fates of trillions of people and of the Universal Soul are far more important than I am. It's alright."

The Guide turned back to Edric Yan, "Well, Edric?"

"Takar, there are at least two others. You and Malin are familiar with both of them. They are Paya and Alana. Paya is in the Cathedral, and Alana is on the University Planet to provide any assistance that the primary Controllers' Researcher, a scientist named Kieran Llot, needs."

Inara came out of her chair. "Who? Kieran Llot?"

"Yes, is that a problem?" asked Edric Yan.

"No. No. Uh, no. It won't be a problem."

"Good. It is vital that Kieran come on board. The others would be helpful, too. Naturally, they will have to pass muster with you, Inara. I would be surprised if they can't."

Recovering her composure, Inara commented, "I'm sorry. I knew Kieran years ago when I was at Andromeda. I should tell you that we were emotionally close. He is one of the best people I have ever met."

While exchanging glances with Pren, the Guide asked Edric Yan, "What do you propose?"

Yan responded, "I will leave you for a while and return to The Cathedral. Inara and I should stay connected the entire time via an extremely private secure telescence link. She will be in the background with her identity concealed, and she will have full access to all sensory facilities and information that pass between Paya, Alana and me. Just as you have done here, she will have full opportunity to stop the discussion, or alert us to a problem at any time."

Turning to Pren, he said, "I will protect Inara as if she were my own daughter."

All Pren could do was helplessly nod.

* * *

The University President noticed a misty blue frame appear between them and understood that Secretary-General Perg was being summoned by one of her peers.

Alana apologetically said, "President Frax, I'm sorry, but I must excuse myself for a private side conversation."

"Of course, Secretary-General"

A shimmering privacy room appeared around Alana. The others could see a shadowy presence of Edric Yan and Paya Lachlan in Alana's virtual room with her. What they weren't permitted to see was Inara's cloaked presence.

Edric began his explanation to Alana, "I'm sorry to intrude on you, but I need to bring you up to date on some important things I have just learned from The Guide and some of his team." Secretary-General Yan began to play a recording of the meeting he had attended to bring them both up to date. Alana quickly stopped him. "Edric, I am with University President Gareth Frax. He needs to see this also."

Paya quickly agreed. After a moment's delay for a background discussion with an unseen Inara, Edric also agreed and the semi-private blue frame disappeared. Alana made introductions and the recording restarted.

After they had all viewed the recording Edric Yan said, "I think it is essential that you all attend the next part of this discussion in The Guides' chambers. Will you join me?"

"Of course", Paya, Alana and Gareth answered simultaneously. Alana added, "If there is no objection, I think it is important that Sector Minister Monz Ingra join us."

Again, after another discrete discussion with Inara, Edric agreed saying, "I think that will be necessary. Bring him along."

As that meeting ended Alana turned back to Gareth Frax. "President Frax, it looks like we will all have to be quick on our feet for the next couple of days. Do you mind contacting your friend, the Sector Minister, and ask if he will join us?"

Gareth responded with no hesitation. "I'll be happy to. Let's call Minister Ingra together and bring him up to date. I'm sure he'll agree."

* * *

One hour later, Edric Yan rejoined those in The Guide's chambers. The group included University President Gareth Frax and Sector Minister Monz Ingra. Edric introduced Paya and Alana. Alana in turn introduced Gareth and Monz. As agreed among them all, Inara brought those who had remained at The Guide's Hall up to date.

"So it appears," said The Guide, "that we have an improbable team with an unexpected mission of saving as much of the galaxy as we can."

"I agree," said Paya Lachlan. "However, what about this horrible evil Inara has told us of? These people will certainly want to destroy you and the Pilgrims, and Inara in particular."

The Guide commented, "Inara, perhaps you should show a little bit more."

Inara launched into the same two presentations she had previously given to The Guide, Edric and Pren. She showed how she saw the galaxy in space-time and then in space-time-soul. She showed the brown clouds and the sewage smell connected with the presence of great evil concluding with, "That is a sampling of how I see everything."

She then paused for a second, looking in turn at everyone in the room and finally settling her gaze on Paya Lachlan. "You are being told this because I know, without any doubt, that you are all good people and that you will do the right thing with the information I'm sharing with you."

143

At that moment Inara's demeanor changed as she became a bit tense. "Now, I must tell you something horrible. Oh, no. All of a sudden I understand." Inara paused wide-eyed, "The Universal Soul can't wait any longer. It is reckoning time. Oh, no! No!"

* * *

Inara announced to the group, "Something is going to take place immediately that we can't control but we can assist with. Everyone, will you each please remove all emotional filters you have remaining in place. You must each know without any doubt at all that you are dealing with each other in perfect honesty. If you do so, then you will each perceive immediately that there is no dishonesty involved in any way in this discussion.

"I think we all understand that good and evil are always at some level of war with each other. It can be a struggle within ourselves between desire and duty, or it can be something much bigger between massive groups of people. I have just shown you long term evidence of one struggle that has had immense effect, but been invisible to us.

"Before humans even existed, this struggle was taking place and is alluded to in the most ancient of documents as a massive combat of the spirit. It will go on forever, and humans will have a part in it for as long as we are around."

With extreme sadness in her voice, Inara continued, "Now, the spirit, the Universal Soul, has no choice but to enter combat again on a galaxy-wide scale as it has done at least once, even before life had appeared on Earth. Sides have been chosen, and we must help in the only way we can. A war beyond our comprehension will soon begin, and the results will be quickly visible all across the galaxy."

Inara observed quietly, "I understand even more clearly now that the recent disruption to our entanglement systems was a spasm of pain from the Universal Soul. It was the Universal Soul's uncontrollable reaction to harm that had been inflicted on it for so long. But, what is about to happen next is deliberate warfare. The Universal Soul is entering a massive, galaxy-wide battle with evil that it must engage in to prevent evil from gaining total control in this extremely small part of the universe. It is a battle for the soul part of space-time-soul and it is already starting. Guide, I think that you also can sense what is coming."

"I can, Inara. I just have no idea what it is going to be. However, I have the overwhelming sense that it is a time for prayer."

"It is. Guide, you are more a part of the Universal Soul than anyone alive. You also have an army at your disposal that cares for that soul and can help it fight and recover. You must send an immediate message out to all Pilgrims everywhere, particularly those who work as part of the Pilgrim church to pray for the strength and health of the Universal Soul. It has no choice but to do some immediate and important work. It is my impression that evil people who have done the Universal Soul so much harm for so long are about to die in disturbingly large numbers. We are part of that soul and must help give it strength. I suggest that the prayers start right now."

The Guide responded, "I'm sending a neural command to my chambers to direct all Pilgrims across the galaxy to pray for the strength of the goodness in the Universal Soul."

Guide Takar Cillian, but none of the others, fully understood what was being asked. With determination and sadness in his eyes, he nodded his head. The room responded, and the message was sent out immediately to all Pilgrims everywhere across the galaxy.

As that was being done, Inara asked the room to display a real-time three-dimensional image of the galaxy with the evil brown clouds and tendrils overlay. Just the action of sending out The Guide's message caused many of the tendrils to quiver. Inara, on impulse, zoomed in on Secretary-General Edric Yan's office.

Inara announced, "Secretary-General Yan, if you check your office you will find that your female assistant is rapidly becoming gravely ill and is near death."

The Guide interjected, "Paya, Alana and Edric, this is a desperate time. Other than energy and communications transfer needed to keep people alive, can you gracefully shut down all animate and inanimate entanglement transfer all across the galaxy immediately? If entanglement weakens the Universal Soul then we need to stop all the entanglement activity we can while this battle rages."

Paya replied, "That will strand millions of travelers at entanglement stations and cause massive problems for the government as well as for the controllers. But, you already know that."

Turning to Edric Yan, Paya stated, "Do as The Guide has directed."

Edric responded, "I'm taking that action now."

Inara then said to all in the room, "The Universal Soul has begun its battle. We are already doing all we can to assist."

Inara continued, "We can't be deceived into wishfully thinking that this battle between the Universal Soul and evil ends our problem here. The disruption that Kieran fixed was just an indicator of the extreme technical disruption in the balance of space-time-soul and the spiritual pain being felt by the Universal Soul. That technical disruption and the spiritual pain are closely related, and have the same source, but they are distinct from each other.

"The Universal Soul will do what it needs to do, with our prayers, to restore its spiritual health through the open warfare it is engaging in right now with evil. The Universal Soul must do that if it, and all of us, are to survive in our galaxy.

"But that does only little to fix the technical disruption that has been building for one hundred thousand years. We are still facing a disaster of a scope that may spell the end of our civilization."

Inara then said to Paya, "With The Guide's permission I offer my assistance to work with your best technology team and, of course, with Kieran. I will be available any time you wish."

Paya turned to The Guide. "Takar, as a person with a long history of great leadership responsibility, I have learned how to evaluate people and situations even when there is a minimum of time and information. That experience, this meeting and the dropping of all emotional filters tells me that we must listen closely to what Inara is explaining to us."

Speaking to The Guide, Secretary-General Yan added, "In addition to being a secretary-general in The Controllers I am also a devout Pilgrim, and you are my Guide. I will do what you ask."

Takar Cillian simply nodded. He seemed to be becoming sadder by the minute.

Looking at Inara, Edric Yan said, "I have a team for you to work with. It is already being led by Kieran Since you have already met, and were close at one time, then I am sure you trusted him then. However, I will pay close attention to your reaction in case you sense any change in him." Speaking again to The Guide, Edric said, "That is, of course, only if you agree."

"How could I disagree?" responded The Guide.

* * *

The telescence session ended quietly. Edric Yan found his female assistant already dead and a few other members of his operations team terminally ill. Some of the others also found team members dead or dying.

Pren Bodhi had already started praying. Against the orders of The Guide, his prayers were for Inara.

* * *

At the end of the session, Gareth, Monz and Alana were all left in a similar emotional state. Gareth looked out the window across the beauty of the University. For each of his lives he had worked toward this job. He had never wanted anything else and had reveled in his last hundred years as University President. In his mind, there wasn't a better job in the galaxy. He had never analyzed too deeply why he loved this job so much. It was an emotional thing and he learned long ago from a good friend that emotional things shouldn't be examined too deeply for fear of destroying them. She had told him at the time that he was so driven by analysis that he would destroy a rose to learn what made it so beautiful. His drive for details and hard facts led him to be just as analytical in his personal relationships. Eventually, he destroyed his friendship with her before he learned too late the lesson of the rose. Today, he kept fresh roses in his office all the time as a reminder to not get too deeply into analysis and to guide his staff to discover beauty as well as knowledge.

Now, this disruption was threatening to destroy civilization, and perhaps create the need to participate in a revolution against his incompetent Prime Minister in the midst of catastrophe. He pictured the beautiful galaxy with spots of cancer spreading out to consume the whole. He also saw his university combined with the Guide's Pilgrim technologists as the possible magic bullet in the long term healing process.

Gareth, Monz and Alana moved to a round table near the window. Each knew that there was really no choice about what to do next. The new team must start work immediately in the remote hope of fixing the disruption, or perhaps reducing it in scope. In the worst case, they had to preserve knowledge for whatever future generations might survive the horrible errors of previous generations.

Gareth asked, "Why is it that after so long it is the generations that come after, the generations we love and build so much for, that are the generations who suffer for the sins of those who come before them? It seems we never learn and it never changes."

After a couple of minutes of reflecting on this rhetorical question, Alana broke the silence. Looking at Minister Ingra she asked, "I assume you will now want to brief the Prime Minister?"

"Not quite yet. Esha Arza is the Sector Minister for the sector in which The Guide's Hall is located. She is extremely competent and we have worked with each other from time to time over hundreds of years on some complex and difficult projects. I trust her completely. We need to bring her on board since it is now clear that the Guide's Hall needs to survive, if at all possible, along with University Planet and The Cathedral.

"Will this day never end? It looks like it is going to be a long night."

"You are absolutely right about contacting Minister Arza," replied Alana. "Do we need to leave you alone with her?"

"No, that isn't necessary. It is important that government, education, the Pilgrims and The Controllers act as, and are seen as, a single team in all of this."

Seeing nods of agreement from Alana and Gareth, Monz transferred control of the telescence session they were in to his office. He expanded the conference table creating another seat for Esha and requested a telescence conference with her.

* * *

Esha Arza, the Sector Minister for the area of the galaxy in which the Guide's Hall resided, couldn't believe what was happening and how utterly out of the loop she felt. Without preamble, she answered Monz's call.

"Monz, even under these outrageous circumstances it is good to see you. Secretary-General Perg, the last time we met was at a reception in The Cathedral. And President Frax, it is good to meet you.

"Now, at the risk of being abrupt, Monz, do you have any idea at all about what is going on? I'm totally in the blind out here and getting more than irritated. My staff and I are deluged with alerts that the entanglement transport stations have stopped operation all across my sector and, it seems, all across the galaxy. Furthermore, something horrible seems to be happening to portions of the population. My entire sector is in near panic, and I don't blame them. I've received no information at all from the Prime Minister since yesterday evening's briefing. It frankly looks like the central government has collapsed. It seems like the only ones who might have some semblance of coherent action is The Controllers. At least, I hope they do. And, Alana, that brings my short tirade to you! I really hope you can enlighten me, so I can inform my population and perhaps save a few lives."

Monz interrupted, "Actually, we can all answer your questions, Esha. Will you please join us around my table?"

As she moved to the table Esha pressed, "I could really use some answers, and some help, the sooner the better."

Avoiding even brief pleasantries they got down to business.

"First, Esha, I'll confirm what you already suspect. The Controllers have shut down all matter transfer across the Galaxy." He held up his hand in a gesture to ask patience. "Second, many people, all of whom are extremely evil and many of whom are extraordinarily powerful, are dying or will soon die all across the galaxy. I know that you aren't a strong practicing Pilgrim, but I will also tell you that these people are in essence, being killed by the Universal Soul. Now that I have given you the bottom line, let me show you the details."

"These had best be great details", commented Esha. "It is pretty strange to hear anyone say that evil people are being killed across the galaxy by the Universal Soul."

"It is definitely a story never told before," Monz responded. He immediately played back for Esha the most essential telescence projections of the pertinent events of the last couple of days.

Forty-five fast paced, information packed minutes later Esha quietly remarked, "You have just turned all that I know upside down. In my three lifetimes I have never come close to conceiving of this."

"I understand, Esha. It is probably much more difficult for you than it is for me because you are getting the condensed version and you haven't been in the middle of it here."

"I assume you have been able to bring the Prime Minister up to date?"

"Esha, I have tried to get through to him with telescence sessions and messages. All attempts to contact him have been rejected. I guess I could assume that he is swamped with calls," he said with some skepticism in his voice.

For the first time in a while Alana spoke up. "Perhaps I can help. Monz, may I address your chambers?"

"Of course."

Alana began to speak her access request to Sector Minister Monz Ingra's chamber. "This is Secretary-General Alana Perg demanding full system penetration authority."

The room responded, "First Step Granted," while the rest looked on in some surprise. Alana smiled in return, "What good is an ancient woman with a little power if she doesn't use it once in a while?" She continued, "Request final step agreement from Secretaries General Paya Lachlan and Edric Yan."

"Please wait," said the room.

Not more than sixty seconds later the reply came back "Full system penetration authority granted without reservation. What is your command?"

"Examine the Prime Minister's telecommunications logs and tell me if he has accepted or sent any calls since his meeting yesterday with Paya Lachlan and me."

"The Prime Minister is refusing all calls. He has not placed any calls."

"What is the emotional state of the Prime Minister?"

"The Prime Minister is near catatonic with fear. He is unable to make decisions required of his current situation."

"Thank you. Full system penetration demand canceled."

"Uh, do you do that often?" Esha tentatively asked.

"Actually, that was the first time. Pretty scary, isn't it?"

"Definitely."

"That's why it was the first time and hopefully the last. There were many more checkpoints in there than it appeared."

"Hmmm."

Alana continued, "Monz, Esha, and Gareth, I suggest that we all try the Prime Minister together. Perhaps a joint call from all of us will get him to answer."

Suddenly, Monz stood bolt upright in alarm as his room announced a major alert and displayed what was clearly a galaxy-wide battle of epic proportions. Seconds later, Esha gripped the edge of the table. Monz made a command gesture and images of his sector and Esha's sectors materialized beside each other in the room. It was as if a silent wind was snuffing out certain lives as it blew through the galaxy. Monz commanded that the devastation numbers be displayed.

Monz quietly said, "I hope this means the good guys are winning. All I can tell from this is that hundreds of millions of people are dying -- fast."

* * *

Now that it was reaching its climax the retribution being initiated by the Universal Soul had Inara in a condition in which she could barely think. When she reached her room, she was essentially in a zombie state. More than anything else she could feel what she sensed as a massive turmoil of space, of the Universal Soul. While the initial disruption was occurring, it was as if every nerve ending in her body and brain were feeling a mild burn with flashes of random pain. It was not nearly as intense as during her transport several decades ago, but it was still painful and a surprise since she wasn't in a transport node.

She leaned back against the wall of her living area and sank slowly to the floor. Once there, she stared at the opposite wall with its image of her home on the Jungle Planet. For a few minutes, her mind was trapped in the beauty of the scene which was really a garden her father nurtured and which she would sit in for hours at a time when she had lived there. She understood that, with the potential collapse of galactic civilization, she might never go there again, and that she might never have another real or telesence contact with her parents.

Her emotions began to burst through without restraint. At first, her breath just heaved, and then she began to shake and shudder. Finally, she sobbed great gasping sobs that seemed to come out of depths that couldn't possibly exist. After an hour, she passed out on the floor exhausted from the intensity of her emotion.

In the meantime, the Pilgrims were praying.

When she awoke, Pren and Malin were there with her. She asked them to go with her to her laboratory where there was a large room in which free space three-dimensional images of experiments, graphs and charts could be projected and manipulated. With Malin supplying the passwords and permissions, she tied all the Guide's Hall computers into her laboratory. Since almost all ofthe Hall was in prayer for support of the soul only a few computing systems were in use. She commanded the system to display evil as they had all earlier been able to perceive it within The Guide's chamber. All they saw was a few hundred remnant cinders. Out of pure self-interest, she looked at her home planet. To her surprise, an entire enclave in a remote section of the jungle was just a hole in the ground. She noted with satisfaction that all around her parent's home was intact.

Then she commanded the system to display the galaxy in its entirety. What they saw shocked them all. Areas displayed in the brown that represented evil were rippling. The most prevalent initial areas were in the stellar systems close to humanity's origin around the star, Sol. As they watched, the ripples crumbled seeming to dissolve. It was clear that the centers of activity were beginning to disperse to include the twenty-seven Earth-identical planets, and it was evolving at a rapid pace.

They decided to look at Earth's region more closely. They activated an override protocol supplied by the Controllers to link into video systems in the public areas on Mars, Earth's moon and Earth. At first, they didn't notice anything, so they drew back to some high-altitude cameras so they could look at a broad area. Suddenly, they noticed sparks in various locations. In most areas the sparks were just quick flashes. When they zoomed in on these locations they saw only charred carbon deposits. They looked at a mountainous area on Earth's largest continent and saw intense activity in one of the large valleys where there was a huge estate. Initially, the activity was just at the fringes. Then there were small flashes at what looked like random locations inside the estate. Finally, the estate simply disappeared, leaving only the granite rock that anchored the mountains.

And so it went all across the galaxy. Individuals, groups, buildings, transports of various kinds simply turned to cinders or winked out of existence. It was a reckoning one hundred thousand years in the making. This was a war that was going to be won or lost in the span of a day and with what looked like a massive loss of human life.

After a few hours it was over.

That was the good part.

The bad part was yet to come.

Intentions

Before dawn the next morning The Guide was praying in his private sanctuary. Malin sent a small bird to flutter in front of The Guide to get his attention. Since only something critically important would cause Malin to interrupt The Guide's meditation Takar signaled the sanctuary to mutate into an office.

"Yes, Malin."

"I'm sorry to interrupt, Takar, but Inara says that it is important she talk to you."

"Thank you, Malin. I'll contact her."

Takar Cillian took a few minutes to prepare, and chose to meet with her in a normal office setting. He waved for the meeting to start and for their offices to be merged.

Immediately, Inara appeared in her lab and just a few feet in front of The Guide. There was an elegant, wide archway connecting her work area to the Guide's office.

The Guide noticed that Inara had lost weight overnight. The dark circles around her eyes and her stooped posture betrayed her fatigue. Inara saw the concern in Takar's face, but without preamble launched into her discussion.

"Please forgive my lack of ceremony. I'm so tired and my entire body, my soul, sense the galactic turmoil. I understand even better now what the Universal Soul is going through and it is important that we talk".

The Guide leaned forward in this chair and nodded to indicate that Inara had his full attention.

Inara began her explanation. "It is now clear that each transport that has been done since the first experiment by the Ancients just after they left planet Earth has tortured the soul. The question is 'Exactly why does it torture the soul'?

"Malin and Pren have given me the opportunity and encouragement over the last few months to exercise my gifts. In that time I have paid closer attention to my integrated senses in a somewhat different way. Consequently, yesterday's events revealed much more to me than they would have before I came here. So, last night, in spite of being exhausted, I reevaluated the evolution of my pain over time. I began to probe more deeply the idea that the damage was not just a physics issue. That is just a symptom. I followed that thread of thought and early this morning began to understand more clearly what is indeed an ancient problem.

"Through my research and my conversation with Malk Kring I have learned that others have sensed what they called The Pain in the distant past. I'm almost certain that I was the only one in our time to sense it decades ago. However, by now I wouldn't be surprised if some others who are deeply contemplative and close to the soul might have been affected by it recently to varying degrees."

The Guide had begun pacing across his office as he listened to Inara. He stopped, turning to look at her in the doorway of her laboratory. "Inara, what are you leading to?"

"Guide, from a technical perspective, people who study systems know that all systems are the same. The equations look different but they are just tools that we use to help us define with great specificity the particular system we are focusing our attention on at that time. A systems engineer will tell you that each equation can be generalized into cross variables, through variables and a constant. The systems engineer must be taught to think that way. For me, everything is the same. So, this systems perspective is something that it is inconceivable for me not to have. It is not a reach to say that the soul part of space-time-soul is a mathematical part of the overall system.

"I have told you that I now understand that the Universal Soul is intrinsic to our physical systems in ways we don't fully understand. The soul is, as we have known since long before we left Earth, nurtured or hurt by our thoughts and actions toward each other.

"However, and this is extremely important, all of space-time-soul is also affected by our intentions whether or not we complete an action. Two different people might take identical actions. However, one might take an action with good intentions. The other might do exactly the same thing with evil intent. On the surface, and perhaps in many situations, people may not perceive any difference in the immediate, or even perhaps the long term outcome, because they can't see that secret and hidden intention.

"Guide, we now know that the technology of entanglement, and eventually telescence, was at some point in the beginning controlled by evil people with the profound intention to make them powerful and give them total control over everyone else. They performed horribly evil acts to maintain and increase that control and also just because they enjoyed it. As they did so they had no idea that they were having an extremely negative impact on what a few of us now understand is space-time-soul.

"That negative effect caused by their evil intentions showed up initially in a variety of ways. As the soul was damaged it affected the associated space-time. The change seemed, and essentially was, sudden at first because it was a rapid shift from a balance that had been achieved over billions of years before humans arrived on the scene. The change was abrupt because of the massive effect of terribly evil people suddenly having such powerful space-time technology under their entire control. Their intentions were evil and the result was damaging to the soul. But, space-time, or more exactly space-time-soul, tries to achieve balance.

"That sudden initial shift finally reached a tentative balance that we perceived as stable until recently. In the last few decades the suffering of the Universal Soul finally attained a level at which space-time was thrown into a great imbalance. That shift, that increasing imbalance with resultant pain, is what I have been experiencing all my life. If I had been born five thousand years ago I might never have noticed it. It is the reason for the disruption we recently experienced.

"The important point in all of this is that evil actions are just periodic, no matter how frequent. Intentions are continuous and therefor have a greater cumulative effect on space-time-soul than actions. Intentions are the reason for our disaster."

Inara noticed with appreciation that the Guide understood what she was saying and, more importantly, accepting the information. As the environment sensed her increasing exhaustion the doorway to her laboratory retreated and the environment morphed so that she was now sitting close beside the Guide.

Her integrated sense of The Guide was changing. They were becoming close friends. At the same time she sensed, and appreciated, that the Guide had a duty to fulfill and that he would use her as necessary to meet that obligation. The Guide touched her shoulder in a gesture of comfort. She was surprised by the healing in his touch that quickly spread throughout her body and soul.

The Guide gently said, "Take your time, Inara. I am learning much from you. But I need to know, are you also telling me that what you are sensing was perceived by others in previous times?"

Inara took a shaky hand to wipe the moisture forming below her eyes. "Yes, Guide. I am not totally unique. Others have had my abilities to varying degrees. Understanding that, I wondered if there was other evidence back over time to support my theory.

"My research took me back to the period when humans were just starting to move outward from Earth and making the initial discoveries about entanglement as a communications and transport system. What I learned was more than enlightening.

"The scientists and the entrepreneurs in those days were ecstatic at their discoveries. They were totally innocent of any understanding that damage was being done to the fabric of space with each transport that took place. Almost all were unaware of the intentions of the people who ultimately controlled that transport technology. The scientists and business people had no way to know about, or measure the physical effect of intentions. They had no idea that they were doing more harm than good. We still may not be able to measure the effect of intentions in a fully scientific way.

"However, as Malk Kring has revealed to me, the most religious of people on planet Earth, its moon and the nearby planet of Mars were experiencing simultaneous feelings of anxiety. Some sensed what they described as evil that created in them a latent sense of foreboding. A few of these people were the leaders of the most introspective religions. Most were from the rank and file with no particular stature in their organizations and wanting none. However, even these normally quiet people were so moved by what they were feeling that they aggressively pushed their superiors to report their concerns to their highest leaders. These leaders became so concerned that for the first time in human history they felt they had no choice but to put aside their differences and gather together to try to understand what was happening. Each time they met only briefly, in tremendous fear and in the greatest of secrecy because they had no clue at all about the source of what they perceived to be great evil."

Inara noticed a difference in The Guide. His numbers showed a sudden shift and his flavor changed at bit. She had touched on something that perhaps had allowed The Guide to gain even greater understanding. She paused, waiting for him to make a comment.

"Inara, through my studies of the ancient origins of the Pilgrims I am aware of this meeting and that these ancient people never discovered the source of their concerns. Most of us have simply put their concerns down to some primitive superstition or mass hysteria. Are you telling me that the initial entanglement experiments were the undiscovered cause of concern for these people and the reason for this meeting? The reason the Pilgrims met in the beginning may be the cause of the end of our civilization! That is an astounding revelation!"

Inara nodded.

The Guide continued, "You already understand that this unique meeting of the highest religious leaders resulted in an investigative arm called the Pilgrims who evolved into what we are today. They never did discover the source of their great concern because they didn't associate the kind of damage to the soul they were experiencing with the arcane and secret experiments of a few distant scientists. They never had a chance to understand.

"Let me show you something that is in the Guide's Hall files. It is closely related to information that Malk Kring gave you. There is only one copy. It was made in great secrecy and handed down over the millennia. It is a file accessible only by each Guide and their assistants. This file is one that Malin found for me and contains critically important information that occurred about six months after the meeting in Atlanta on Earth that Malk told you about. This meeting is of top religious leaders of that time."

From The Guide's Private File

Only a few thousand years after humanity was springing out from Earth and exploring their neighborhood of the galaxy, Coptic Pope Cyril X, Metropolitan of Egypt, stood quietly off to one side of the great hall in the Atlanta convention center. From his spot next to a twenty foot high blue curtain in front of a cold beige wall, he looked with fascination and humility at this unlikely group deliberately dressed in inconspicuous street clothes. He thought carefully through the words he would use to open the afternoon session. He had been given the honor of chairing this secret gathering of humanity's top religious leaders only six months after the general meeting in Munich where the subject of The Pain had been the main item on the agenda. He had barely spoken so far except to provide a few short words and a prayer during the opening. Frankly, he hardly knew what to say. Nevertheless, it was now after 1:30 PM and past his time to open the afternoon session.

Pope Cyril walked over to the podium. Once all in the room had quieted he opened the afternoon meeting with a prayer. Still not quite knowing exactly how to start, he silently said a second prayer for God's guidance. Then he began.

"When our rabbi friend from Jerusalem suggested, or should I say demanded," some laughter broke across the room, "that we thirty-seven discretely meet I had no idea that I would experience a morning like we just had. Perhaps it is good after all that our brother is so persuasive. However, I should be careful that he doesn't convert me." Pope Cyril paused as the laughter which he hoped would, to some extent, relieve the palpable tension continued.

"I'm frightened by the education I received this morning. I worry that my fear may indicate insufficient faith on my part. We've heard much evidence about a growing, strange perception of sporadic pulses of evilness and danger that seem to come from everywhere at once. This feeling is so strong among a highly respected few that, for the first time in history, it has caused us, the leaders of humankind's largest religions, to gather together in one place. We are here to discuss only this one subject.

"Brothers and sisters, we are tied together by the bond of belief in, to put it generically, a Higher Power. We also agree that there is a horrendous evil that hates our Higher Power. There are people on Earth, Luna and Mars who either hate or don't believe in our Higher Power. Of course, evil has always been with us.

"However, something new is happening. Over the last few decades, many of us gathered here today, as well as others, have felt the same increasingly unbearable and undeniable sense of foreboding and evil. That almost tangible sense of dread has recently escalated so dramatically that it is oppressive with an intensity that can't be ignored. It is what has driven us together for just a few hours today in as close to total secrecy as we can get.

"There are a number of theories for this continuous increase in the perceived intensity of evil. We can't prove or disprove any of them. All of us in this room, because of our leadership positions, receive reports of horrible evil much too frequently. Sometimes we are able to help with the suffering caused by this evil, and sometimes we can't. I have felt especially helpless in recent years because no one in my church has provided even a remotely close explanation about a tangible source of the massive intensity of evil that is being sensed. The closest anyone seems to come is to correlate it with humankind's accelerated venture to, and development of, our moon and Mars, or possibly the horrible interplanetary corporate war that ended a few years ago. Frankly, I am at a loss and am hesitant to believe that humans are supposed to remain only on Earth. Humankind has always expanded and war has always been with us.

"I also know that an increasing number of religious people in my Coptic Church are experiencing unexplainable physical pain and spiritual anguish. The reports have been coming to me with ever greater frequency over the last few years. Naturally, I have taken the same action as many of you. I have invited doctors to look for a physical explanation while asking some of my more sensitive senior religious people to do interviews. I have brought in skeptics in an aggressive attempt to uncover potentially fraudulent stories. As the months and years have gone by, it has become clear that this evilness surge isn't a physical ailment or hysteria or a conspiracy. The intensity of evil on our worlds really has increased, and it is evident that some of the more sensitive among us have been feeling a surge in what might be called the soul's pain."

Pope Cyril X paused to maintain his composure.

"I am so sorry that I didn't understand that this was happening within many of your beliefs as well. I am eternally grateful, perhaps literally from the perspective of my soul, to Rabbi Cohen's broader view and for his suggestion that we all meet and work together. I have learned so much from the presentations this morning. I am, frankly, intensely frightened by this new knowledge I have received today.

"During lunch I had the opportunity to meet with several of you. Clearly, we all feel the same way. We have to find a unified response to this evil that is increasing so dramatically. Rabbi Cohen has offered a suggestion, and I now turn you over to him."

* * *

The Rabbi who, until recently, had been energetic and spry approached the front of the room gingerly. All were extraordinarily silent as they watched this man for whom each had great respect. With slightly shaking hand, he took a small sip of water.

"Sons and daughters of our Higher Power, I am thrilled that we are all together here in mutual respect. I am, as you can see for yourselves, sickened by the reason we have gathered. I am too tired to take long at this podium this afternoon. My flock in Jerusalem, who has sometimes had to listen to me at length, would tell you to be thankful for that."

By this time, the feeling in the room was so solemn that this attempt at humor was only met by nods. The Rabbi understood.

"People like us cannot all, at the same time, simply disappear for long from our normal lives and locations without the media and others finding out and asking intensive questions. So, the only time we have together are these few short hours. You all give me strength, and I wish we had more time. I suspect that we will never meet like this again during my lifetime.

"We have many of the same questions that the media might ask because we are not fully certain either about what has caused all of us to assemble for the first time in history. We just know that the intensity of evil in the world has increased dramatically and we want to understand better why that is happening. It is an evil that kind of feels like that which is present during demonic possession except more diffuse. It seems to be spread out and come from everywhere in sudden waves. I, for one, have no understanding at all of what is happening. I just know that it is frightening and horrible. It feels like it is torturing my soul with blast furnace flame when it takes hold of me. It leaves me constantly tired.

"We differ to varying extents in our specific beliefs. We all have to admit that those differences have caused some damage over time. I am not naive. Those differences are not going to disappear. But what drives us together today is something we all agree on without exception. There is, quite simply, good in the universe and there is evil. Good enhances the soul, or the spirit, or the essence, or whatever we want to call it. Evil damages it and all of humanity. We must work together to fully understand this evil which we sense so strongly. To that end, I suggest we each appoint one person who is extraordinarily brave and good, and who we trust with the future of good, to be on one team to learn what is happening. We will let that team work out the details of how they will operate and tell us what they learn."

Another hour of discussion ensued. Many differences were discussed, great friendships established, and the recommendation of Rabbi Cohen was readily accepted.

Over the next month, a group of thirty-seven investigators was chosen. They were to become collectively known as "The Pilgrims" and they were directed to meet in secrecy within six months.

* * *

Six months, later the thirty-seven appointed Pilgrims, as well as six individuals who had a special contribution to make, met in Berlin. There was a feeling of even greater urgency in this meeting than in the previous ones. The representative of the Dalai Lama, Denpo, was selected to chair the gathering.

"My friends, those who have an unusual closeness to the spirit continue to sense a growing burden of evil that in the past has come in unpredictable waves. In just the last six months since the leaders of our congregations met together in Atlanta those waves have transitioned into an increased level of pain that is persistent.

"Rather than continue myself, I'll let our Russian Orthodox brother describe what he is feeling. The only additional thing I will say is that when I first talked to Father Demetri about this subject he told me that his initial feeling of "The Pain" came on him quickly and unexpectedly. Others have told me the same. I find it interesting that the first feeling of this evil for most of them seems to have come at the same time. The only loose correlation we can make is with humankind moving more aggressively to the moon and Mars. Frankly, that correlation still doesn't make spiritual sense to any of us, and the relationship appears to be extremely weak. We have researched independently and together to try to find a specific source of what feels like an intense evil agony but can't find a credible focus. Indeed, the agony as described by these holy, sensitive people is one that somehow penetrates the soul and comes from all around us.

"Father Demetri, the podium is yours."

Father Demetri was a young man only in his early thirties with the walk of a person one hundred eighty years old and near death. There was softness in his eyes that clearly showed through the pain etched into his face. With surprising strength in his voice he brought himself to stand up straight before the Pilgrims.

"Brothers and sisters, I am only a humble representative of perhaps two hundred people around the world who are experiencing what we call "The Pain". It came infrequently at first, but at the same time for all of us. It is now happening almost continuously and with gradually greater intensity. It is a pain that penetrates our entire bodies to the marrow and sometimes makes us pass out from the agony. At first, there was relief between the agonies. Now there is only a temporary lessening in the amount of The Pain between each episode. I stand before you with every cell in my body in a moderate amount of continuous pain. At least once a day I collapse. At the same time I collapse, others of the approximately two hundred may do the same. Or, at the least, they will experience an agony that drives them to their knees. Many others, who don't experience The Pain, live with the sense of foreboding that brought all of our top religious leaders together for the first time six months ago.

"We have learned much from each other during that our previous meetings and the last six months. Perhaps we learn more from pain than we do from pleasure. I don't want to complain, but right now I could do with a little less knowledge," he said as the softness in his eyes was joined by a twinkle of humor.

"Some Christians have conjectured that The Pain could be similar to the stigmata. Those of us who have this pain don't believe that. There is an evil feeling that comes with The Pain. All of us feel that the entire world is enveloped with an invisible cloud of something that wants to push goodness to small corners. I wish I could explain it better than that. I'm sorry. I am exhausted."

Father Demetri then returned to his seat beside the other five intense sufferers who were attending. All showed the same fatigue caused by the constant pain. Each stood briefly to share their experiences.

After they were finished Denpo went to Father Demetri and the others with him to say a few words and then went to the podium. "We Pilgrims have a special obligation placed on us by the leaders of our various religions to understand the source of this evil. We have worked with each other in teams and shared information among all of us. Sometimes we come together in smaller groups, just as we do this week in a larger assembly, to understand and fight what we see as intense and growing evil and perhaps impending disaster. The good that has come out of this is that we continue to learn much from each other. We understand the beauty of our differences based on culture and background and history, while affirming that we all want the same basic things in life and for the soul. We are making friends and breaking barriers. I hope I don't offend when I say that our willingness to embrace each other's beliefs sometimes makes religious leaders uncomfortable. And I include my Dalai Lama in that."

That last comment brought murmurs of agreement all around since more than one of them had been counseled within their religions about remembering the reasons for their own beliefs and adhering strictly to them.

Denpo concluded, "As spiritual people, our primary mission has been to understand what we perceive as an evil growing at a rapid rate all around us. We are approaching this in a number of ways, including meditation, historical research, as well as philosophical and psychological investigation. At the other end of the spectrum, we are tasking a dozen of our Pilgrims who are also technologists to see if science can be used to understand what is happening. I'm afraid we all may be returning to our religious leaders only with a greater understanding of each other but no additional knowledge of the evil that seems to be penetrating our world. Even that is great progress."

Intentions Explained

Inara exclaimed to The Guide, "This makes increasing amounts of sense. Those first sensitive religious people felt what they described as a sudden evil simply because it was indeed sudden in the great scope of things. What they didn't have any chance of understanding was that their pain was caused by entanglement transfer because it was developed and controlled by evil people. As a tool of evil it was causing injury to space-time-soul which was being contorted by people with evil intentions.

"Over the centuries the foreboding and pain of these sensitive people disappeared. because some semblance of stability in space-time-soul had been achieved. The soul's pain became an ever present background that was seen by succeeding generations as so natural that it wasn't paid attention to. It was like the difference between an unexpected thunderclap and a background ringing in the ears on a normal day. The concern simply disappeared into the environment. All of this fits closely with what Malk Kring has revealed to me."

The Guide contributed, "Eventually, while the initial reason for assembling the Pilgrims faded away, the Pilgrims remained a coherent group dedicated to being more tolerant of, and even embracing some of, the differences between religions and concentrating on the basics that really mattered."

Then Inara observed, "So we are their spiritual descendants and have come full circle because I now sense what was felt by the most sensitive of the religious ancient people.

"Only now I understand what they had no hope of knowing. There is a connection between the evil intent and evil control of entanglement and the destruction of the soul. Entanglement communication and matter transfer has been an absolutely innocent thing in which we have all participated. However, the fact that it was controlled by a small and powerful, shadowy evil group is what caused The Pain."

The Guide placed a hand on Inara's arm and commented, "Inara, you have helped me to understand things that no one ever knew. Let me now help you. The leaders of all of Earth's major religions decided long ago, when humans were just beginning to spread across the galaxy, to maintain the heads of their churches on either Earth or planets that could sustain human life without any terraforming at all. Some wanted to do this in part to stay closer to the Creator and to creation. There was also the practical reason of survivability on worlds that wouldn't need outside support in the event of a major disaster. Almost all of these discrete religions, as you know, still exist. The popular conception is that these religions are subsets of the Pilgrims. The truth is that the Pilgrims are just a mechanism for promoting harmony among all religions and religious people under one principle. That principle is that there is one Creator and everything in the universe is part of that Creator through one Universal Soul. The Pilgrims are also the technology and investigative arm for all religions.

"As Guide, I work for and report to all the heads of these religions. I am their servant as well as leader of the Pilgrims. My job is to work to understand the evil that is in the world so that all of the religions can be protected. While my position is highly visible it is also invisibly subservient. The religions are protected, evil is investigated full time and our technology teams do scientific research for all religions. We have done this in a manner to confuse evil and evil people. It hasn't always succeeded. And, unhappily, we ourselves may have been manipulated by some outrageously evil people.

"I do believe in the subtle, and sometimes not so subtle, intervention of the Creator. I understand more clearly than ever that the Creator, or the Universal Soul, intervened to create and preserve the Pilgrims. You and I were not brought together by accident."

Inara observed, "The Universal Soul has a purpose for us. We have been through a disruption caused by the cumulative effect of evil intent. We have prayed for the welfare of the Universal Soul while it went to war with evil so that good could win in our galaxy. But great harm has been inflicted on space-time-soul and the technology that was the tool of that damage may soon be useless to us. We quite possibly have a terminal disaster facing all humans in the immediate future. No one, least of all the Controllers, should assume that yesterday's event was the worst of our problems. That was only the opening act. The vast majority of the Five Families have been eliminated. But the damage they did remains and may result in the end of our civilization."

Inara and The Guide simply sat together for a while tiredly lost in their thoughts.

After a few minutes the Guide said, "Inara, if you are up to it then it is time for you to join Kieran on the University Planet. You have helped us to better understand, nurture and love the Universal Soul. Now you must lead us as we all work together to save humanity."

* * *

The Guide made his personal transport available to Inara and Pren Bodhi for the five astronomical unit trip to the local entanglement node which was temporarily put in operation for this special trip. Pren noticed that Inara experienced no discomfort this time, and that she seemed much more at ease than on previous occasions. Edric Yan had arranged for express transport from the University Sector entanglement node to the University Planet, and to the office of Gareth Frax where they were met by Dammar Corday, Kieran Llot, Gareth and Alana Perg. Pren couldn't help but notice Inara's unusual reaction as soon as she saw Kieran.

Gareth made the introductions. He concluded with, "Inara, Kieran is the Researcher who helped to reestablish operation of the entanglement system when it failed yesterday. As you know, it is our hope that your new knowledge of the interconnection of space-time-soul combined with Kieran's detailed knowledge of entanglement may be able to help us bring our systems to balance."

Inara abstractedly murmured, "Yes, Kieran and I have worked together before."

As Pren watched with great concern, Inara slowly walked over to Kieran. She reached out to take his hand. Kieran, offered his hand and was clearly surprised to have Inara take it and quickly withdraw. Inara stood quietly for a moment then reached out both of her hands to take Kieran's right hand in hers. The room was quiet as she held Kieran's hand for a least a full minute. Finally, showing some sudden embarrassment, she let go of Kieran's hand saying, "I'm pleased to see you again. It seems we have a lot of work to do."

Kieran replied in little more than a whisper. "It's been a long time. I didn't think we would ever meet again though I have thought of you from time to time. I was only recently told we would be working together."

Turning to the rest of the people in the room Inara said, "If you'll give me fifteen minutes I'll be ready to start."

Gareth, looking a bit puzzled responded, "Yes, of course. You and Pren have a large suite in our guest area. You have been assigned your standard cheetah droid to show you the way. We will await your return."

Alana, with almost a millennium of observing human interaction was the only one in the room who looked more amused than confused by what had just transpired.

When Inara and Pren entered their suite Pren said, "Inara, what just happened in there? Are you sensing evil or any other kind of a problem? Or, is this just a natural response to again meeting someone you once cared for deeply?"

"I was simply taken by surprise. I have never had the kind of combined sensory perception that I just had with Kieran. When I knew him before I knew him as a good and terribly troubled person. We were immediately attracted to each other and I found more pleasure, of all kinds, in being with him than with any other man. Eventually, we went different ways. I told you part of the story before. He left to continue his work and I was confined at the time to Andromeda. Telescence meetings weren't enough to keep our relationship going. It broke my heart. It broke his, too.

"He is still good and troubled. But he is strong and he has learned so much about life since we last saw each other. He is less naïve. Of all the thousands of people I have met I've never seen numbers like his. Or taste or smell. It isn't bad. In fact, it is quite pleasant. And when I touched his hand our numbers seemed to meld and become continuous. In fact, the individual essences of our souls seemed to merge slightly. It is quite confusing and totally unique."

Inara rushed through her words. "Don't worry. He is a good man. And strong emotionally and spiritually in spite of clearly having suffered more than his share of personal pain on several occasions. You don't have to be concerned. We will work well together. I just needed some time to collect myself after that surprise."

"In that case, I'll leave you alone for a while and return to the others."

"Thanks, Uncle Pren."

Ten minutes later, Inara returned to a much larger group wrapped in lively conversation about the events of the previous morning and evening. The added members of the group were Contoller Technologists who had been thoroughly briefed while Pren and Inara we making their way to University Planet. The catastrophe of the morning was technically far more understandable to them than the event of the evening that was focused on fewer people and seemed to the general population to be mysterious in its origin. Dammar Corday, with his strong scientific approach and lack of participation in the previous evening's meetings was clearly suspicious of the story.

When Inara entered, Dammar quickly opened the discussion with her. "Inara, a lot of powerful people across the galaxy died under strange circumstances yesterday. Many of them were well known. Others, while extremely rich, lived deep in the shadows. These people who lived so much in the shadows give indications of having worked hard to stay that way. It is beginning to be apparent that they may have been quietly powerful almost beyond belief. It seems from the discussion in this room that you may know more about this than anyone."

"I'll be happy to explain all that I understand." Dammar happened to be standing by some poured refreshment and Inara took the opportunity to get closer to Dammar by walking over to get a cup. By standing close to him, she could put all of her senses to better work at understanding the full intent of his question. She could tell that, while skeptical, he just sincerely wanted knowledge. She also sensed his closeness to Kieran.

She explained, "As Kieran, his team, and I work together, I hope to be able to understand this even better myself. In short, and as we all know, there is both good and evil in the galaxy. It seems that there was, until yesterday evening, a few number of families who worked in the deep background to control all the business and financial activities of all humankind. Before you say that this is impossible, please know that they have been doing this since before we all began our emigration from Earth. They have had a long time to get it right. These people were evil in the extreme. They did not believe in, and many of them were entirely separated from, the Universal Soul. They took pleasure in killing, and they would kill wholly without reason. They would do, and did do, anything to attain riches and power. Through a long chain of contacts, they controlled, and were enriched by, entanglement technology. Less than one-millionth of one percent of all the good people in The Controllers organization had a glimpse of an idea that this small number of ruthless, incredibly powerful families existed. I only found out about just one of them by accident a little over eight years ago, and I had no idea what I was really observing. Happily, I told only a few people who I totally trusted, otherwise I would be dead today."

All in the room listened in silence as Inara paused to take a sip or her drink and collect her thoughts.

The silence was accompanied by the unannounced entrance of Malk Kring who stood in the doorway to the room without saying anything. As each noticed his appearance they turned quietly toward him. Inara was the first to speak.

"Hello, Malk. It has been a while since you visited."

"Only in your frame of reference, Inara," Malk responded. "For me it was yesterday, will be tomorrow and was now. It seems that I am here because I am needed."

Inara replied, "Yes, you are definitely needed. I can tell that you are frustrated by your trap as well as being fulfilled by your mission. In my limited perception of space-time-soul I can only hope that you will somehow find escape from your confinement."

Inara continued, "I am aware that you already know everyone in this room." Turning to the others, she said, "Please permit me to introduce Malk Kring who you already know about from the information I have given you."

Inara then faced Malk and said, "I was hoping you would visit again. We need all the help we can get."

Malk began, "I'm going to tell all of you a little more about the evil that you are battling. Inara has already learned much that has been helpful but you must know more because you are still naïve about the truly evil nature of the Five Families and the injury they have inflicted since truly ancient times. Until you understand their evilness you will not have even a remote chance of saving even a vestige of our civilization.

"As Inara knows, and as she has in turn told you, the Five Families kept an incredibly extensive history on themselves. They kept this amazingly objective and accurate history because they knew how important it is to learn from the past and that it is essential to be unsparingly honest about events even when they are not flattering.

"In addition, they have always known that ruthless behavior always has an advantage over the activities of good people hampered in their actions by morality and ethics. These have never been people with whom you can negotiate. Their attitude has always been 'We win, you lose'. This is a difficult concept for good people to understand. Some never understand and naively assume there is always an opportunity to reach an agreement.

"Here is an example from the time when humans were just leaving Earth and when entanglement experiments led to the infancy of telescence. What you are about to experience is disgusting. However, it is necessary that you fully understand what put us into our current situation."

The Shadow Masters

Chairman Gordon Bailey, impeccably dressed and resplendent with flowing and powdered white hair, prepared to open the Meeting of Twenty-Five. Taking a casual sip of a rare, expensive green tea, he savored the faint aroma and exquisite flavor that only a few in the world were given the opportunity to sample.

It was now precisely 8 AM in Hakone, Japan in the Spring of 2178.

He rose quickly from his seat at the head of the highly polished, donut-shaped, teak table surrounding the central arena. As he did so his family members immediately ended their conversations. His attentive eyes took in each one, stopping momentarily at the opening at the far end of the table through which he would soon be walking.

When he was sure that all were ready, he turned to stare directly at the three people bound to their chairs behind him. With a smile, he noted the terror in their eyes. The drug they had been given from a laboratory-bred widow spider had selectively frozen their muscles. They could sit on their chairs but do little else. The eyes in their unmoving heads frantically darted around the room. Their mouths strained to scream through paralyzed vocal chords. He could barely hide the excitement he felt about the next few minutes and the performance of a two millennia old tradition.

"Thank you. Well done." He addressed that compliment with even more than his usual gentleness for her to his youngest adolescent child, Melanie, who was now standing at his side. She had been afforded the privilege, honor and pleasure of briefing their guests three days earlier, and in great detail, about their fate. The effect of that knowledge was exactly what the Twenty-Five wanted. After facing the prisoners for a few seconds, Gordon Bailey slowly walked to a table behind their chairs. The workmanship and balance of the ivory handled knife surprised even him as he picked it up from that ancient carved table with its scene of rice paddy workers.

He glanced at the prisoners and took pleasure in the visible quiver of fear that appeared to be vibrating through each of them. They had been told, in detail, to expect death to come from behind. However, if he had to endure the potential consequences of this day, then they would suffer just a little longer.

Bailey took a lingering look around the room, enjoying its antique Japanese woodblock prints, vases and bamboo plants. He had dictated that life-size statues of samurai be placed in each of the four corners because he had such respect for the fierceness of those honored warriors.

He relished the rewards of being rich beyond the imagining of all those outside their families. Such riches bestowed power, secrecy and security. He was committed to using all of that to protect what was their rightful heritage. But, could he protect the one he loved the most or would he lose her before the end of this day?

His gaze settled once again on his twenty-four relatives seated in massive leather chairs. They represented humankind's oldest continuous line of power. All were closely related to five couples, The Patriarchs, who were so discrete that they were never present at these gatherings. The power and true identity of those ten Patriarchs were absolutely invisible to all others, including every one of the world's governments.

It was time to return to the pleasure at hand.

He walked around ever so casually to stand in front of the three guests who had, as usual, been chosen at random from around the planet. He used the knife to dispatch two of them himself and gave Melanie the pleasure of the third. He knew that if he failed in his mission today it might be the last joy she would experience.

The family members stood and applauded enthusiastically. It was a good start to a fearsome day.

Bailey returned to his seat as the applause subsided. He nodded to Melanie and watched as several members of the ever-present security team, under her direction, removed the bodies through the rice paper doors near where she and Bailey had killed them. They quickly rolled up the carpet on which the guests' blood had been spilled and took it away. The bodies would disappear, and no one would ever know what happened to them no matter how diligently they searched.

ENTANGLED SOUL

Thus it had been since Philip of Greece had set the stage for the creation of their five families in Cairo when the pyramids were only beginning to show some age.

At 8:06 AM Melanie and the only remaining security guard were ready to leave. Melanie took one look around the room, gave her father an affectionate kiss, and then eagerly departed for a long-anticipated shopping and sightseeing trip. At seventeen she was beautiful and so happy. Her guards, who might become her executioners if he failed today, left with his daughter.

He shoved aside the sudden ache that always surprised him. Bailey had been prepared for his own death for years. However, the thought that his failure today could result in the death of his daughter was horrifying. Within their families he was required to see her as just a tool for continuation of the family line. Somehow his Patriarch had deduced that he loved Melanie in the way that most fathers loved their offspring. Now that knowledge might be used to punish him if he was defeated today.

Bailey watched the final guard take up his station at the far end of the hardwood-floored hallway. He was one of hundreds of a private army from all over the world dressed as tourists visiting Mount Fuji, the surrounding scenery and sacred shrines. Each was a martial arts expert and, in violation of Japanese law, carried at least two concealed weapons.

To complete the security precautions, near and distant relatives of the Twenty-Five from their five families occupied every room in the hotel as well as each hotel in a three block radius. It had taken over a year of planning to make it appear that these family members had arrived as tourists normally would at random times from all over the world. No one had any clue that they were related to each other. Most of the relatives didn't even know about the meeting of the twenty-five people in the second-floor conference room with its transparent force field view of Japan's sacred Mount Fuji.

* * *

Finally, at precisely 8:07 AM, Chairman Bailey broke his silence.

"Ladies and gentlemen, the standard briefing team will now enter the arena to present our plan. You have seen the agenda. We are now going to defend our recommendation for a new way of ruling the world and assuring the financial health of our five families. It is a large evolutionary step forward from how we have constructed world power in the past. This has been made clear in the briefs that were provided to you last month. Lydia Templeton, Yori Tanaka, and Ibrahim Faruk will be the proposal defenders. However, I retain full responsibility for the adoption of the plan we are putting forward."

Bailey then stated, "I assume you are all satisfied with the identity cloaking arrangements that have been made. We will now step to the middle of our conference table circle to defend our proposals."

Chairman Bailey and his three team members walked through the opening in the table into the central arena. Standing close together they faced outward as a solid cylindrical wall was lowered around them. As soon as the rest of the room was shielded from their view, the twenty-one remaining participants moved randomly to exchange seats. When they were ready, a special holographic display rose to the top front of the conference table to hide the twenty-one from the four in the arena. Subtly, and constantly, morphing images represented, but did not resemble, the people behind the video wall. The image that was speaking might not represent the person at that location. In this way, the identities of those challenging the four in the arena were fully disguised. Once the display was in place, the cylinder surrounding the four standing in the arena was lifted.

Chairman Bailey announced, "We have two core topics and a supporting topic today. Each proposition will have a champion, and I will be the second for each of the champions. I retain overall responsibility for today's results.

"Yori Tanaka, our current Chairman of Infrastructure, and our host for today, will defend our proposal on the political transition from nation-states to corporate-states. Lydia Templeton, the chairwoman of technology will address the scientific developments that she and her team are involved in, and will eventually control, to facilitate this transition to the corporate-state. Ibrahim Faruk, the

Chairman of Operations will discuss the supporting security procedures in this future world. Let's begin."

* * *

Bailey's first proposal defender, Tanaka-san, in traditional Japanese kimono and wearing a samurai sword that was a family heirloom, bowed to the group and said, "It is indeed an honor and a pleasure to have this meeting held so close to my home. I hope you will enjoy this presentation and the associated events we have prepared for you."

Yori Tanaka acknowledged the greetings from around the holocircle. He paused shortly to look above the surrounding images and through the room's transparent force field at Mt. Fuji. He noted the cherry blossoms floating through the trees in the warming breeze. The freshness of the morning after a night of cleansing rain drifted in to permeate the room. It was indeed a beautiful day; fitting for these people who controlled unwitting presidents, prime ministers, kings and queens without their knowledge through a discrete chain of power.

He resumed, "We have honored our ancestors. Those financiers and rulers who came before us would be proud of what we have done. We have used the secret, preserved assets of Alexander, ancient elements of the Japanese monarchy, the craftily concealed financial resources of the Medici and the Fugger families from the Middle Ages as well as others to fund our empire. The political knowledge of our forefathers from the Qin Shi Huang dynasty and the ancient wisdom and long hidden riches of the original Indian regimes is in our blood and in our brains. Our family ancestors used these accumulated riches and wisdom to orchestrate the demise of the city-state and the evolution toward countries. They, and we, created periodic disruptions meant to keep those countries sufficiently off balance so as to be readily manageable. However, the model of geographically defined political entities is beginning to fall upon hard times."

An anonymous image with disguised voice interrupted, "Yori, we only suspect, and we can't confirm, that the model is showing flaws. There are cycles in government just as in everything else. I must say that I see great risk in our Chairman's plan that you are supporting. The way our five families have secretly ruled the world for over two thousand years works. Why must we change what has succeeded so well? Please explain."

Yori Tanaka politely bowed while responding, "With pleasure. Everything is temporary. This transition is needed for a number or reasons. I will explain, in as much detail as necessary, why we must end the power of national governments and establish corporations as the ruling powers."

Tanaka-san paused to collect his thoughts. "Everyone in our five families knows that not long after the dawn of written history our blood ancestors, other forebears, and those who came before them have been able to recruit the masses and, in particular, self-serving, ambitious government leaders to unwittingly accumulate wealth and power for us. We have used our invisible positions of influence and associated riches to catalyze wars fought by the general population at our discrete direction. Through those wars we have, over a great deal of time, gradually eliminated those who are not part of, or have challenged, our empire too aggressively. We have created the world we desire. The tactics we created so long ago have served us well.

"Hundreds of years ago we, and our immediate families, stopped fighting in these wars. We have become masters at stirring up patriotic fervor to get others to fight wars on our behalf, so we can build our massive wealth and power. Those who didn't fight were branded traitors and killed or imprisoned. Their families were ostracized or eliminated. All of that taken together influenced the populations to follow the directions of the government puppets we permitted to exist. We encouraged laws that made it illegal to kill the heads of government who started these wars for us. At the same time, we made it legal to encourage the slaughter on the battlefield of the general population forced to fight for these leaders who we controlled."

Another disguised image said, "Get to the point" with obvious irritation.

Tanaka replied, "The point is this. The current model has become increasingly difficult to manage over the last hundred years. Almost all the world population has become highly educated through universal communication and computing. With this education and communication has come vague and general recognition of the real situation we have created.

"People are demanding greater accountability from their governments. If a minister or secretary of state fails in a negotiation that leads to war there have been demands that the leadership of that country be put on the front lines of the war. Astoundingly, the populations are showing signs of actually refusing to fight unless that happens.

"These and other issues threaten to cut into our wealth and power. This old system which served us so well is developing some weaknesses. It is time to move to something better suited to our present and future situation."

Chairman Bailey interjected, "As we move outward from Earth, we are taking pains to avoid a freedom initiative like the one that occurred in the eighteenth century. The European colonists of North America worked hard, and almost successfully, to upset the visible, and thus our shadow, power structure. Poor and slow communications across ocean distances were great aids to their near success. It took tremendous, patient and subtle effort over more than two centuries to quell that dangerous freedom initiative. Even then, our full recovery was almost derailed by our impatient senior government puppets who were more passionate than logical about the beliefs in which we slowly indoctrinated them.

"We had to keep these leaders from realizing that they essentially lived in a borderless world with our Families as the real one world government. We orchestrated and perfected ethnic and religious wars without boundaries. We spread around massive amounts of money provided through temporary intermediaries like Jorge Rosor to advance our political agenda. We created worldwide marketing programs using the compliant news media to sell emotional objectives that discretely and deceptively undermined society rather than logical ones that steadily promoted stability and peace. Since we controlled these emotional cycles we made vast amounts of war and investment money from the trends we created and therefore more firmly established control of the unsuspecting masses. Even so, there were, and are, many who opposed us to a degree sufficient to slow our pace."

Yuri continued, "Now we are in the process of crossing the ocean of space. It only takes days to reach Earth's moon, Luna, but it takes months to get to Mars. We can't make the mistake of the 1700s. At the same time we can take the opportunity to create a new set of governments using an entirely new model that, by its nature, blurs traditional physical borders."

A more aggressive image challenged, "You are both making invalid comparisons. The situations are different. Travel may be as you say but communication is only minutes long. Any agents we have on Luna and Mars, or even on Mar's moons will tell us immediately if there are problems brewing. The model change you are suggesting is extremely dramatic."

"You are, of course, correct," Tanaka-san responded. "However, I'm not willing to assume that we will have the luxury of taking months to reach Mars to fix a situation that is going wrong. Diplomacy and negotiation are the provinces of only those who don't have the strength and position to act. That is the practiced tactic of the fools we place in command of governments. I am not ignoring the fact that the immediate, discrete and ruthless use of force is what helps keep us in power. Our families don't take three months to apply prompt, necessary action."

A calmer image suggested, "State your solution."

Yori Tanaka continued, "Some of what you have brought up will be addressed by Ibrahim. More to the current point, I believe that we must make a significant adjustment. Here are the details." Tanaka-san displayed a set of free space holographic images around the arena and launched deeply into his presentation.

Thirty contentious minutes later, and with a bit of sales flare in his voice, Tanaka-san concluded. "We are introducing the era of the corporate state. The current geographical governments will, within the next couple of decades, begin to exist only to handle necessary and basic Maslovian infrastructures on a socialist model. As has been repeatedly proven, this will result in dependency of those easily led and lazy. In this way, we will readily identify the less productive members of society and eventually eliminate them, or let them prey on and destroy each other. This will increase class warfare. The human population will be more strongly focused on each other and have fewer tendencies to discover any of the control we exert.

"Our five families will more strongly manipulate the corporations with key commodities being under our total command. We will decide the mix of corporate dominance over time with power shifting in the manner we permit just as we have done with geographical entities over the last couple of thousand years. We will establish a world in which corporations, and to a more limited extent the legacy countries, will be permitted to create laws as well as police and military forces and declare war. As is always true, the laws will give the image of creating order and preserving freedom. Naturally, we will use the increased number of laws from fluctuating corporate states to create legal traps for those who oppose us. No one will be able to obey all the laws that will be created.

"In short, corporations will be the ruling entities as humankind expands beyond Earth. Some Mediterranean countries will be the first to make the transition to a weaker role. The rest will follow in short order. The evolution will be mostly bloodless, but examples will be made within the corporations and states that don't follow our subtle, inflexible influence. As usual, we will be discrete but merciless."

An image leaned forward menacingly, "Yori, this had best be well planned. If we fail, then the legacy of our families is dead."

Tanaka-san simply said, "As you continue to listen then you will understand that this is a strong plan with many interlinking elements."

Chairman Bailey interrupted, "Yori has stated the overarching goal. It is one that the four of us in the arena strongly support. I assure you that any challenge against Yori is a challenge against all of us."

Another shifting image spoke from a different place in the circle, but it was clearly the same person, "I am simply stating that I fully understand the gravity of this massive change. It is disturbing to think about removing a model that has made us so rich and powerful. You must convince me that all the proper elements are in place. We still have the issue of distance that has created such large problems in the past."

* * *

Lydia Templeton, black-haired and regal looking, put a comforting hand on Bailey's shoulder. She stepped forward speaking with authority. "As chairwoman of technology, that sounds like my cue. Technology in various forms has always been the underpinnings of the growth of economy. Historically, that technology might have been just a better way to farm or hunt. New instruments of war have always been the result of technological innovation. The predominate progress in business technology in the last three hundred years has been through electronic information and communication. We will make sure that we take full financial and operational control of one emerging technology in particular as we make the structural transition that Tanaka-san has described. That technology is called quantum particle entanglement.

"It is one of our core beliefs that technology without business application has no value. In our case, there will be visible and invisible control of business applications of entanglement technology. In support of Yori's plan we will be the discrete controllers of entanglement technology and siphon off a great deal of money from its use.

"It will become possible to use entanglement to transfer information, inanimate matter and living plants, animals and humans anywhere humans live. We will use it to avoid the problems of the 1700s.

"I have been told that my previous information on the subject of entanglement technology, and many of the technical writings, may have been a bit difficult to muddle through, especially for those who find technology boring. I'll summarize the capabilities in clear language in less than three minutes. Please observe my holographic displays as I explain.

"We are all aware that the traditional speed limit of the universe is, simply put, the speed of light. Nothing can go faster than that including all forms of telecommunications. So, a round trip message to our moon takes three seconds. That's no big deal for humans. However, a round trip message between Earth and Mars can take anywhere from six minutes to forty minutes depending on where these two planets are relative to each other in their orbits. These time lags are significant impediments to human and computer transactions.

"Nothing made of matter can even approach the speed of light. In fact, our fastest space ships, for reasons of both physics and economics take six months in the best case to reach Mars from Earth. When Earth and Mars are farther away from each other we don't even attempt the voyage because it doesn't make sense.

"But there is something else special that can happen across long distances. In fact, this special thing can happen between two physical particles instantaneously regardless of how far they are away from each other. Even if they are clear across the universe from each other, two particles can be entangled. Simply put, this means they are related to each other such that if we make a change in one of the particles the information about that change is sent instantly to the other particle. The speed of light is not a limit for entanglement.

"We are making great inroads in understanding this technology. We have long been able to control entangled communication between anything as small as sub atomic particles to as large as complex molecules. Over time, the plan is to use entanglement technology for instantaneous communication between any locations where there are humans or our devices. Eventually, we will be able to use this technology to transmit matter instantly between any two points. At first, this will be inanimate matter. Over the longer term, it will be live plants and animals, including humans."

Another hologram interrupted, "That is all well and good, Lydia. However, this technology is still in the early stages. You and Yori are risking our long-held family power on its eventual development in the manner you describe. I'm finding it hard to support this."

Lydia quickly responded, "All of you know me intimately. Have I ever failed to deliver to your satisfaction?" That double entendre brought shuffling and a few chuckles from around the room.

She pressed on with her argument. "Look, when the project to develop fusion power was initiated by one of our predecessors in the mid-twentieth century it was set up as a near one hundred year plan. Our families knew, without any doubt, that it would be successful because it was an application of science that already existed in nature. Today, the entire planet uses safe fusion power, which is ultimately controlled by us. It is an amazing revenue stream for our families. Entanglement is also an application of science that exists in nature. We now fully understand how the process works. Development will be a step by step process with an outcome that we are just as confident of as we were with fusion."

A quickly shifting image interrupted, "But what about the timing? If I understand your written brief, any application of entanglement to transporting people will lag populating Mars and Luna by perhaps centuries. There is a big technology gap between transporting people and molecules!"

With a conciliatory nod Lydia countered, "That's true, and I understand the concern. However, Mars and Luna are quite different from the America's in the 1700s. All we have to do is shut off, or even just subtly disrupt, the lifeline to those off-Earth colonies. They will then be so consumed with survival that they will forget all thoughts of any independence. Furthermore, because of the political changes Yori has described, their allegiance will not be to a country on Earth. It will be to a corporation they are part of at both their location and Earth. Perhaps we can see that situation as just another form of entanglement."

Lydia waited for the wry chuckles to subside and turned to Ibrahim Faruk. "Ibrahim will now tell you about population controls that are well-proven."

* * *

Ibrahim Faruk, the Chairman of Operations, was sure that he had enjoyed the presentation that morning more than anyone else in the room. It helped that he felt that he had much less at stake than Chairman Bailey or the other presenters. Grinning broadly, he moved to the center of the arena.

"Thank you, Lydia. This has been an excellent education today as well as much more enjoyable than the usual meeting.

"Yori and I are perhaps bookends today. Our families first started all this in the country of my ancestors. It is good to be gathered together on this beautiful, sunny and refreshing morning in Yori's homeland.

"My team and I have been working in close cooperation with Yori and Lydia. We have a series of actions planned to take place over the next couple of decades. You will find some of them quite interesting. These steps will ensure that we have the appropriate operational systems in place to support and control the development of entanglement. We will position the right internal people and establish the proper organizational structures to ease the transition from geographically-defined to corporate-defined states."

With Gordon's help, Ibrahim spent the next hour describing the flexibility they had available to maintain the control they were used to having. The twenty-one who were watching were clearly interested as was evidenced by their excited and probing questions. Ibrahim finally had to cut off that part of the discussion.

He continued in a different vein. "There are some, right now, who are aggressively opposing our objectives. Several of them are only tens of miles away from us. If you please, direct your attention toward the right of Mount Fuji. You will see an intercontinental hypership approaching at high speed with two engines on fire. The ship's radios have failed due to some chafing in the wiring systems. A complicating factor is that the autopilot has been programmed by some of our people to run the rockets up to full speed and crash into the mountain about one-third of the way up its side."

As if by Ibrahim Faruk's command the plane smashed into the sacred peak at almost six hundred miles per hour exploding into a huge fireball that a few seconds later shook the building they were in. All in the room erupted into applause for Ibrahim Faruk who nodded his head in thanks.

"It goes without saying that only people who we approve of and appoint will be on the accident investigating team."

Ibrahim concluded by saying, "My dear relatives, if I can control that, then I, and my successors, can do whatever is necessary to maintain security and control until entanglement is fully developed."

He then nodded to Chairman Bailey who announced, "It's time for a lunch break and some entertainment. You will be shielded from our view as you retire through the doors that I have just remotely opened. We in the arena will join you within a minute.

"You will also notice a change to the agenda. We have a recently provided opportunity to invite a guest to lunch. A few of you know her."

* * *

Bailey, taking a bite of sushi, scanned the room in which they had gathered for their mid-day break. From their beginning, the five families had been clinically careful in their selection of marriage partners. Gordon Bailey smiled as he admired the result. All were handsome and beautiful, robust and taller than the average person. Intellect and strength showed in their faces. All looked young for their varied ages.

As he looked to his left he was surprised to see an item in the room that he had not ordered. Only his uncle, the male Patriarch of his family, could have directed that it be put there. The gleaming pure gold skull on the polished silver staff was a blunt reminder of his daughter's fate if he failed today.

When all were comfortably seated, another set of doors opened and the guest that Chairman Bailey mentioned was invited in. She was the head of the TriNational Bank of North America.

In confused outrage, the banker shouted, "Why have I been hijacked like this?" Turning to a family member she said, "I know you! We were at a cocktail party together in Toronto. I'll have your head for this," which drew a smile from Gordon Bailey and a quiet chuckle from Yori Tanaka.

Bailey nodded to the security guard accompanying the bank executive. The guard applied a medical agent sufficient to make her compliant and paralyze her vocal cords. She was then guided to a seat of honor near Tanaka.

Bailey stood and bowed to her. "Thank you for joining us today. I know that you had the opportunity to watch the plane you were supposed to be on crash into Mt. Fuji. You should thank us for making sure you weren't on it and that someone else was chosen to die in your place."

She weakly started to rise but the guard put a firm hand on her shoulder.

The Chairman turned to the two guards at the far door. "Please bring in the rest of our guests."

The guests were ethnic entertainers from various places around the world. None were well known outside of a small region. Nevertheless, they were excellent. They would be greatly missed in their widely dispersed villages and cities. However, no one would ever question why they all went missing at the same time.

It was a glorious hour filled with a total of ten comedians, dancers and singers. At the end, Gordon Bailey invited them to the front of the room to receive appreciation from the group. Yori Tanaka, as the country host, joined them. They were standing directly in front of the national bank executive. Tanaka, in an excellent demonstration of swordsmanship, decapitated them all so quickly that none had the chance to respond in any way. The relatives cheered as the bank executive stared in speechless horror.

As soon as the mess was cleared away, Ibrahim Faruk approached and stood in front of the executive.

"You were given your position in part because of your intelligence, your education and your connections. You knew that you were expected to follow the direction provided to you through a long string of messengers. You failed to do all you were told. That cost us money and power and compromised part of our distant operations. That cannot be tolerated. You conspired with the President of the United States to put country first and bank affairs second. For that you will die within the next few minutes in the manner you have just witnessed. Tanaka-san will be your executioner."

Ibrahim continued his explanation. "Your head will then be frozen and put into a secure pouch. Your youngest son will deliver the pouch to the White House following standard procedures. He won't know what is inside. One of the White House staff will deliver the package to the President. The pouch will be marked

"Eyes Only: The President of the United States". Through a channel we have to the President, and that he trusts, he will be told to open the container in private. A self-destructing message will tell the President that the next pouch will contain the head of his brother if he continues to put country ahead of international finances. He will also receive instructions to reseal the pouch and return it to your son who will be waiting for it. Soon after your son leaves the White House grounds he will be intercepted by one of our people. He will then disappear. Your son will join our cadre of slaves and serve us until he is no longer useful."

Chairman Bailey nodded to the bank executive's guard who administered another injection that reversed the effects of the sedative. The executive jumped from her chair and ran toward the door that was again open. Tanaka beat her to the door. He smiled at her as she froze in her tracks. Before she could move again he cut her head off and caught it by her red hair before it touched the ground. All stood and bowed to Tanaka-san as he held the severed head up for all to view. He then placed it in a chest for freezing.

Chairman Bailey addressed his family members, "The four of us in the arena will now return to the conference room to conclude our meeting. You will be told when we are behind the central barrier."

* * *

Chairman Bailey had no idea if he was succeeding or failing as they entered the closing discussion. His thoughts returned to the gold head on the silver pike. He knew exactly why inner-circle members of the Five Families always remained clinical in their relationships. Children were supposed to just be a tool for continuity. Loving them was a dangerous weakness, and his Patriarch knew his weakness.

He began, "During peacetime, which we have always strived to keep a little disturbed, we permit the populations just enough belief that they can succeed through hard work. And some people do greatly improve their lot for a few generations. Then we change the rules to crush their wealth. We continue to experiment with different societies. Some we permit to be rich. For others, we create conditions for extreme poverty. We pit them against each other to increase our knowledge and control.

"Regardless of their great wealth or grinding poverty, each country or society has always been taxed at gradually higher levels in manners so complex that we can easily and secretly siphon off massive amounts of money into our personal treasuries. The wealth of our five families has long exceeded the combined wealth of the entire rest of the population. These taxes have sometimes been obvious and sometimes subtle. On the average, they have resulted in over half of the earnings of the population. Amazingly, we have even succeeded in taxing people for dying."

This brought a round of laughter from all present.

"We experimented with creating national banks in the seventeenth century and were pleasantly surprised. We increased the number of those banks across the world over the next couple of hundred years. Each time we created a new national bank, we increased our control over governments, corporations and the general public. We amassed so much money through these banks that we had difficulty hiding it. Sometimes, like today, we have had to discipline those who strayed from our plan.

"Our families have learned much in two thousand five hundred years. Our discrete wealth has given us secret and absolute power over everything humankind does. Every action we take is with the objective of dramatically increasing that wealth to maintain total control."

Bailey finished his short historical review and moved into his summary of the new plan. "We will now change the psychology and loyalties of the population. The ocean of space will create a temporarily uncomfortable situation for us. We will avoid geographical or planetary allegiances by moving the populations toward corporate loyalties without regard to location. The threat of isolation from life-sustaining resources will also be an interim control mechanism that will prevent revolts by off-Earth populations.

"In the short term, entanglement is the next massively disruptive technology we must absolutely control. We will work toward that control over the next two hundred years. I can't stress the importance of this technology enough. Yori Tanaka and Lydia Templeton have provided more than the necessary arguments. According to our plan, we will have the proper elements of entanglement technology ready at the right time. This technology is vitally important to us because it will be used to ensure that all of humankind is bound tightly together for the continued success of our five families. It will be used to provide instant communication and, eventually, immediate movement of materials and people between Earth, Luna, Mars and beyond. We must control everything through entanglement, or we may lose control in the longer term.

"Ibrahim Faruk has shown that we have the tools necessary to exercise whatever control is required with great discretion.

"Everything we have discussed today is part of a well-integrated plan.

"It is clear, and it is essential, that we operate at an unfair advantage over everyone else. We have written the rules of engagement for humanity, and they must live by those rules or be punished by fines, imprisonment or death. The big change for the masses is that corporations will replace nations as the rulers of humankind.

"Our five families live with only one rule. We must never be compromised in any way. Those who break this rule, and all of those close to them, will die horribly. We have absolutely no compunctions about creating misery, inflicting torture or causing death. As a consequence we can't lose. Our children who don't display the proper characteristics are quickly dispatched or used in complete isolation as we wish until they die. With these rules and with money, and the power that comes from money, we will secretly stay in power forever. As we always have, we will stay deeply in the shadows as we remain the masters of humanity.

"Almost everyone outside of our families professes to believe that total control is an unachievable illusion. We are proof that they are wrong. Each of our generations has attained incrementally greater control over the expanding mass of humanity. We have made freedom and personal success the real illusions. We will keep those illusions real for the masses as we cement our control even more strongly in the thousands of years ahead of us.

"Other than natural disasters of planetary or multi-planetary magnitude, the only unplannable disruption we have to be concerned about is an encounter with alien life. We are still working on that problem, but the unknowns are keeping us from defining the full set of events that such an encounter might bring."

Bailey concluded, "Now, it is time to vote. If you accept our plan then please press the green tile on your side of the holographic display. If you reject it, then obviously you should press the red tile. A yellow tile is available for those who are undecided."

Seconds felt like minutes. Then one display turned red. Bailey had trouble controlling his breathing. Where was Melanie?! He saw Ibrahim become uncharacteristically tense. Yori almost imperceptibly moved away. Lydia stood her ground close by his side. A green display appeared. Then another red one. Five more green. Then yet another two reds.

Bailey knew that by now Melanie's guards, turned potential executioners, had been alerted for action. Bailey imagined the guards closing in around Melanie. Perhaps his plan was just too radical.

Blood pounded in Bailey's ears as nothing happened in the room for a full two minutes. Only a lifetime of self-discipline kept Bailey from groaning in frustration and agony. Others saw him as professionally impassive. He wanted, but knew it was useless, to bargain with his life for Melanie's.

Then five yellow screens appeared. The voters must be caucusing behind their holographic wall. He just couldn't fail!

Another eternity and then four more screens lit up at the same time. Three more reds and two greens. It was a tie! He had failed!

In his mind's eye, he saw Melanie being pulled from whatever store she was in and herded into a secure transport. No one would be answering her questions. He knew that her death would take place in front of him and that there was nothing he could do!

Maybe there was. He must find a way to die before she was brought to him.

His body relaxed into immobility from the designer drug that seeped through his skin from the surrounding air. How ironic. He was doomed to watch his daughter's death unless the vote progressed in his favor. Ibrahim Faruk moved farther away. Lydia, still by his side, laid a comforting hand on his shoulder. Tanaka-san remained stoic. Bailey held no rancor for what needed to be done. He long understood and embraced their closed secret society. However, that didn't take away his torment.

Then two yellows turned red while two more turned green. It was still a tie. The one yellow gave him hope.

Melanie entered the room flanked by her guards. She happily ran to Bailey. Then comprehension dawned on her. She knelt before the father she loved seeing tears in his eyes. She knew her father was going to be executed for his failure. That was her last thought before the remotely controlled poison coursed through her body and she collapsed into his lap.

All the screens turned green. Bailey's mind screamed with the lesson his Patriarch had just taught him.

Shadows Uncovered

Inara and Malk stood in front of the silent group.

Malk continued, "Now all of you know much more clearly who we have all been quietly and discretely ruled by since long before humans left Earth. These people had no idea that they were sowing the seeds of their own destruction one hundred thousand years in the future. Of course, it is also the potential destruction of all humanity.

"The rest of what I am going to tell you will be validated through the work that Kieran and Inara will be doing. Keep in mind that I can't perceive everything. Strangely, though I live simultaneously across all time, some of what will happen in your near future is not visible to me."

Malk turned to Inara as an indication that she should address the group. Inara proceeded.

"Let me put it this way for now and provide a quick summary that will assure that we all have the same information. The next few minutes of what I am going to say has already been explained to the galaxy's leaders. The technologists in the Controllers organization who work the mathematical details of entanglement technology will be hearing this for the first time.

"In summary, entanglement has always been managed as a space-time concept. If that is all it was then we would not be having a problem today. In reality, it is a space-time-soul manifestation. The Schmidt constant compensates for the interaction with the Universal Soul."

As Kieran and Dammar began to ask questions Inara cut them off. "Please let me explain just a bit more. This is important and is the essence of a discussion The Guide and I had just before I left his hall to come here. We all know that two different people can take exactly the same action with different intentions. One person's intentions may be totally honorable. Another's may be horribly malicious. The immediate perceptible outcome may be the same. However, over time the effects may be quite different. Those of us who have strong religious views will tell you that we believe different intentions have a different effect on the Universal Soul. Even the ancients believed this. Some believed in

Enlightenment, others in the Universal Self, and still others in The Great Spirit. The bottom line is that harm done to one is harm done to all. The same is true of good."

Malk interjected, "Let me show you a file you have never seen from the Five Families private archive. You need to know before this part of the story starts that the famous Dr. Marianne Schmidt was a high level member of the Five Families. She understood perfectly, and fully agreed with, how the Patriarchs of the Five Families intended to use her work."

Exploitation and Expansion

Researcher Marianne Schmidt forced herself to sit quietly on her favorite stool in the lab. She absolutely knew she had succeeded. However, scientific protocol required that she had to wait for confirmation from others who worked with her in the dome-covered crater on the far side of the moon.

Her laboratory was easily the busiest place on Luna these days. As she strived to keep from fidgeting, a storm of activity continued all around her. She was the cause of that storm. Equipment streamed through the entanglement pipeline into her many laboratories.

Dr. Schmidt was the quantivity genius of Quantum Controllers Interplanetary which was secretly owned by the Five Families. She managed ten interconnected laboratories on Luna, seven on Earth, five on Mars, and two in high orbit around Mars and Earth's moon. Everyone at each of these laboratories was working on the same top secret project for their company.

Finally, the word came. "Dr. Schmidt, the amoeba you just transmitted lived and there is nothing wrong with it." The message arrived instantaneously at the Luna offices from the huge space laboratory high above Mars.

An amazingly simple statement. It came after one hundred fifty years of research, trial and error, and the solution of massively complex equations across multiple integrated disciplines. They had finally graduated from transmitting inanimate matter to sending living protoplasm instantaneously between two widely separated places in space high above Mars and high above Luna.

On the outside, Dr. Schmidt maintained her professional decorum. "Humph, to be expected." She then called to her assistant in his adjacent office. "Johannes, get Roger for me."

Johannes was accustomed to his boss's gruff and abrasive attitude. "Yes, ma'am," he responded, erroneously suspecting she was already immersed in her equations and not listening.

Roger Huber arrived within a minute. "Yes, doctor. What can I do for you?"

"You can check my work. Call me at the lodge when you finish."

Doctor Huber could only watch in surprised silence as Dr. Schmidt left the lab. Marianne Schmidt never asked anyone to check her work. What the hell was going on?

Johannes walked in with a puzzled look. "Roger, Dr. Schmidt just left, said she was going to the lodge, and told me to have a nice day. She is never cordial at all in any way. I'm stunned."

"Johannes, it gets even weirder than that. She just asked me to check her work and call her at the lodge when I finish. Extremely strange."

"I guess I'd better leave you alone," he observed.

"Not that alone. Send in my entire team. Set up a sleeping area in the adjacent room and have food appear at regular intervals. This is so unusual that I don't want any of us to leave until we have finished this review. I don't intend to disappoint the boss."

Minutes later Roger learned about the successful transmission of the amoeba and understood. His level of urgency instantly became greater and was joined by nervous excitement.

* * *

Three almost sleepless days later, Roger had checked the work of Marianne Schmidt every way he could think of. He had made sure it was verified many times by individuals, groups and massive computer analysis and simulations. Finally, Dr. Huber called Johannes. "I understand exactly what Dr. Schmidt has done. We have validated her work with repeated successful tests from high-Earth and high-Mars."

"I assume you will tell Dr. Schmidt yourself," observed Johannes. "After you tell her, please meet me in the bar."

Roger left the lab and walked through the passageway across the lunar crater to the lodge. He went up to Dr. Schmidt sitting in her favorite leather chair facing a view of the distant crater wall and said simply, "Congratulations, ma'am."

"Thank you, Roger." The response was clearly a dismissal.

That was another surprise. Doctor Marianne Schmidt never thanked anyone for anything. "You're welcome, ma'am."

Still puzzled, Roger Huber went to the lodge bar where Johannes was sitting at a table in the far corner. He had anticipated correctly, and a fruit drink was already waiting for Roger. They sat together in silence for a few minutes. Finally, Roger spoke up. "Where is the rest of the team?"

Johannes responded, "Right after you called me, I reserved the room behind us and had it set up for maximum security. The team is rapidly assembling and had best be ready in five minutes. They will be waiting for you and, most especially, for Dr. Schmidt. The room is outfitted with audio-video briefing equipment, and a full summary of Dr. Schmidt's equations has been prepared. All members of the team are exhausted but too wired to sleep. Closure on the last three days will be good for them. Frankly, I think it would be good for all of you."

Dr. Huber took a large sip of his fruit drink. "I guess I should go back to Dr. Schmidt and invite her."

"No," Johannes responded. "You need to join the rest of the team. Protocol requires that all of you be in that room when Dr. Schmidt arrives. She already knows that you will be there. I'll escort her."

"You're assuming that she will grace us with her presence," remarked Roger.

"Roger, you're a great scientist and generally surprisingly good at leading a team. However, sometimes you amaze me with your lack of recognition of protocol. Not only will Dr. Schmidt be there, but she is expecting this.

"She has made the greatest set of scientific and mathematical advances since Einstein. She knows it, and we all know it. When she enters that room, you had all better be there and give her a standing ovation that lasts for five minutes. She is an introverted, ill mannered, inconsiderate excuse for a human being. She has also just derived the greatest set of equations of the last four hundred years. Behind that controlled, and frankly shy, exterior is a human being who is bursting with pride and joy. If you all acknowledge her amazing achievement when she walks in that room you will be giving her everything she wants and more than she feels like she has ever had. Finish your drink. In fifteen minutes I will be escorting Dr. Schmidt into that room."

Johannes took one more sip of his drink, excused himself as politely as ever, and went to see Dr. Schmidt.

Roger, somewhat nonplussed, took just a couple of minutes to finish, sign the tab and walk the few feet to the conference room. To his great surprise, he was greeted by hearty backslaps and handshakes all around. Clearly, this tired team was proud and excited.

"Thank you, all," responded Roger. "We are all highly impressed by what Dr. Schmidt has accomplished. She has made the first successful entangled transfer of a living organism across planetary distances and has provided the full mathematical description of the Grand Total Unification Theory; the Grand TUT."

Dr. Huber paused for the cheering to subside. "If Johannes adheres to his legendary punctuality he will be bringing Dr. Schmidt through that door in about ten minutes. I understand that he has already worked with a few of you to set up an audio-video presentation of Dr. Schmidt's work and that one of you will manage the presentation for her. In the meantime, I suggest that we await our guest of honor."

The scientists excitedly chatted with those nearest them. A presentation by Dr. Schmidt was a considerable honor on top of the privilege they already had of working with this demanding, driven genius.

The door finally opened, and for a few seconds the room fell into total silence such was the impact of her presence. Then, almost as if on command, they all erupted into thunderous cheers and applause. This group of normally reserved, introspective scientists couldn't contain themselves. Dr. Schmidt at first looked surprised, and then perhaps a little embarrassed, as she walked to the front of the room nodding her thanks as she moved through the crowd. She stood there for minutes accepting the honor. Finally, she held up her hand. All became silent and sat down.

"I'm going to keep this short. We are all tired. And you, because of the work you have done for the last three days, already know most of the story.

"To transport the amoeba required solving a massively complex set of equations and the use of enormous telecyber power to manage all the variables in picoseconds. Transporting larger biological material will require vastly more telecyber power which, of course, will be developed. From this point onward, it is a matter of increasing computer power to manage the greater set of variables that comes with managing more complex biological matter.

"I must tell you that there is a piece of the story that eludes me, and that none of us should take for granted. You noticed that I used a special constant to make the Grand TUT equations work. I'm frustrated to have to admit that I don't know why I had to use that constant."

That unexpected revelation brought a sudden murmur across the room. As quiet returned, Dr. Schmidt continued.

"I'm confused by the need for this constant. It really doesn't make much sense to me, and your validation team should have questioned it more energetically."

That slight rebuke created what was clearly an uncomfortable shuffling in the room.

Dr. Schmidt continued, "All I can suggest to myself, and to you, is that it accounts for something not quite part of space-time that affects space-time. I am choosing my words carefully here. Note that I said that it is not quite part of space-time but affects space-time. What I believe, and what you probably did not notice, is that this constant, this fudge factor as I see it, may not have been needed a few hundred years ago. I emphasize that there is something that is not quite part of space-time that has affected space-time to make this constant necessary."

Dr. Schmidt had to wait again for the murmuring to cease. "I learned this when I overlaid my equations on top of detailed data that has been collected since the beginning of mankind's entanglement work. There is a trend line that shows that the constant is needed less and less as one goes backward in time to the first days of entanglement work by our predecessors. At the same time, there is no measureable difference in the constant over the last twenty-three years. It seems to now be staying flat. On the other hand, there is a hint in the equations that there is also something other than a change in space-time affecting this constant. So, there is still work to do. Perhaps we should expect more change in this constant."

Dr. Schmidt then abruptly left the room with Johannes following closely.

Evil's Effect

After the scene ended, Malk continued, "In the beginning, entanglement technology was seized by, and controlled by, the small group of horribly malicious people I have shown you. They managed it to create power and riches for themselves while inflicting great harm on others. They were absolutely evil people who performed heinous acts. Their intentions with respect to the powerful entanglement technology were inherently wicked. It was not for the betterment of humanity. It was to control humanity. Dr. Schmidt was a senior member in their organization though the top several layers of the Five Families were hidden from her. However, she knew that entanglement was to be used to control humanity while benefitting people whose desire was to control more than serve."

Inara stepped in to press home with great emotional intensity the point that Malk was making. "At the risk being repetitive, we must all understand that these evil intentions damage the soul in all of us. As a result, the intentions changed space-time and its relationship with the Universal Soul. This is what created the mathematical necessity for the Schmidt constant. If entanglement had been developed and controlled by other than horribly evil people, there would have never been a Schmidt constant. After the immediate effect, space-time-soul settled into a change that was so slight that it was imperceptible to humans until recently. The Schmidt constant, after its initial evolution, reached what looked like stability. In reality, the change over time during this falsely stable era was so minuscule that we didn't detect it with our monitoring systems. Over the last hundred years it has become more imbalanced. Some evidence of that is the disruption we have experienced to the entanglement nodes as well as in some very recent mathematical analyses. That imbalance was less than we could perceive until the last year or so except for the effect it had on me."

At this point, Kieran gestured a virtual computer into existence and made a neural connection with it. Inara noticed that he was frantically working and could tell that he understood what she was revealing.

She continued. "Yesterday morning's disruption was a symptom of that imbalance which has become worse since then. Kieran's genius effort compensated for that imbalance. Yesterday evening, the soul portion of space-time-soul could no longer tolerate The Pain and had to exterminate the evil if space-time in our part of the universe wasn't going to, in effect, emotionally, spiritually and physically collapse. My suspicion is that the work we are all going to do together will eventually reveal the mathematics behind all of this."

Dammar began, "Assuming this is all true . . ."

"It appears that it may be," Kieran interrupted.

Dammar paused, a bit irritated. Then began again. "Assuming this is all true, does that mean our entanglement systems will soon begin operating properly?"

With a look, Inara diverted Dammar's question to Kieran. She and Kieran were already beginning to operate as a team.

Kieran, looking concerned, waved his virtual workspace away. "I can only give you a generalized answer. I've just quickly adapted what Inara has told us to my recent discoveries. Inara's information has helped resolve some of my technical confusion and heightened my sense of alarm."

Kieran paused to gain composure, looking to Inara for assurance. She nodded for him to continue. "It took one hundred millennia to create the damage. It won't come even close to taking that long to fix it. But," he continued quietly, "it isn't going to be fixed in weeks or months or even a few short years. In the meantime, most of the population of the galaxy is going to die because our entanglement systems will not be able to carry the energy transmission load necessary to maintain planetary environments in the narrow zone capable of sustaining life."

With a bit of a tremor in his voice, Kieran said, "Please, Inara and I and our team must start work as soon as possible."

Dammar was clearly surprised at Kieran's intensity. "That's a pretty dramatic and negative assessment."

Kieran was a bit embarrassed by his mentor's comment. "I'm sorry, Dean Corday. Please take my emotion and frankness as an indication of my sudden understanding of what is truly happening, and my recognition that this is so much more complicated than I ever realized. I'm stunned by Inara's revelation of space-time-soul. However, as I just mentioned, her explanation appears to resolve the mathematical dilemma that I have had."

Dammar relaxed a bit, saying, "I understand, Kieran."

Looking at Kieran and Inara, Gareth offered, "All of the resources of the University are obviously at your disposal. A special laboratory environment has already been established for you only a minute's walk from this room. As long as our entanglement systems are operating, you will have direct telecyber links to any and every educational resource in the galaxy."

Alana, who had been in a quick but discrete telescence conversation in a far corner of the room, returned to the group and said, "I have just been talking with The Guide, Paya Lachlan and Edric Yan. They are providing full telecyber links of all Controller and Pilgrim resources to your laboratory here. It is safe to say that you will have more combined computing, analysis and research resources at your disposal than anyone anywhere has ever had."

Monz Ingra chimed in, "I have just ordered a multi-layer security cordon around University and Cathedral. My entire sector is now under strict martial law. I continue to be unable to reach the Prime Minister, so I have again directly contacted the Sector Minister for The Guide's Hall. At my request, she is taking a similar step in her sector. Although she is still working to digest what is happening, and by my request, she has been in touch with The Guide and offered intense security around The Guide's Hall. He has accepted."

Dammar walked over to Kieran and unknowingly echoing an earlier comment to Inara by The Guide said, "It isn't fair, but the future of the galaxy is now in your hands and Inara's hands."

Kieran and Inara turned to go to their laboratory.

On the way, Kieran simply commented to Inara, "It is good to see you again." Inara understood that it was a great understatement and was warmed by that thought.

Malk followed them at a short distance.

Discovery and Countdown

One day later, they all assembled again in a meeting area adjacent to the laboratory. To his own surprise as well as Inara's, Malk was still with them having spent the night in a nearby suite.

Kieran and Inara had conjured up a large circular pit around which they were all seated. Kieran began the presentation.

"All of us are physically and emotionally spent. Inara and I will get to the bottom line immediately, and then we will tell you why we have reached our conclusion. In front of you is the countdown clock to total collapse of all of our entanglement systems across the galaxy. You can see that we have a little over two days left. And, no, there is nothing we can do about it. The worst case will be realized."

There was no uproar; just profound silence. All in the room were intelligent people who hoped for the best but frankly expected the worst. Each knew that an emotional outburst would be of no use. Nevertheless, Inara could see and feel the hope aura diminish in the room. She was gratified to recognize courage, determination and unity in all of them. She had noticed the same thing taking shape in and around Kieran over the last day as their team discovered the outcome through their technical analysis. It was surprising to her that she still had such great love for this young man in whom she could see much personal pain yet was so steadfast and so full of concern for others. He was a strong and admirable individual.

Inara took up the presentation.

"Neither Kieran nor I, nor our team or anyone else working independently without our blend of talents or experience could have fully understood what is happening. Please don't take that as braggadocio. We are simply fortunate to have been thrown together again. On the other hand, I am beginning to believe it was by design. I guess that brands me as a bit of a mystic. I am certain that the Universal Soul has been interceding for perhaps a century on behalf of life and itself."

Inara turned to Malk as if to ask for confirmation of this last statement and received a slight nod in response.

Inara felt an increasing calmness and certainty inside her as she prepared to continue. She could see in Kieran many sensory indications of pleasure and thankfulness at her comment. "Kieran has force-fed me all I can absorb about the technical side of the space-time equations concerning the entire science, infrastructure and applications involving entanglement transmission. I have employed every sensory capability and every ounce of intellect I have to learn and understand. It has been a stretch. I have in turn combined that information with my knowledge of the full integration of space-time-soul and taught Kieran all I know about that. With that new knowledge we have been able to have our technical team work toward the conclusions we are presenting to you."

Focusing directly on Dean Corday, Inara remarked, "Kieran, as you know, Dammar, has the advantage of having been exposed to this technology, for better or worse, since he was a young child. It is second nature to him. He also has the kind of mind that can readily look at things from different and new perspectives."

Inara then redirected her words to the entire group. "Through our exchange of information, Kieran led us in the development of a full set of space-time-soul equations. These equations mathematically and in great detail explain, for the first time, the reason for the ancient Schmidt constant. That, by itself is an amazing accomplishment. Beyond that, these equations actually show that there is a mathematical relationship between intentions and results."

That comment caused some stirring and puzzled murmuring in the group and an amused expression from Kieran, who continued the presentation.

"Inara and Malk have told us that results may look the same in the short term when the intentions are different. On the other hand, the results will definitely be different in the long term. What I can show you, through Inara's and Malk's teachings over the last day, is a set of equations showing that results are in part changed if the intentions behind identical actions are different. Here is the core group of those equations. Dean Corday, you might be the only senior individual in the room at present to understand these equations. I'll give you a minute to look at them. For the rest of you, there is a plain language explanation beside each line of equation. Even moderate changes in intention produce differences in the result. The change in intention produces an initial result only in the soul portion of space-time-soul. There is a follow-on effect that ripples out of soul into space-time.

"Through Inara and Malk, we know that extremely evil people came to be invisibly in control of the entanglement technology that is the glue of our galactic civilization. The rest of us have, for the most part, been innocent users.

"As Malk has shown us, these shadow masters killed and tortured many people every day for sheer pleasure. We have now identified old and current centers of torture where they kept thousands of people in agony for tens of years."

While Kieran was talking, images of some of the innumerable people who had been tortured were being displayed by Malk for all to see. A pictorial of the money and power path was also being shown.

Turning directly to face Dean Corday, Kieran emphasized, "Given what Inara and I have learned together it is plain to see why entanglement is moving toward collapse."

Everyone listening to Kieran and watching the simultaneous displays of information were in stunned, guilty silence. Kieran was close to being emotionally exhausted. Inara walked over to hold his arm. When she did so, she again experienced a combining of their beings which caused her to gasp in surprise. It was clear that Kieran felt it also. As she let go it was like they were still connected, and as if they had literally left of piece of each of them with the other.

Inara continued the presentation. "All of this information is now in the University information systems. Others should begin analysis of our work immediately. Kieran told you that we have a little over two days left until total collapse of our entanglement systems which are the glue of our civilization. The equations, and our recent experience, tell us that the collapse took a long time to reach this point of sudden and dramatic change. It will take decades to recover. Our estimate is that it will be at least thirty years after the impending full collapse before we can begin to put part of our entanglement systems back in operation. If we are right, then little of our civilization will remain. We both hope we are wrong. The work of our team needs to be checked."

Inara concluded by saying, "I know you each have an unspoken question. The answer is, Yes, and I reiterate, if entanglement technology had been implemented and used by good people with good intentions there would never have been a need for a Schmidt constant, and we would not be in our current situation."

Malk interjected, "You need to know that good people were also working on entanglement communication and transportation. One group in particular was close to success. Let me show you who they were and what happened to them.

"This information is also from archives of the Five Families that I have access to. You will note the extensiveness of their reach, with the help of intrusive governments, into the private lives and discussions of people they considered to be a threat to them or who they could learn from. If humanity survives, then I stress that it is important that everyone know that the negative impact of just a small number of evil people is disproportionately large. Future generations must understand that if good people like I am showing you here had been in charge of entanglement technology we would not be going through this painful contortion the entire galaxy is experiencing today. One massively evil person can in a short period of time undo the work of thousands of good people working tens of years.

"What I am showing you here is from the years leading up to the invention of entanglement transport technology by the Five Families. The APS that Frank Simmons refers to is Advanced Projection Systems. It was the public face of the much more secretive Quantum Controllers Interplanetary that I just showed you."

Good Intentions

Walking back and forth on the unpainted concrete floor in front of his brother's cheap desk at their Earth-based office, Frank Simmons shook his head. "I wonder what I'm missing as a businessman. Our scientists were among the first to succeed at matter transfer entanglement, and we did it from the Earth's surface without distortion. Granted, it took computing power that almost drove us to bankruptcy and set up time was an hour, but we did it. APS couldn't even come close. Heck, I'm astounded that APS had to go to a high orbital laboratory to make it work. This is beyond belief!"

His brother George commiserated, "You aren't missing anything, Frank. We know that APS stole a bunch of our work and the work of others. How, we don't know, but they got it. They combined that stolen knowledge with that of their own admittedly great scientists, threw a bunch of money at it, and finally perfected instantaneous transmission from their high laboratories."

Frank retorted, "I understand all that. What I don't understand is why APS can't make physical entanglement work from the surface of a planet and why they have problems from low orbit. Any of us, if we had the money they have, could do what they do and better. Speaking of money, I'd sure like to know where that money comes from."

George paused, looking at his older brother. "Frank, in this universe, and perhaps in any universe, money comes from power. Massive amounts of money come from massive amounts of power. If we knew where the kind of money APS has comes from we might not want to talk about it too much. If we did talk about it, then we might not be talking about anything much longer. Best to let it go, Frank. Take what we have learned and perhaps just become a supplier to APS. We can make a good living that way.

"By the way, entanglement transmission from the surface has become almost unworkable in the last few weeks, even for us. I have been given a trend line by our scientists which shows that entanglement from Earth's surface will become impossible in about three months. The problem seems to be directly related to the size of a planetary body. I doubt that any of us will be able to use entanglement transport from Mars in about four to five months and from Earth's moon in about seven or eight months. Our lab rats are puzzled and keep mumbling something about a shift in transmission parameters. I wonder if there will eventually be a change in high orbit capability."

George concluded, "What continues to be most interesting, and has always been true, is that anytime an APS person joins us in the test it fails completely."

All George received from Frank in response was a despondent grunt.

Six months later, after asking a lot of questions and aggressively pushing to compete with APS, Frank was found dead from snakebite while on vacation exploring the Australian outback.

* * *

As the years went on, George shut down their entanglement development efforts and instead became a wealthy supplier to APS and a few other companies adept at entanglement transmission. He took it upon himself to take good care of Frank's wife, Ann, and his son, Frank junior, who was fifteen years old at the time of his father's death. George made sure that each had a significant share of stock in the company. They lived on property in the same secure community as George and his family. Frank junior became adept at the family business and, in addition, showed an almost natural talent as an investor and speculator. As a consequence, the fortunes of the entire family rose, and they all lived comfortable lives.

About twenty years after the death of his father, Frank junior and his uncle George were sitting in their Adirondack chairs on the back porch of their family cabin overlooking the lake in Dillon, Colorado.

Frank broke the silence. "Uncle George."

"I can tell from the tone of your voice, Frank, that you're going to start in again about your dad's death. There are some things people need to let go for lots of reasons."

"I can't do that, George."

"Look, we've been through this a million times. It's a painful subject for both of us." Pointing a finger at his nephew, George continued, "I sense something different in you this time."

"You're right. I have more than enough for my family to live on for generations, and Frank III is off to college in a few weeks. I've learned a bit more, and I'm convinced more than ever that dad's death wasn't accidental. It's time for me to find out what happened."

"Frank, I love you like my own son. I know I can't talk you out of this. Just make sure you don't poison your legacy. Don't be like Greeks who still hate Turks for having stolen Helen."

"Isn't that analogy a bit of an exaggeration?" responded Frank.

"I hope the lesson isn't pertinent. Generational anger is poison."

***

Even though humans had spread to Earth's moon and to Mars, the core members of the five families had never left Earth. The Meeting of Twenty-Five was still always on Earth, and Quintus Gordon was the current chairman. This day they were meeting on a cloudless summer morning in a conference room on the four hundred thirteenth floor in the recently completed high rise one and a half miles above Grand Central Terminal. Quintus was taking a few minutes to admire the clear view north along Park Avenue in downtown Manhattan, New York. Central Park, Long Island Sound and the great length of the majestic Hudson River lie before him. He couldn't help thinking that it had the clarity of a quantum resolution photograph.

At exactly two in the afternoon Quintus Gordon walked to his place at the conference table, put down his coffee and opened the meeting by spreading his arms wide and announcing, "This is a day of celebration of power and success. Our Dr. Schmidt has successfully transmitted the first living biological matter across interplanetary distances using entanglement technology. In the process, she has made discoveries about the laws of physics that, over time, will someday put the entire universe within our grasp. Our vision statement for over two thousand years had been "We will be unconquerable rulers of the planet." Our current vision statement created about four hundred years ago is a major step closer to realization. I have no doubt that someday "We will be unconquerable rulers of the universe"! And what better way to enjoy what we have than to demonstrate our capabilities and enjoy them immensely. Ladies and gentlemen, this is a day to relish power!"

Quintus waited for the applause to subside then continued, "For the first part of this celebration we have with us today five special guests. They are the two men and three women seated behind me, and they will help us open our meeting in the traditional manner established by our founders. I think it is fair to say that each is in a state of stark terror. In fact, you can see that for yourselves. If they were not injected with the appropriate drugs to regulate their heart rates each would probably be having a heart attack. That is because they were shown three days ago the horrible way in which they are about to die. Four of them are random selections from different cities in the world. Soon their families and the authorities will give up any hope of finding them. I love how good we are at making people disappear without a trace. The fifth is a woman who has simply become too curious about the power behind the world's visible rulers, all of whom we control. She will die last.

"We all know that entanglement transmission has to take place in high orbit to avoid the effects of space warp caused by physical bodies like planets. It is also currently true that biological transmission only works with one-celled creatures. Nevertheless, we have two specially constructed entanglement machines here today that are large enough for human-sized transmission. They are managed by the massive computer network we own far beneath this building. Let me show you the results of human transmission on the surface of a planet."

The guards took one of the men, and the chair he was firmly bound to with metal clamps, and put him in the first machine at one side of the head of the conference table. His bulging eyes filled with tears. Quintus smiled at the man and pushed a button on the conference table. Immediately, the man disappeared from the first machine and appeared in the second one.

Quintus observed, "You can see the results of transmitting a human at this stage of scientific development. The parts just don't come out quite right. This clearly demonstrates what we have learned about needing more computing power and being able to transmit only from high orbit."

The attendees watched entranced as the man who had just transferred to the second machine appeared as a distorted mess. The rest of the guests were executed in order and in the same manner with varied effects but the same general result.

At the end of the demonstration the twenty-four around the conference table stood in applause as the guards removed the five distortions and the machines.

Quintus Gordon then continued with the meeting. "As part of our celebration of the first biological entanglement transport we have some other guests we have been expecting. We will now all be participants in an amusing play."

Quintus made a small gesture by slightly extending the little finger of his right hand. The large doors to the conference room opened and a family of four entered. Quintus walked across the hardwood floored room to shake the hand of the man and accept the offered hand of the woman. He greeted the gentlemanly young boys and said a few quiet words to all of them. Spreading his arms to the rest of the Twenty-Five, he ushered the husband and wife to seats that had been left vacant for them at the table. As young boys would do, they immediately ran to the ceiling-to-floor windows to look in wonder at the New York skyline.

A young female member of the core family had come into the room with the new guests. As soon as the boys were over their initial excitement of the view, she took them to a small table. There she sat with them to read books and play some games.

As things became calmer, Quintus turned to rest of the Twenty-Five. "Please allow me to introduce Frank Simmons III and his wife Akinji. Mr. Simmons has been tenacious at trying to solve a family mystery. His efforts came to the attention of one of our Patriarchs, and I have been asked to help him. I thought it might be best if we put our combined resources to work."

Each of the Twenty-Five politely murmured a welcome. Quintus turned to Frank and said, "Please let the group know what we can do for you and your family."

* * *

Frank took a few seconds to look around the room then said, "Thank you, Mr. Gordon. I'm not sure how I came to be so fortunate to receive your help. My family and I greatly appreciate your interest in our situation."

Quintus nodded his head and stretched out his hand, palm up which Frank took as a gesture to continue.

"Ladies and Gentlemen, I have a problem that perhaps only powerful people can help me with. And it is clear from the elegance of this room in such an expensive location that you are powerful people.

"Many members of my family have long believed that my grandfather, Frank Simmons, may have been murdered and his death made to look like an accident in the Australian Outback. I don't know if that is true or not. Frankly, that is a one hundred fifty-year-old issue, and it is too late now to dig into it. However, it is interesting to note that since his death his descendants, including myself, have been repeatedly plagued by strange and strong reversals of fortune whenever we have accumulated wealth and achieved great success. I come from a long line of talented and aggressive business people, and these periodic problems just don't make sense. I believe that someone wants my family to suffer for some reason. It isn't something we can go to the police with, but we have hired investigators over time. They have turned up nothing. Their only comments have been that we must have made terrible errors of judgment to have suffered such huge financial losses from time to time.

"These losses have twice driven my father to bankruptcy. I have also suffered strange reversals from which I have recovered. My family and I are now in a good position. We have great distributed investments and enough money to launch a much larger investigation and perhaps fix this problem.

Frank paused for a moment before finished his opening "I found my way to you through a friend of a friend. I hope you can help me. I understand that you each have the file in front of you describing in some detail the history of my family's situation."

Quintus responded for everyone in the room, "Yes, we are familiar with your file and your situation."

Frank noticed with some alarm that one of the male members of the Twenty-Five stood so suddenly that his chair rolled back several feet.

"Ah, Quintus, I apologize for the interruption. And please excuse me, Mr. Simmons. I've just received an alert that there is some news we should all watch. Apparently, it is something urgent. Do you mind?"

Frank took that as a signal to sit down as he heard Quintus's reply, "Of course not, Jacob. I know you wouldn't interrupt unless it was of extreme importance."

Quintus nodded while pointing to a section of the window. Frank redirected his attention as the scene of New York disappeared to be replaced by a three-dimensional image of a popular news anchor who was clearly a bit agitated. All turned in their chairs to watch. Only the two boys and their temporary nanny were oblivious to the urgent information being presented. At the same time, the doors to the conference room opened and about twenty armed men entered to take up positions along one wall.

Frank Simmons looked at Quintus wondering what the sudden activity was all about. Quintus smiled in a manner which Frank took to be reassuring and said, "The guards are just a precaution. As you have said yourself, this room is filled with powerful and influential people. As a result, we are always cautious. I'm sure you understand."

Frank answered with only a bit of hesitancy, "Yes, of course. I understand" he replied as he felt his wife, Akinji, reach for his hand.

The newsman was showing a hastily assembled graphic. "As you can see, some diverse segments of the International Stock Exchange have been battered by this series of massive and sudden sales by a wide variety of investors. Unrelated to this, a mega space ship on its way to Luna has done the impossible. It has fallen from space while exiting orbit. It has crashed onto Indianapolis causing an explosion and fire that have flattened over half the city and devastated much of the rest. The shock wave has been felt over one hundred miles away. Satellite video of the Indianapolis devastation is now being displayed on the left of your video. The segments of the stock market that have virtually fallen to zero are on the right."

Frank gasped as he immediately recognized that all of his wealth had just been extinguished.

At a nod from Quintus, the senior guard approached him for orders. Frank heard him say, "You must take us all to our safe havens immediately. Take me and Mr. Simmons to my Patriarch's home. Take his wife and children on diverse routes with other teams so we can help keep them safe. Make the assumption that we are all in danger."

Turning to Frank and Akinji, he said, "It would be best if you followed the directions you are given immediately and without question. If all of us who you are meeting within this room are in danger, then so are you. Your children of course will be kept safe as well."

Frank responded, "I don't see the need . . . ."

He never finished the sentence as an explosion blew out a far wall of the conference room as well as an adjacent pane of glass. Five men coming through the wall were immediately killed by the guards who then quickly began herding everyone in the room through the doors. Quintus, Frank and his family, and the woman assigned to the children left just in front of the last guard. Frank looked back to see even more attackers coming through the opening created by the explosion. The guard who was directly behind him opened fire on the new attackers until he was killed himself. Frank felt himself roughly grabbed by his collar and thrown into a small escape elevator with Quintus. With a massive surge, the elevator shot upward causing Frank and Quintus to sag to the floor.

Frank managed between gulps of air to ask, "Where is my family?"

Quintus gasped back, "We have all dispersed for safety. You will see them as soon as we reach our haven."

Quintus finished that last sentence just as they came to a bone jarring stop at what Frank, in his disoriented state, assumed had to be the roof of the building. With another surge, Frank felt them shoot upward for another second. Then the acceleration resumed and for a full minute they were apparently rocketing upward again.

Frank and Quintus were still sitting on the floor against one wall of the elevator when the door opened and two uniformed people entered.

"Mr. Gordon, are you alright?"

Quintus, moving gingerly to his feet, replied, "Yes, this is Frank Simmons. He is our guest. Our destination will be the third intermediate home. We will be using the "Ultimate" protocol to cover our path. We will be in the lounge. Please check on Mr. Simmons' family and make sure they go to the same destination. As soon as you know their status please let us know."

Turning to Frank, Quintus said, "Mr. Simmons, please follow me."

After only about fifteen paces Frank and Quintus arrived at a wood paneled lounge outfitted to look like an English gentleman's club of old.

Quintus turned to Frank and said, "Please allow me to offer you a drink."

Frank stood just inside the doorway taking in the room for perhaps thirty seconds before taking a deep breath and responding, "Whiskey, please."

Quintus nodded to the steward who seemed to come from nowhere. He listened for a moment as the steward spoke to him in a low voice that didn't carry to Frank. Quintus by way of invitation motioned Frank to a deep dark leather chair.

Quintus took a sip from his own drink and then observed, "Perhaps, sir, you have encountered more than you bargained for."

"To put it mildly. But, what about my family? Are they safe?" Frank asked with great anxiety.

"They are. That whispered conversation, for which I apologize, was to tell me that everyone escaped successfully. You will see your family before the end of the day."

"Where are they?" Frank pressed.

Quintus fixed Frank with a stern gaze which slowly softened. "You may have noticed that we were well organized and successful in our escape. There are many in the world who would like to see us all dead because they are jealous of our power and wealth. We know we have to be ready to scatter or defend ourselves as necessary. In the past, we have been attacked at times of unusual crisis. Today is clearly one of those days. I have some concern that those who attacked us created the financial diversion and the mooncraft crash on Indianapolis. The hope was probably that these twin disasters would have distracted us sufficiently to divert our attention from the danger we all live with constantly. However, such disasters only serve to send us to a higher alert level which is why the guards entered the room before the attack. We have layers of protection, Mr. Simmons, and our enemy today was also attacked from the rear as they approached us. Our guards practice protection and escape all the time. Today's escape plan involved scattering to a wide variety of vehicles and escape to many destinations. If I told you where your family was right now it would compromise our security methods. I will only assure you that they are safe and will join us."

Frank leaned forward in his chair to say with some strength. "I'm not reassured and won't feel good about all this till I have them with me again."

Quintus raised his drink in salute, "I admire that, Mr. Simmons. And you will see them again shortly. For now, you are widely separated from each other. The last minutes have taken us from the meeting we were in to the roof of our building. Our elevator was then taken up into my surface-to-high-orbit ship where we are right now. You are approximately forty thousand miles above the Earth."

Frank took a few seconds to absorb that information then pressed on, "And do you seriously mean to tell me that someone could arrange for the simultaneous crash of specific segments of the stock market and a Luna bound mega ship? That's preposterous!"

Quintus slightly smiled as he replied, "No, Mr. Simmons, it is not preposterous at all. Perhaps it was actually you who was the target and the rest of us were just collateral damage. After all, from examining the file you provided to us, it may have been your portfolio that was specifically targeted in the stock market crash. I may end up being sorry that we took an interest in your situation."

At that moment the steward reentered the room. "Mr. Gordon, it's time for the next transfer. Please come with me."

Quintus stood and looking at Frank said, "Please follow the steward, Mr. Simmons. We should move quickly to maintain stealth and safety."

The steward, followed by Frank and Quintus returned to the capsule that had first served as their elevator and then transfer module to the spacecraft they were in. Frank and Quintus entered the capsule, and the door closed behind them. Quintus gestured toward what looked like an acceleration couch. "Please lie down on that couch and buckle in."

After they were situated in the couches, Quintus commanded, "Mr. Simmons, the ride is going to get a bit rough now. Modules have been attached to this capsule to propel us to another ship at higher orbit. We will be invisibly cloaked so that no one will know we have made a transfer if they are still watching us, which we assume they are. In just a second you will experience some large acceleration forces"

Frank raised his head and said, "You can't be serious!" barely getting the words out before his head was jerked back into the cushion.

Thirty minutes later the acceleration stopped. There was a sickening lurch, and before Frank had a chance to say anything else there was an even stronger acceleration that lasted about ten minutes. Then a jolt.

Quintus began unbuckling his harness and said to Frank, "Follow me quickly. Stay close behind me, do exactly as I say, don't be surprised by anything, and don't ask anything."

The door to the capsule opened again. Frank dizzily got to his feet behind Quintus. Feeling extremely disoriented, he quickly followed Quintus and the two guards who were now in front and behind down a corridor that looked familiar. They went through a set of double doors that he knew he had seen before and found himself in the conference room he had been in only a couple of hours before overlooking Park Avenue. All the same people were there, except for his family. Each was on their feet smiling and clapping; offering shouted congratulations to Quintus Gordon. The conference room was in perfect condition.

As Frank's confusion increased a guard walked up behind him, and Frank felt a pinprick in his neck. The guard helped him settle into the chair he had been in earlier that day as Frank felt his legs go slightly weak. Clamps were fastened around his arms and legs. Frank's weakness began to disappear as the clapping and congratulations died down and everyone else resumed their seats.

"Where is my family?" demanded Frank.

"Ah, perfect!" Frank heard Quintus exclaim. "You said the command phrase we were waiting for. I told you that you would see them again today."

Instantly, two of the windows became three-dimensional screens. One displayed Akinji with tears in her eyes and tied to a chair. The other showed Frank's children happily playing with the woman they were with earlier. Akinji and Frank could see each other. The children had no idea they were being viewed.

"What is happening?" Frank screamed as he struggled to get up.

"I'll explain everything. You, your father and your grandfather have been great fun for us. We have especially enjoyed watching you and your father repeatedly raise a fortune only to see it collapse at our will. You see, we are powerful beyond any possibility of your understanding. You have just seen a small example of that. We have run everything on Earth for thousands of years. And now we are in full control of Earth's moon and Mars and its moons. We can do anything we want. Today you have been great sport for us. However, you crossed a line somewhat distant from us during your investigations, and we felt it was time to put an end to this piece of our enjoyment. But not before we planned this elaborate hoax which the other members of this room got great fun out of watching this afternoon.

"Now, we are going to teach you a lifetime lesson. In just a few minutes you will be sent to a dungeon three miles under this building. You will never see daylight again, and you will toil for us as our slave for the rest of your life. You will find that you will have no choice because we can control your mind as well as your body.

And we will make sure you live in mental anguish until you die. Your wife will become a slave to one of our families. Your children will be raised by us and be told that you and your wife died today. They might possibly make great contributions to the wealth of all of us in this room."

Quintus continued with enthusiasm, "I want you to know that you have been part of a great celebration for us today. Our scientist, Marianne Schmidt, has perfected biological entanglement transport over which we have full control. Your grandfather's work contributed greatly to that success, and we are thankful. Of course, our ancestors killed your ancestor, but we are still grateful for his contribution."

Tears of anguish and regret roll from Frank's eyes as the clamps that constrained him made him incapable of any but the smallest movements. He looked from Akinji to his children as he struggled. Akinji's screams rang through the room as the Twenty-Five laughed. The laughter increased as Akinji was removed from her room and beyond Frank's sight. He watched his children play with their new nanny as two guards lifted Frank to take him to his underground dungeon.

They paused for only a moment for Quintus to say to Frank, "By the way, the news program was a hoax, the assault was a hoax, and the trip we took was an elaborate work of art by our special effects people. You have been magnificent entertainment, and we all thank you."

"You are evil people," Frank yelled. "How can you do this?"

"I will grant you a few minutes of enlightenment since I am in a celebratory mood. Good and evil are your fantasy. It is a fantasy that we promote for you and for all outside of our core families. Our reality is that there is either power or subservience. You have seen a small demonstration of our power in this play that you have participated in today for our enjoyment. For thousands of years, we have started and ended wars. We create and destroy economic bubbles. We experiment with entire societies and pit them against each other for our education and pleasure. Look out the window, Frank. Everything you see to the horizon and beyond is our design. All of you who think you are in control of your own destinies are really just our pawns. We are powerful beyond your comprehension, and we can end your pitiful existence, and that of billions of others, anytime we wish. I am sending you to a dungeon that will crush your spirit as you slave for us. We will take good care of your wife who is now our slave. Your children will be raised as members of our family unless they decide to be difficult. Then we may have other uses for them, or not. Good-bye, Frank."

Through anguish so strong it left him dizzy and weak Frank could hear cheering and laughter as he left daylight for the last time.

Survival Planning

Sector Minister Monz Ingra looked across his desk at the grim, determined faces of Secretary-General Alana Perg and President Gareth Frax. The three were meeting separately from the others to discuss what they had just learned from Kieran, Inara and Malk.

"I suspect that we are still in total agreement that the University planet and the nearby Cathedral must be preserved for posterity. The knowledge carried in these institutions will be critical in the rebuilding of our civilization. If there is one to rebuild."

Monz continued, "Naturally, I have some thoughts about what we must do next, and I understand that we are under unbelievably tight time constraints. However, I'm open to suggestions."

Alana's mind ran rampant with all she had learned in the last two days. Technically, her world had just been turned upside down. Her belief that The Controllers could use technology to fix anything that came their way had been destroyed. They simply couldn't fix this problem that was perhaps going to end all civilization as they knew it. Islands of humanity would remain. Certainly, Earth would remain. Planets much like Earth that could sustain life on their own would remain. Technology would help others like University to hang on through a combination of brute force and intellect. Some people would survive in stasis pods.

There was also this new knowledge presented to her and many others by Inara and a few of the Pilgrims from The Guide's Hall. Alana had always accepted the linking of all things through the Universal Soul. It was an old belief with its roots in ancient religions. It was faith, not knowledge. And faith was sufficient.

It was becoming horrifying to her that she had at no time conceived that what she had dedicated her multiple lives to for a millennium was secretly and discreetly run by horribly evil people who had put themselves outside of that soul. She had helped provide leadership of a technology that, because of its ultimate intent of use, had terribly damaged the Universal Soul and was threatening to end all civilization. She wondered if, as a technologist she had done more to people than for people. All this rushed through her thoughts as she said her next words.

"The galaxy is lost. And I agree that the University Planet and The Cathedral must be preserved. Not for the people who populate those places but for any humanity that may remain across the galaxy and eventually find a use for our collection of knowledge at some future time. We must do that for a lot of reasons, not the least of which is to help some future generations, or rebuilt civilization, avoid our horrible mistakes. For the same reasons, I believe we must also preserve The Guide's Hall, and all the lessons associated with it. What they do, what they will preserve, and what they have to teach is vastly more important than anything that will happen even in our sector. We must also try to preserve as many of the Pilgrims at The Guide's Hall as we can. The moral compass they provide will be much more useful to our rebuilt civilization than our technology knowledge."

Alana's words provided pause for both Monz and Gareth. Gareth was the first to respond. "Alana, I have to confess that I have been so tied up in the details of survival of knowledge for posterity that I gave no thought to what amounts to the survival of character. You are, of course, correct."

Again, a few moments of silence. During that silence, Alana and Gareth could see that Monz had been making subtle retransmission gestures to the room. Finally, he stopped and looked at both with sadness and resolve. "I have been trying repeatedly since the end of Inara and Kieran's presentation to reach the Prime Minister. He has blocked my access to him. And it appears that he continues to block all access from anyone. Since this is no longer a time for political politeness. I have to assume that the weakness that we all know is in him has left him incapacitated. We will have to take action without him. Unhappily, I believe it is now necessary to invoke martial law all across the galaxy for all the good that will do. We are also obligated to let the galaxy know what is happening. Based on what you have just said, Alana, the message to the galaxy needs to be totally open and honest. It must be a joint communication from the government, from The Controllers and from The Guide.

"Given the situation, and in spite of the discomfort I feel in acting above my pay grade, I'm going to make some requests of each of you. It is my reluctant intention to assume the role of

Acting Galactic Prime Minister. While I am reticent, I will be necessarily aggressive in doing so.

"Alana, please talk to Paya and bring her up to date. Gareth, please continue the leadership role you have taken with Kieran, Malk and Inara. You don't have to come to me for anything. I will talk to Pren Bodhi and Malin to ask them to brief the Guide on my intentions. I will contact Esha Arza, the sector minister for The Guide's sector and request her help. I will also contact other ministers and ask them to support me in making a declaration of martial law for the galaxy.

"Within a few minutes, I will direct that we divert all resources in this sector to the preservation of the University and the Cathedral. I will ask Esha to divert all of her sector resources to The Guide's Hall. If Esha agrees, then we will each take the necessary preparatory actions within the hour.

"I suggest that the three of us as well as Paya, The Guide, and The Guide's sector minister meet for breakfast. If nothing changes as a result of that breakfast discussion, I will address the galaxy with Paya, The Guide and Esha. Are there any objections or suggestions?"

Gareth looked at his best friend and said, "You should transfer to University. Where you are in the sector won't last long, and you need to continue leadership. You already know that the Prime Minister will not respond."

"Under other circumstances I would object to that. But, if our Prime Minister fails to take proper leadership I will do as you suggest."

Alana offered, "I know that you are understandably reluctant to do so, but if you have to take over as Prime Minister I know you will have the support of the Controller Council."

"Thank you, Alana. I will see you both in the morning. In the meantime, I have a lot of back-channel work to do. There are people to brief and support to garner."

* * *

Kieran and Inara returned to the laboratory that had been created for them and which they had repeatedly expanded as their needs increased.

"Inara, it is clear from our conversations that you have felt risk to your life since long before we first met. I never knew that before. Are you feeling safe now?"

It was a question Inara hadn't thought about as they rushed through everything they were doing. "It is interesting that you ask that, Kieran. Yes, I do feel safe now. It also seems like there is something missing around me. Now that you bring it to my attention it may be the absence of an oppression that I never quite noticed because it was constantly there as part of the background I always felt. On the other hand, we all may be dead in a few days."

Kieran said, "Please wait a minute." Working too quickly for even Inara to follow, Kieran created a specialized, massive telecyber interlinking of all major computing systems across the galaxy using all the override commands that had been provided to them by The Controllers and by The Guide. He took the output to an amazingly detailed telescence display of every element of the galaxy. The image filled their laboratory and enveloped them inside it. With a show of frustration and urgency, Kieran gave a quick combination of oral, gesture and neural commands and expanded the size of the laboratory ten-fold and moved it about one mile above an open spot on the campus.

"Inara, this is the most intricate and complete telecyber link that has ever been created. It is overlaid with virtual telescence paths that you can open to anywhere in the galaxy. In effect, I've tried to bring access to the entire galaxy to you inside this room. Please tell me what you sense."

Building on Kieran's work with her own set of commands, Inara added additional sensory information that Kieran could not initially see. Remembering that she wanted Kieran to sense as much as possible of what she perceived she translated the output in a manner that Kieran would be able to absorb. She knew she was successful when she heard him gasp. She turned to look at him in alarm. "Are you alright?"

"Yes," he said a bit breathlessly. "It is just a bit much to take in immediately."

"To put it mildly you have managed to put me into a bit of sensory overload as well," she replied with a double meaning that he was a bit too naive to catch.

"Perhaps you should look around to see if you can learn anything else that can be of use to us," he suggested.

Inara observed, "What you have done is amazing. I can, in a virtual manner, go anywhere. Please follow me. You'll notice that there are no longer any intense brown smudges with interlinking tendrils. Naturally, there is still evil and some of it intense. And, of course, there will always be sinful people. But I am not sensing the integrated, organized, pervasive evil that was there before."

Kieran pressed on, "OK. There is something I want to try. Let's focus in on the Controllers organization." Together they worked through a set of filtering commands that showed only those segments of the galaxy and integrated Universal Soul that had to do with the Controllers organization.

Kieran continued, "Let's build a further filter to focus in on the most evil twenty percent of the Controllers organization."

Inara was catching on and finding it exciting to be working with such a fast and strong intellect. She paused to look closely at this man whom she had once loved so intensely that it broke her heart when he left Andromeda. If only she had told him then why she couldn't leave with him. It was clear that he felt the same way but never recognized the depth of her feeling in return. What a horrible mistake her secrecy from him was. But then, how was she to know? She looked at him more closely with all of her senses and recognized that his heart had fractured as much as hers. But she also recognized that his past pain had held him back from saying more and acting more strongly on his feelings. Her sense of loss blended with a resurgence of her love would have been overwhelming if her obligation to the present situation wasn't so compelling.

Kieran suggested some further modifications, "Now, if the galaxy looked like this, what would be the effect on the Schmidt constant?"

Wow, she only thought she was keeping up.

"Uh, you'll have to help me with that," she slightly stuttered.

"Then get out of my way, slowpoke," he teased.

Kieran took the multi-sensory conversion to visual presentation he was working on and made an interface to create an equation output that showed the current and future trending health of the Universal Soul depending on the filters applied.

For the next few minutes, he toyed with the settings until he gave a small grunt of satisfaction. Inara could see that he was searching for some kind of optimum point. Next he took the settings that he had developed for the Controllers subset and applied them to the entire galaxy. Kieran played the system through time at a rate one thousand times normal. The result was surprising. Perhaps there was hope after all.

Inara moved over next to Kieran and he, much to his own surprise, automatically put his arm around her. They stood like that in silence until Kieran finally said, "We have to take this work to our team. It is possible that we are only seeing what we want to see. We wouldn't want to do more harm than good."

"No, we wouldn't," Inara said quietly.

Kieran was too intensely into the equations to notice the new tone in Inara's voice.

* * *

Kieran felt a tentative surge of hope as he looked at the galactic display and the equations. He had a new faith that perhaps they could fix this problem. Over the next few hours, Kieran and their team expanded the University laboratory yet again and created permanent telescence links with the Cathedral and with the research Pilgrims at The Guide's Hall.

Dammar Corday and Pren Bodhi took on the leadership tasks of integrating the technical teams along the lines that Kieran and Inara needed. This new analysis required a more extreme amount of precision. At Kieran's request, Inara did a thorough sensory analysis of every person added to the team to make sure they were a positive experience, rather than a negative effect, on the Universal Soul. Inara was impressed that Kieran had internalized so readily the need for good spiritual as well as technical people on the team.

Since Kieran had the greater technical skill for this part of the project she went off by herself to immerse into what she called the essence of the galactic presentation that Kieran had created.

Inara was repeatedly stunned by the detail and the functionality of Kieran's galactic presentation. She would have loved to understand the elements behind how he had done this, but accepted the fact that his training was far beyond hers in that regard. Instead, she just learned how to use it. With only a small loss of detail she found that she could place herself on the surface of planets, float in space or hover above the tenuous surface of stars.

She went to Earth and explored the scar left behind in the mountain valley where one of the evil families had lived. The edges were precise and the innocent people nearby had been unaffected. She played the scene back in time to before the destruction of that place and felt the full impact of the disgusting sensory perception of evil. She saw the brown tendrils snaking off into space and to a couple of other places on Earth. The tendrils were almost like a highway or a network. The thicker, more distinct ones connected the islands of greatest evil. The thinner ones led to peripheral groups or individuals.

She followed the thickest one leaving the Solar system to a nearby star system and found an entire planet run by the evil ones. She again moved backward in the recording to yesterday to watch everything be carved off that planet down to the granite core.

Eventually, she went to her home planet to see the couple of places there that had been excised from existence by the Universal Soul. When all the actions across the galaxy had been taken into account, it was indeed the most massive reckoning of all time.

Out of curiosity, she followed a thin line to an individual in a remote location. At that point, she found some gray lines and smudges indicating a lesser degree of evil but people who still lived in some secrecy. She had the perception of a hierarchy of evil. This was obviously a shadow government. Evil clearly went hand in hand with secrecy.

Then, on a whim guided more by emotion than intellect she followed a thickening brown line back tens of thousands of years and met Malk Kring and observed him when he was held prisoner by the evil people Malk has shown her.

Finally, after more time than she had realized, she removed herself from the system to go to the office that she and Kieran had created for themselves. Pren and Dammar had offices beside theirs, and Pren saw her coming across the laboratory floor.

* * *

Pren reached out for Inara's hand, "I was watching you from over here. I could barely keep up with your movements as you wandered across Kieran's galaxy."

"Kieran's galaxy! That's amusing. Do you realize how brilliant he is? He has produced an amazing tool. It will be a great help to us if we have any chance at all of solving this problem."

Pren ignored Inara's euphoria focusing instead on her last comment. "Whoa, I thought you two had said that disaster was unavoidable. Do you really think we have a chance of avoiding disruption?"

"Probably not. But Kieran seems to think we have some slight chance. I am trying to have hope, and we can't just quit looking for a solution." Then as a quiet afterthought she murmured, "I wonder if living without hope is actually the greatest sin of all."

Pren studied her carefully. This young woman, only in her 60's in her first life was again learning so much. Thinking back to when he first met her as a baby, he reflected that she was going through more than many people absorb in an entire first life. Even when she was just a few years old, her experience input had been phenomenal. What a journey it had been since then. What a privilege to know her and have her regard him as a dearly loved uncle. He was truly a fortunate man. Now, even though she didn't realize it herself, he was watching her fall deeply in love in the midst of disaster. He wondered if this love would last only for a moment or be one of those rare, almost unique relationships that kept people together lifetime after lifetime like Inara's parents.

Inara's parents!

"Inara, you must know how your parents are doing! Are they alright?"

With sudden tears, Inara buried her head in Pren's shoulder. Then, composing herself, she pulled back to look at him. "They are fine, Uncle Pren. Except for one major, and some minor, locations that belonged to the Evil Ones everyone on their planet is safe. The Evil Ones were excised by the Universal Soul. For now, mom and dad are well. But, I have little hope for them after the next few days no matter what preparations they make."

She continued with greater firmness, "In the meantime, though, we have other things to take care of. What has happened while I have been wandering around Kieran's galaxy?"

* * *

Kieran worked all that night and asked for a meeting before the breakfast gathering that he had been told would take place between the top leaders. He had awakened Inara to ask her to join him in the laboratory two hours earlier to help him verify what he had learned

They all gathered again in the briefing auditorium at one end of their laboratory. The Guide and Malin Nowl, all the Controller Secretaries-General, the Sector Ministers and their immediate staffs from the Cathedral and Guide's Hall sectors, Pren Bodhi and a few others were present. Kieran and Inara were standing in front of them ready to present. Malk stood slightly to the side of them. Their laboratory staff was behind them. It was clear to everyone who had been asked to come to the briefing that all work in the laboratory had stopped and that the entire laboratory team was either physically or virtually present.

Kieran began. "I have asked for this meeting only because I wanted Minister Monz Ingra, Secretary General Paya Lachlan, The Guide and other leaders to have the latest information before they meet at breakfast.

"We have done everything we can as a combined team of scientists and as caretakers for the Universal Soul. This team that you directed us to put together and permitted us to lead has made some headway, but we have not had the success that we hoped for. I must tell you that my view of everything has changed. That seems to also be true for this entire team. This has been a life-changing experience beyond anything I could have ever conceived. While you may be anxiously waiting for me to get to the point, the comments I have just made are perhaps the point. I will be less vague.

"This night has been a jumble of expectations and emotions. At one point, I thought that we were within a couple of days until annihilation of all life in our galaxy. At other times, I saw the glimmering of a solution. Then there were points at which I felt that Earth-identical and Earth-like planets might be the only survivors.

"In short, we have been learning much and each new piece of knowledge encouraged us to either grasp at straws of hope or think the worst. What Inara and I and our entire team now conclude with great certainty is that enough healing of space-time-soul has taken place just in the last day to allow us to pump a minimum amount of energy and inanimate items around the galaxy to temporarily preserve a few thousand planets throughout the Milky Way. We don't know about the long term for those locations. Earth, of course, would have survived anyway as well as the twenty-seven essentially Earth identical planets we are all familiar with. But, we had previously thought that even that would be relatively short-lived because they would eventually run out of supplemental imported food and other resources needed to take care of basic necessities. Instead, we believe that a majority of the people on those planets will survive, but their lives may be difficult for a long time. They will have only the minimum necessities of life to survive.

"That is much better than the worst case of total annihilation, but there will still be a horrendous disaster. Trillions of humans, animals and plant life on the remainder of the planets will soon be extinguished and there is nothing we can do about it. Closer to home, we can put our greatest intellects helpful to the future of humanity in stasis here, at the Cathedral and at The Guide's Hall. Most others in these two sectors will perish."

Kieran went on to explain, "At one point we hoped that the destruction of the Evil Ones by the Universal Soul might cause a dramatic reversal in the situation we are facing. Unhappily, there are elements involved that might be considered analogous to mass and velocity. Eventually, the situation that we are facing will be reversed and entanglement technology will again be able to be used provided the intent is good. But the inertial rush to destruction is so great that it will take decades or longer to reverse the trend."

Turning to Inara and nodding, he sat down. Inara gently put her hand on Kieran's shoulder as she took her turn to speak.

"Kieran mentioned that we are a combined team of scientists and caretakers of the Universal Soul. As we have poured through analysis and equations we have learned much from each other. Perhaps if we had combined our thinking one hundred thousand years ago we would not be where we are today. It's a lesson for the future. Simply put, we now understand considerably better the science, equations and emotional implications of space-time-soul. While everything looks different to each of us at present than it did before, it also looks much more the same today to all of us. We have a common understanding. It might be called an integrated understanding because we now have a merged set of equations leading us to a better comprehension of space-time-soul and its past and current condition. That has had two results.

"One result is that we can see that the Universal Soul is beginning to heal, and we can actually measure that healing progress. The second result is that we have been able to slightly adapt our entanglement systems to this changing space-time-soul. This will perhaps give us the opportunity to help a few more of the people in the galaxy survive.

"An unexpected benefit is that we can now see, through these changing equations, the increase or decrease of evil in the galaxy. Naturally, the equations are showing us a tremendous recent decrease in evil. However, there are degrees of good and evil. The less evil the faster the healing. The more good the quicker the healing."

"Inara," exclaimed The Guide, "That last part is astounding information. Are you telling us that we can now technically measure good and evil?"

"That is exactly what I am telling you," Inara replied quietly. "And I am not sure we are to be trusted with that kind of knowledge. What will we do with it? At the same time, look at what we did without it. Perhaps we should just rely on a Guiding Hand and do the best we can."

Inara continued with her subject. "Kieran is a genius who was in the right place at the right time. I think he had help in being there. In fact, I know he did. That wasn't an accident. It was a cry for help from the Universal Soul which penetrates all of us. Kieran fixed the problem and actually saved the galaxy from an immediate disaster. We didn't fully understand that, or exactly what he did, until a few hours ago. He is a good man with nothing but good intentions. He is one of the best persons I have ever met. And that is partly why he succeeded. His intentions were actually a tool to success. Through the soul part of space-time-soul he was nudged by the spirit that links all of us toward the solution.

"In that regard, we have all been nudged. This team didn't come together by some grand coincidence. It was guidance."

Kieran again addressed the group.

"I can't tell you that I, or the rest of our team, understand this to the degree that Inara understands all this. She senses things that are beyond the rest of us. She goes beyond the equations to give the rest of us guidance. Malk has been doing the same. Perhaps in the same way I was guided the day this disaster so blatantly manifested itself."

Kieran continued. "What I can tell you is that we have a fresh set of tools to help guide us. We also have a new way of thinking that we had better never forget.

"Now it is time for all of you to prepare the galaxy for the inevitable in whatever way you feel is right. The clock that we set up for you has been reset a bit. You have about eighteen more hours than we initially thought and none of us on the laboratory team believe that will change again. You leaders have a horrible task and set of decisions ahead of you. We will help you any way we can.

"For now, I want to leave you with one thought. Entropy causes everything to want to go to its lowest energy level. We understand entropy in the realm of space-time, and we understand its direction. We are learning to understand the Schmidt constant in space-time-soul. However, we may yet have to learn a great deal about entropy in that broader domain. Is evil the lowest energy level for space-time-soul and is that the direction that entropy pushes us? Or is it more complex than that. We still have, and always will have, a lot to learn."

* * *

Inara and Kieran returned to their suites of rooms, which were adjacent to each other. As Inara turned to walk to her private area, Kieran grasped her hand. He pulled her to him and kissed her lightly on the lips. It had been a long time since they had done that. Inara felt the effect through all of her integrated senses as well as through her increasingly strong connection to the Universal Soul. She knew she had literally found her soulmate. If only evil hadn't gotten in the way. As she forced herself to pull away she could tell that something unusually special had just happened for Kieran as well.

"Inara, we have only had a few hours together again, but I know that I want to spend much more time with you -- alone. I don't want us to lose each other again."

"I feel the same way, Kieran."

They stood holding each other for a while. The area they were in sensed a need for a couch and one appeared beside them. Sitting together, holding hands, Kieran said, "I was hoping you would say that."

Inara fought them, but the tears flowed anyway. Finally, she composed herself.

"Kieran, I have been blessed with many gifts. An amazing brain combined with interlinked senses that let me see and understand an astounding amount. I know so much because of these gifts. You also have great gifts that you use to work beyond emotional pain to do such good things. You are smart, compassionate, driven to help others. You also have something I don't have. That is faith. You don't believe just because the facts are so clear to you. You believe in the future simply because you believe in all of us. That is something I don't have. It is something that I would give up all my other gifts for right now just to have the faith that you have. I have never needed faith, so I don't have faith."

"What are you trying to tell me?"

"I know what you want because I have this gift. I can sense in every way that you have such strong feelings for me. I also have those strong feelings.

"But there is something important I have to sort out, and it may take me a long time to do it. And I'm not sure that sufficient time exists for me anymore. Millions of evil people just died. They were killed because they were outside the soul and faithless. Trillions of others will also soon die, and our civilization may end because of actions other faithless people took over one hundred thousand years."

Inara gently raised her hand as a signal for Kieran to continue to listen. She continued, "Those people were raised to be evil and faithless from birth. I know that I am a good person. But, I am also faithless. I have certainty about much including the Universal Soul that I love so strongly. I have never needed, have never had to develop, faith. I have every gift except the gift of faith. And I worry about my faithlessness. Because of my certainty, I had no problem with the annihilation of the evil ones. I rejoice in it with no hesitation. I feel no remorse for them at all. And I worry about that, too.

"When, and if, it finally comes time to be in a serious emotional relationship with someone, I would like to have what my parents have. They had more than an unusual lasting love. They had absolute total faith in each other.

"If it is someday possible, you should go with Pren to visit them. You would all like each other. It is unusual in this time of extremely long lives, but when the time comes I want what my parents have. I want to have total faith and love so that I can be with someone forever from life to life. And that requires what I don't have. Faith. It is faith that permits the reckless abandon that those who are truly in love have. It is something I see in the people I admire the most. Most of all, you. And it is surprising to see it in you because I also see the pain that you have suffered in your life. It is pain that often permanently submerges feeling that you had lost and fought so hard to rediscover. You are so unusual."

Kieran felt a despair that left him dizzy. It was far beyond what he had experienced after the death of his sister, Tra and the collapse of his family when he was still so young. It eclipsed the loss of all his community and friends when his planet was destroyed only a short time after he had left it. He could hardly breathe, but finally found the strength and courage to ask, "What are your plans?"

Inara was almost unable to comprehend the hurt she could see, taste, hear and feel in Kieran. It amazed her that she could see the core of strength in him stand fast against the staggering emotional pain displayed to her with such blast furnace intensity. Her resolve to do what she knew was right almost failed. It was as if she could hear cracking sounds of emotional destruction inside his body. The pleasant, optimistic music that normally defined him was suddenly silent. She couldn't believe what she was causing. But she also knew she was right, and that staying together would cause more pain than pleasure in the long run. She saw and felt in him the strength that he had fought so hard for, and earned, over such a long time. She also knew his friend Dammar Corday would help him through this.

Inara quietly finished, "I have to learn faith. I will return to The Guide's Hall where I hope he and others will help me with that. If I survive all this, I hope to not merely know, but to faithfully accept. When, and if, that day comes, perhaps I will be ready to make different decisions. You should not wait for that day because it may never arrive."

Alana, who had just happened to pass by, watched from a distance.

Intentions' Result

The Galactic Prime Minister's room and throne tried frantically to get his attention about a highest priority message from the ministers of the sectors for The Cathedral and The Guides Hall. These were arguably the two most important and most politically powerful sectors in the galaxy aside from the one in which he had his government offices. He still needed time to think and gestured all systems into mute. His assistant unceremoniously burst into the room. Totally out of character, she addressed him by his first name.

"Callum, the situation is critical, and you have to answer this call. Why aren't you responding?"

Prime Minister Callum Seph simply shook his head and waved her out of the room.

* * *

Galactic Prime Minister Callum Seph continued to ignore the various and increasingly urgent signals which kept reminding him that there was a telescence image in his mail box which needed his immediate attention. His dawning realization of what was happening to all mankind during his rule had left him completely without the capability of responding. Through the fog of his mental anguish he knew that millions of people had died in the last day. His First Secretary told him that all life throughout the galaxy might end in the next two days. He was vaguely aware that his First Secretary was unofficially running his office telling all callers that the Prime Minister was occupied with urgent matters. He knew that he should do something but didn't know what it was.

The signals were totally insistent now, and a new alert was coming through. From his fetal position on the floor in front of his throne, he again commanded all alert systems to shut down. The room responded, "An urgent message for the Prime Minister is stored in the telescence mailbox. This message has override instructions attached to it sealed by the council of Secretaries-General and a Sector Minister using martial law authority. This mail will be delivered in thirty seconds. Any refusal to receive will also be overridden."

A light-blue border formed ten feet in front of the Prime Minister's prone body. The border signaled a one-way telescence message. Callum Seph would receive full sensory impact of the information being transmitted but would not be able to respond. The room spoke again, "Your mail will be delivered in ten seconds." The Prime Minister reached up to the arm of his throne and pulled himself upright so that he was leaning against its base. He stared with fascination at the telescence mail image of University Sector Minister Monz Ingra flanked by Esha Arza, Secretary-General Paya Lachlan, Guide Takar Cillian and other galactic leaders in the background. A code in the comer of the image of Minister Ingra's message let Callum Seph know that this was being broadcast to all sectors of the galaxy. What was Monz up to?

* * *

"Fellow ministers." The image of Monz Ingra was grim, his voice subdued, yet firm. The brown eyes in dark skin tired, yet determined.

"This is an extremely important message to all sector ministers across the galaxy. It is a message that must be relayed to all the citizens in your sectors so they can prepare for the inevitable. I apologize to my mentor and Prime Minister, Callum Seph for sending this message to each of your mailboxes without consulting with him first. However, he has not responded to repeated attempts to reach him. His First Secretary admits that the Prime Minister is refusing all contact. Time is running out, and it is urgent that we act immediately.

"We have become aware over the last couple of days that the transport glue of our trans-galactic civilization is slowly dissolving and that there is nothing we can do to prevent its near-total dissolution.

"Just to be sure that each of you understands the situation, and its gravity, let me explain it to all of you. I am sending to you right now transcripts of meetings that have taken place over the last two days that give the detail behind what I am telling you. Scientific data is also being sent to you.

"We have made a drastic mistake which is going to spell the end of our civilization as we know it. In the last one hundred millennia, we have put all the precious eggs of civilization in one fragile basket. We thought that this basket was indestructible, but now we know that it has been slowly deteriorating without our knowledge.

"Our entanglement transport system is that basket. The same system that makes telescence and this session possible is the system we use for moving energy, and people in the form of energy, around our galaxy. It is our transportation, communication, and energy transmission system all rolled into one. And in a couple of days, if we do nothing, it will stop working completely. As you know, it recently ceased transporting unexpectedly for a few short hours across the galaxy. The result was large scale panic and loss of life of about two percent of the people in the galaxy. That was followed later by a sudden deliberate shutdown by the Controllers for another few hours to prevent a potentially greater catastrophe."

Monz paused. It was obviously taking a supreme effort to control his emotions. Though he continued with dignity and strength he looked terribly old.

"Within two hours each of your sector's main transport nodes will be shut down to about one-tenth of one percent of their current power level. It is now my understanding that at that power level only Earth, Earth identical planets and less than two hundred Earth-like planets will be able to survive. Even they will suffer dramatically. Software has just been loaded through the galactic telecyber system to place control of all of your nodes at the Cathedral. If we don't exercise these measures, we are fully convinced that all the systems supporting our civilization will completely collapse. As it is, little of humankind and other life in our galaxy will survive past the next few days. Even Earth, Earth-identical and Earth-like planets will suffer since they are heavily dependent on importing food from agricultural planets. Again, the data to support this action and these conclusions is being sent to you right now.

"I have learned that it is important to nurture the Universal Soul with complete honesty. I am still not sure that total honesty is always helpful, but in this case it may be essential to the health of our galaxy. It has been made abundantly clear that we are only as sick as our secrets. So, now I am going to tell you something that may seem self-serving. I believe, and those who are advising me believe, that it is important to preserve as much of our knowledge as possible for future generations. Assuming there will be future generations. To that end, we are piping as much energy and basic necessities into University Planet and The Cathedral as we can. We don't know how much that will be and we don't know if it will be sufficient to sustain life. Perhaps it will be enough to preserve and protect our archive of humanity's knowledge and a few people to help with that.

"We are going to do the same with The Guide's Hall.

"The full archive of knowledge from those locations will be made available to all remaining humans in the galaxy even if all of us at these locations perish. Fusion and quantum power will be used to keep our end of these telecyber links running for a few centuries.

"I strongly recommend that each of you review the transcripts I am sending you of our discovery work here, at the Cathedral and at The Guide's Hall over the last two days. Through that information, you will understand what led up to this catastrophe. We are hoping that this graceful shutdown or our systems will be better for humankind and for the Universal Soul than letting everything run for another couple of days toward sudden collapse.

"The final thing I want to tell you is that we did something much worse than put all of our eggs in one entanglement technology basket. That basket was designed and owned by a few evil people secretly working to enrich themselves and gain total power over all of us. The rest of us didn't know this, and we clearly should have been asking more questions. Hopefully, generations that come after us will be more diligent about understanding these things.

"Good-bye. May the God that I believe in more strongly than ever before be with us all."

* * *

Callum Seph, Prime Minister of the entire Milky Way galaxy and all human civilization, and stunned by Ingra's message, climbed slowly onto his throne. As Galactic Prime Minister he should have been the one to direct the activities in the final days, and he realized that he had failed before hardly even starting. It was a failure too large to live with. He looked out at the view of the central black hole with its shredding stars and chanted a secret command. The scent of lilacs filled the room, and soft music began to play. As the lights dimmed, the Prime Minister's attention was fully focused on the rainbow of colors surrounding the black hole. His own vision dimmed with the lights in his room for the last time.

* * *

The next two days were a desperate effort to prepare everything as best they could for the inevitable catastrophe. Line of succession for the Galaxy's political leaders had long since been routine. However, there was no more galactic-wide political structure. Very soon there wouldn't even be sector political structures. Star systems and planets were on their own. As a consequence, the suicide of the Prime Minister was a ripple that went unnoticed compared to the tidal waves crashing at the shores of civilization. Each sector of the Galaxy prepared separately and sent Monz Ingra's message and accompanying files out to all of their planets.

All transport of people across the galaxy was canceled. Even so, there was a crush of traffic as separated family members tried futily to reunite. Many died by being trampled. Soon only information and energy would be passed between entanglement nodes. Then just information would be transmitted. The dying islands of humanity would be able to communicate their distress and messages of comfort but nothing else.

The University Planet had, in effect, become the new seat of galactic government. But it was galactic government in name only because no authoritative power or control remained over other sectors. Minister Monz Ingra became the de facto Galactic Prime

Minister. The University Planet Administrator was the Galactic Deputy for Catastrophe preparation, and Paya Lachlan continued as the Supreme Secretary-General. In her turn, Paya put leadership of all the Galaxy's Controllers under the operational command of Edric Yan. Kieran and Inara, with help from Malk, were temporarily still at University Planet looking for a solution, although the general feeling was that there was none.

Finally, Pren Bodhi went to the laboratory to tell Inara that she was out of time. "Inara, if we are to get to The Guide's Hall we will have to leave in the next few minutes. Otherwise, we will be here forever."

At barely a whisper, Inara replied, "Thanks, Uncle Pren. Give me just a minute."

Pren, and all the lab members, either left the laboratory or moved as far away as they could. Alana Perg observed from as closely as she dared without being obtrusive. Inara and Kieran stood beside each other knowing how they felt but leaving it unsaid. Kieran hugged her, then reluctantly let go. They looked at each other's eyes as Inara slowly backed away. Their fingers finally parted and Inara turned with a sob to join her uncle to make the short trip to the local entanglement node.

Malk, standing a short distance away, waved a silent goodbye and disappeared.

Alana sadly shook her head. As she watched Inara and Kieran she knew there was one more important thing she needed to do.

* * *

For the second time in her life Inara made an entanglement trip without any pain at all. Much to the surprise of both Pren and Inara, The Guide and Malin Nowl were both at the private transport pod landing gate to greet them as they arrived. Uncharacteristically, The Guide rushed up to Inara to hug her as soon as they arrived at The Guide's Hall. "Inara and Pren, I know you have both had a difficult couple of days but would you please join me in my study for a few minutes. I can offer you a little refreshment before you go to your suites."

Pren responded for them both. "Of course we will. Thank you."

Inara walked silently beside the three men as they brought each other up to date on the details of the last couple of days. In a few minutes they arrived at The Guide's study. Inara smiled appreciatively at The Guide as she noticed the setting was her planet. She was surprised to see what she thought was a telescence image of her parents sitting on the hillside overlooking her home. Inara rushed over to them to embrace them too caught up in emotion to speak. Finally, she turned to The Guide. "You can't know how much this means to me. Thank you so much for setting up this meeting. I know it will be the last time I see them for a long time. You make me feel special."

The Guide responded gently, "Inara, you have let emotion override your special senses. Calm yourself and tell me what is really happening here."

With a puzzled frown, Inara turned back to her parents. Nearby, Malin Nowl was smiling as Pren Bodhi slowly began to understand. Finally, Inara said, "Mom, Dad you really are here. This is really you!" Turning around she exclaimed, "Guide, Malin, you did this! Oh, thank you so much. You don't know what you have done for me. This is beyond anything anyone has ever given me."

The Guide responded, "This is nothing compared to what you have done, and what you have sacrificed, for all of us. Why don't you spend a little time here with your family in your home? When you are ready, Malin has prepared a large suite for all of you. Your little droid cheetah will take you there. I suspect you all have a lot to talk about. So, I will say good night."

After parting with The Guide, Inara, her parents and her uncle sat on the grass together. After a few quiet minutes, Inara took a handful of grass and tossed it into the air. After a couple of tosses, Teo, reflecting on a day sixty years earlier, said to her, "What do you see, Inara?"

Sighing strongly, she replied, "I am seeing way too much, and maybe nothing at all. There are things missing."

Jira gently asked, "What is missing, Honey?"

"I'm not sure," Inara quietly answered. "I sense so much, yet I feel empty. And I've just hurt someone I care about deeply. He no longer has music."

Only Teo, Jira and Pren, because they raised Inara, could understand that last statement.

"You broke his heart"? Jira asked while looking at Pren with a questioning expression.

"Yes, I think so," Inara said as she looked back at her mother and then her father, where her gaze stopped in surprise. It was as if she saw him, fully saw him, for the first time in her life. Taller and thinner than the average man, he wore workman's clothes that he somehow made part of him once he put them on. He carried his lean strength quietly and with good humor. His voice was gentle and so sure. And, suddenly Inara found his blue-gray eyes extremely compelling. It was as if they held depths of caring, concern, pride and wisdom that she couldn't reach the bottom of. Why had she never seen that before?

Her father's voice dragged her out of her sudden contemplation. "Do you love him unconditionally?"

"Yes, completely," she said.

Inara felt a gentleness, understanding and strength flow from her father and permeate her being as her senses were overwhelmed by the depth of his feeling for her. She saw her mother take her father's hand as he said, "Then don't let anything in this universe, including the universe itself, get in the way of that love."

Inara sobbed as she said, "I think I already did, and I destroyed it."

Her parents held her as she cried herself to sleep desolate in the knowledge that she had already held, and thrown away, what she had no idea was hers all the time. Then a cloud surrounded them and carried them to the suite Malin had prepared for them.

* * *

By the third day, the only thing the Galaxy's transport systems were handling was messaging exchange except for one special transmission arranged by Alana. Other than that, all entanglement activities ceased. People, animals and plants on many of the trillions on non-Earth-like planets were already suffering from exposure or had died. Even Earth-like planets dependent too heavily on imports from other locations to support their populations were experiencing the massive panic of impending starvation. Resentment at those privileged to live was everywhere. Riots of planetary scale arose in millions of systems across the galaxy, and many deaths were caused by human panic, anger and desperation. Finally at the end of about three weeks the planets of these millions of systems were silent. They became mute testimony to long-term human error. Those left behind were, for the most part, in such a state of emotional shock that they were virtually useless suffering survivor's guilt or unbearable depression. In the end, only much less than one-thousandth of one percent of humans and other plant and animal life remained in the galaxy.

At the University, the Cathedral and The Guide's Hall, the sense of purpose and responsibility was some protection from the shock. All who were there continued work to find a solution and share knowledge over the now slow information sharing systems. However, all that really emerged from their effort was confirmation of Kieran and Inara's conclusion that space-time-soul had been severely injured, and that healing would take a long time. Perhaps longer than humans had available.

* * *

Guide Takar Cillian, Pren, Inara and her parents were in The Guide's chambers. It was a calming setting symbolic of what life was like for primitive humans. They were on a beautiful plain with a wide river running through it. Wild animals were grazing so closely nearby that they could pick up their scent. Meerkats chittered in the warm breeze. To their left, the sun was setting casting a golden glow on everything including them. In contrast, just above the horizon on their right, the sky was a cascade of stars circling and falling into the nearby black hole.

Malin entered to sit quietly with the group for a few minutes. Eventually, he broke the silence. "Inara, your family has told me about the relationship between you and Kieran. It is obvious to all of us that it is a relationship that was meant to be but surrounded by and cast into chaos by events as great as any that have enveloped humankind. We all also understand that your decision to part is something you greatly regret and wish you could change."

In the quietest of voices Inara responded, "Yes, I can't believe what I have done and would change it if I could. But I'm afraid I have done irreparable harm."

Guide Takar Cillian stepped in. "It is clear that you and Kieran share a rare and profound love. So, it was a surprise to all of us that you returned here without Kieran. At some risk of intruding on your privacy, those of us who care so greatly about you have shared our concern about you and Kieran. There is no doubt that you are both profoundly broken hearted. Kieran understands and respects your reasons for the decision you made."

Inara interrupted in a voice that could hardly be heard. "But, I was wrong. And it was even cruel, though not intended to be that way. I hate what I have done."

All gathered closely around Inara as Takar said, "We all know that and so does Kieran. He, and all of us, understand your concern about faith. But I am going to quote for you something that comes from the ancient Christian texts and survives after all this time. 'So faith, hope, love remain, these three; but the greatest of these is love'. Alana Perg, the oldest, wisest and most experienced of those we have been working with knew, as you and Kieran parted, that the emotional stress and sense of responsibility that weighed so heavily on you was affecting your judgement. It appears that she is a true romantic who just had to lend of helping hand. So, here is what she did."

Those around Inara parted slightly and Inara felt a hand on her shoulder. She knew instantly who it was and turned with the deepest of sobs to tightly embrace Kieran who had just been sent to their location by Alana after finishing some last minute essential work. She managed to gasp, "I'm so sorry. I love you. I was so wrong. I want you with me forever."

Kieran responded, "I know. I love you, too."

Malin reluctantly interrupted, "The time has come. All of our stasis pods are ready."

The Guide reflected, "It looks like our job is finished, then. All work at the Cathedral and on University Planet has stopped and everyone there is in stasis. Few people are left alive across the galaxy. Almost all of those are on Earth, Earth-identical planets, some near-Earth planets and a smattering of stasis pods still in operation. The galaxy is a massive cemetery. Hopefully, those who come after us do better."

Turning to his friend, Takar Cillian asked, "Malin, I assume that all information has been transferred to Earth and that they have full access to all archives? Do we have a new Guide?"

"Yes, Takar. His name is Samto Habib."

"Thank you, Malin, for all you have always done. And thank you for being my friend. Malin and Takar looked at each other as men who are best friends do. They coughed and looked away, shuffling a bit, finally moving forward to share a strong embrace. They left unsaid their uncertainty about seeing each other again. Words were insufficient for anything else.

Finally, the man who was no longer The Guide turned to Inara, Pren and her parents. "Thank you for these last months. I brought you to The Guide's Hall, but you brought me into your family. I pray that we all survive stasis to awaken and stay together for many more years. Now, it is time to leave all this for whatever does, or doesn't, lie ahead for us and humankind."

Postlogue And A New Beginning

"Guide, it is time for your presentation."

"Thank you, Demetrius. Would you like to give it for me?"

"No thanks. However, I'll be watching along with a few billion others."

"Humph. Thanks for the comforting reminder."

Guide Samto Habib took a deep breath in an attempt to stop his sweaty hands from shaking. It was the most important and stressful moment of his life. It was only in the last few weeks that full communication had been restored between Earth, the galaxy's twenty-seven Earth-identical planets and to many of the Earth-like planets. It was the first time that he, or anyone, would be addressing all of those who remained after the catastrophe just a few decades ago. It was a new start for humanity.

"Demetrius," he said, "please walk with me to the meeting dome."

Demetrius responded, "You are my best friend as well as my Guide. It will be my honor to walk with you."

The Guide squinted as he and Demetrius left his office to walk across the grass. The late-afternoon sun warmed him and seemed to be offering courage. His mother used to refer to this as the soft time of day when the harshness of strong light gave way to gentle colors. In a few hours, this lovely evening with its salmon colored clouds would be over. Ending another beautiful day would again be like losing a friend.

The Guide felt Demetrius' hand upon his shoulder, stopping him as they arrived at the entrance to the meeting dome.

"Samto."

In spite of their closeness, the two friends knew they had to keep a strictly professional relationship. Demetrius only called The Guide by his first name when they were alone; and then only occasionally.

"Samto, I know this responsibility and this moment weigh heavily on you. However, you must remember that the people you're going to be talking to in a few minutes love and respect you. You are surrounded by friends. I'll be seated close to you."

The Guide looked at the man he had known for most of his seven hundred thirty-two years and loved like a brother. He simply rasped, "Thank you," suddenly too emotional to say any more.

The walk from the dome entrance to the central podium seemed to take forever. Demetrius went to his seat as The Guide continued the short distance to the spot from which he would address most of what remained of their galactic civilization.

Guide Samto Habib stood in the middle of the great dome which was one hundred meters in diameter. He was in the midst of those who were there in person, or in essence. Telescence images of those from distant locations covered every part of the dome and surrounded him as if they also were present. He saw all near and far begin to take their seats as they noticed that their Guide was ready.

"Thank you for giving me the honor of opening this first meeting of our surviving population. I recognize, and am humbled by, my insignificance and the responsibility that you have temporarily given me."

Humbling was too mild a term to describe it, he thought. All of them were indeed insignificant as individuals but incredibly important in their relationships with each other and the Universal Soul. Guide Samto Habib knew that his generation, and those who immediately followed, would not forget the lessons they had all learned. But, he wondered, can those lessons become permanent? He was determined to make that happen.

"It has been thirty years since 'The Great Collapse' of our galactic-wide civilization. Out of hundreds of trillions of people on millions of planets, there are only a few billion of us left on a little over one hundred planets. We don't know how many are still surviving in stasis, but it is certainly not a billion. A few of those stasis systems fail each day.

"It seemed to me, and perhaps to almost all of us who were in the midst of it all, that we had great order and a well-planned balance of power in the galaxy. The government and its subsets were, for the most part, effectively organized. The Controllers were focused on operation and development of our core infrastructure, and cooperated closely with the government on a well-integrated vision of the future. The Pilgrims, completely separate from government and Controllers, saw themselves as working to understand the true nature of the Universal Soul, and they did pure scientific research to that end.

"What none of us knew is that all of our strings were being pulled by five ancient, hidden families so evil that everything they did or touched, damaged all of us in subtle and not so subtle ways. Not only did they injure us, but they damaged the Universal Soul to such a degree that the destruction spilled over into everything around us.

"So, there is an important true story that must be told. We have discovered and assembled a long history from records that go back over one hundred thousand years to the time when humans were still walking or riding horses between villages and cities. Many have worked hard to make that story accurate and real. We might call it a nano-history for now because there is still much to put together. So far, we have only partially assembled a thread that takes us from that ancient time to what has become known as the Great Collapse just a short while ago. That thread comes from the archives of the Pilgrims, government agencies and from amazingly complete and accurate records of the Five Families you are all familiar with.

"We have accurately assembled enough of the first parts of this nano-history to feel safe in making it available to everyone. We welcome critique and corrections if we have made errors. This first release is just a thread. However, it is the thread that we feel best represents what happened and gives clues to how we ended up where we are today. We will add to that history and quickly make it available to you as we pull more from the various archives. What we add to this thread will reveal the full, multi-colored and rumpled fabric of our history.

"The Five Families who controlled everything in the background were fanatical about preserving historical fact and using it to make sure they learned from it and never made the same mistake twice. Their detailed, deliberately objective history was one of their core assets. In a much different way, we hope that what we learn from history will be one of our primary strengths as well.

"The Pilgrims, the various churches and the government also kept histories. Those histories, while not always as objective, are useful in reconstructing the lessons of humankind.

"We've studied carefully the transcripts left by those who fought so hard during their last days to prevent 'The Great Collapse' and who helped the Universal Soul defeat great evil. The wisdom and knowledge gained in those few days by those great people is staggering. We have learned much from them and from their struggle.

"It seems paradoxical to each of us, and it goes against the instinct of good and optimistic people to know that just a few seconds of evil or error in judgment on the part of one person can undo that individual's entire lifetime of love and kindness. We eventually all learn that this is a fact of life even though we don't like it.

"By the same token we know that a small group of people can destroy what a civilization has built over generations.

"Civilization, and its history, cannot be painted in black and white. Even in the face of what I have learned in recent years, I still believe that almost all of us as individuals have character that must be painted in all colors of the spectrum. However, I have also learned to my utter horror that there are those in whom each and every dimension of character is bathed in evil. Their story can only be painted in shades of black and gray because that truly is the limit of their character."

Guide Samto Habib concluded, "We are linked through the Universal Soul with each other, and with stasis survivors across the galaxy. All of us in leadership positions are dedicated to physically restoring our connection with each other while nurturing space-time-soul. We are also in agreement that we will bend every effort to reach and save as many of those as we can at The Guide's Hall, University Planet and The Cathedral who worked so valiantly to preserve knowledge, wisdom and culture for all of us who remain. That work has already started."

The Guide put his hands on his heart and then threw his arms outward with a sweeping motion. "With that meaningful gesture, I have just commanded our storage archives to send as much as we know of our history to you. Anyone will have access to it at anytime, anywhere. It will be displayed in this dome as a total immersion, telescence presentation. It will be available forever to all of us. Our hope is that we will learn from a culture of mistakes to become fully one with each other.

"The story of our past will now begin. More episodes and information will be added to the story as we discover and assemble them. The desire of all of us who have put it together is that this beginning piece will help us avoid past mistakes. I will serve as your nano-historian throughout all episodes."

Made in the USA
Monee, IL
07 April 2021